The Loss of the
MARION

The Loss of the
MARION

A NOVEL

Linda Abbott

FLANKER PRESS LIMITED
ST. JOHN'S

Library and Archives Canada Cataloguing in Publication

Abbott, Linda, 1954-
The loss of the Marion / Linda Abbott.

Issued also in electronic formats.
ISBN 978-1-77117-008-6

1. Marion (Schooner)--Fiction. 2. Shipwrecks--Newfoundland and Labrador--Fiction. I. Title.

PS8601.B26L67 2012 C813'.6 C2012-904185-8

PRINTED IN CANADA

Cover Design: Adam Freake
Edited by Erika Steeves

FLANKER PRESS LTD.
PO BOX 2522, STATION C
ST. JOHN'S, NL
CANADA

TELEPHONE: (709) 739-4477 FAX: (709) 739-4420 TOLL-FREE: 1-866-739-4420
WWW.FLANKERPRESS.COM

16 15 14 13 12 2 3 4 5 6 7 8 9

Canada Council for the Arts / Conseil des Arts du Canada

We acknowledge the financial support of the Government of Canada through the Book Publishing Industry Development Program (BPIDP) for our publishing activities; the Canada Council for the Arts which last year invested $24.3 million in writing and publishing throughout Canada; the Government of Newfoundland and Labrador, Department of Tourism, Culture and Recreation.

FSC www.fsc.org MIX Paper from responsible sources FSC® C103567

Author's Note

Captain Ike Jones is the name used by locals, in song and in folklore, for Captain Isaac Skinner of the *Marion*.

For my sister Joan,
you loved and lived life to the fullest.

For my father, Ronald,
a war veteran who cherished books.

1915

EIGHT PERFECTLY ROUNDED FISH cakes sizzled in the iron pan. The smell filled the air and greeted Harry Myles as he came into the kitchen. He stood behind his wife, Nellie, and watched her flip over a cake and lay it down into the grease carefully. Globs of bacon fat splattered her thumb. She hissed and pulled her hand away, then just as quickly returned it to the handle of the pan.

Harry sniffed, a long, resonate sound. "Smells good," he said. "I'm starving."

Nellie said nothing and slapped over another fish cake, causing fat to sprinkle the stove. The crust on each one was just the right shade of brown, reminding Harry of well-done toast.

"It amazes me how you always knows the exact time to flip over the fish cakes," he said.

Nellie kept her head bent low. "It's no big deal."

Harry clapped his hands together. "Where are the youngsters?"

"In the shed," Nellie said without looking up.

"Playing alleys?"

"S'pose so."

Nellie seemed tense and Harry placed a hand on her shoulder. "Everything okay, love?"

"Grand," Nellie said, still refusing to look at her husband.

The late afternoon sun streamed in through the open window. Even though it was early June, the day had been unbearably hot in

St. Jacques. At five o'clock the temperature had cooled down to the low seventies. The sun's rays highlighted the grey streaks just beginning to show in Nellie's mass of auburn hair she wore in a bun. She shoved away several loose strands from her forehead with the back of her hand.

Harry stared at his wife's back. "Sure there's nothing bothering ya?"

"I already said there wasn't."

Harry pulled out a chair from the oak kitchen table set he'd built fifteen years ago with the help of his uncle Joe. He looked down at the green canvas, faded from too much scrubbing. His eyes travelled over the white painted walls. Nellie wouldn't hear tell of wallpaper. "Gets too dirty and dull in no time," she'd said. Harry's gaze lingered on the eight South American porcelain dolls his wife had placed with tenderness on two shelves over the sink. It was the only luxury she allowed herself.

Harry drummed his fingers on the table. "Come on, Nellie. Tell me what's wrong with ya."

Nellie turned around. "Is Captain Ike gonna stop off at St. Pierre on the way to the Grand Banks?"

Harry's eyebrows rose. "Why are you asking?"

"Just wondered. That's all."

"I knows you better than that, love. Out with it."

"Fine," Nellie said. "You asked, so here it is. Why don't you talk to that old coot of a captain and make him see there's no point in going to St. Pierre?"

"Captain Ike does what he wants. The crew's opinion don't matter none when he's made a decision."

"All he wants is to fight and stir up trouble." Nellie stood on her toes to reach into the cupboard over the sink and took down five plates. "If he really cared about his men, he'd head straight for the Grand Banks and stay away from St. Pierre."

"We gotta stop off for a few more supplies."

"Right," Nellie snorted. "Booze and fags are what he wants. You men would do anything for a swally and a smoke."

The sound of faraway laughter filtered in through the window. Harry recognized his daughter's voice, the only girl and the youngest of their three children.

Nellie sat down facing her husband and leaned close to him. Sweat beaded on her forehead. Harry pulled a white handkerchief from his trouser pocket and smoothed it away. Nellie laid a hand on his knee. After fifteen years together, her touch still sent waves of heat through him.

"Ike Jones is a fool," she said.

"Can't argue with that," Harry said. "He's stubborn and hotheaded as well, won't back away from a fight no matter what the odds."

"The last time a brawl broke out in the *Hôtel de France*, it was all because of him. You ended up with a black eye as thanks for helping him out."

"The French captain and his men had Captain Ike surrounded. Me and the boys couldn't stand by and watch him get pounded."

"Why don't you miss this fishing trip?" Nellie said.

Harry wasn't sure he'd heard correctly. "You want me to miss this fishing trip?"

Nellie nodded.

"What will we eat when the winter comes? How will we put clothes on the children's backs? How—"

Nellie stood up. "Forget I said anything," she said, cutting across in front of him.

Harry gently pulled her back onto the chair and caressed her chin with his fingertips, rough and hardened from salt water and handling burly nets. "You ain't ever been this concerned before. What's wrong?"

"I have a bad feeling." Nellie's eyes glistened as she held back tears.

Nellie had had a "bad feeling" before Harry's father died. She'd had a "bad feeling" before Uncle Joe died. And when his mother died. She never used that expression lightly.

A shiver ran down Harry's spine.

"How long?" he said.

"Awhile now. I was hoping not to tell ya. Please, Harry, don't go. If not for me, then do it for the youngsters."

Harry shook himself. "Your bad feeling don't always come true. Remember young Gilbert Bloom? You warned him about taking the horse and cart to St. John's last Christmas. He came back fitter than a mountain goat."

A tear slid down Nellie's cheek. "I should've known you'd bring up the only time I was ever wrong. Why listen to anything I have to say? I'm only your wife and the mother of your youngsters."

Harry's heart skipped a beat and he reached for her.

Nellie pushed him away. "Your masculine wiles won't work on me this time, Harry Myles."

"Don't be angry with me, love. Fishing is all I knows how to do."

"It's never too late to begin something new. You could try your hand at the lobster cannery."

Harry shuddered. "Them lobsters gives me the twinges."

"Then how about the herring packing plants?"

He opened his mouth to speak, but Nellie interrupted him. "Don't try and tell me herrings gives you the twinges, too. There's two plants to choose from. Both Mr. Burke and Mr. Young would give you work."

Harry opened his mouth yet again to say something, but Nellie barrelled on. "Your Uncle Joe was the one with the brains in your family. Stayed off the ocean and worked in a safe, comfy fish plant. He wasn't a dope. Lived to be eighty. You don't see many old-timers around here who went to sea."

Harry ran a hand through his blond curls. "Love, I . . ."

Nellie jumped in before he had a chance to go on. "My heart throbs in my throat every time you go out to sea. I die inside when it's with Captain Ike." She heaved a great sigh. "I'm real scared about this trip. More scared than ever before."

Black smoke billowed up from the frying pan and rolled toward them like a dense wave of fog. Nellie darted to the stove and threw the pan in the dishwater. Water splashed over the sides onto the counter and soaked the front of her white apron. Harry ran to open the kitchen door, and the room began to clear.

"Supper's gonna be late now," Nellie said after a brief bout of coughing.

The taste of smoke lingered at the back of Harry's throat. "That don't make no mind," he said, hauling out a sack of potatoes from the pantry.

"Go tell the children," Nellie said, scraping away the remains of a blackened fish cake with a bread knife. "I don't want them in here fussing and getting in my way."

Harry took out two handfuls of potatoes and returned the sack to the pantry. "Nellie," he said softly, "me and the men will keep Captain Ike away from the French skipper."

Nellie stood still and stared ahead, thinking over what Harry had said. "Give me your word on that," she said, her voice little more than a whisper.

"You have it, love."

Nellie continued to scour the pan.

Harry walked to the shed, and just as he reached it the door burst open and ten-year-old Bessie ran out. Harry sprang back and splayed his arms like a shirt left on the clothesline in a high wind. "Careful, maid," he said with a laugh. "You nearly knocked your old man off his feet."

Bessie giggled. "Go on, Pa. You're all right." She looked toward their two-storey house. Pale traces of smoke drifted from the window and door. Her laughter died. "Is something on fire?"

"Na," Harry said with a flick of his wrist. "Me and your ma were having a grand chat and she forgot about the fish cakes."

Bessie patted her stomach. "I loves fish cakes and drawn butter. Makes me hungry thinking about it."

Harry stared into Bessie's sea-green eyes. His father's eyes. Eyes he hadn't seen since he was ten, her age. "Go help your ma peel more potatoes. I'll keep the boys from getting under your feet."

WITH SUPPER OVER AND the children in bed, Harry and Nellie sat by the fireplace in the living room. Their pantry was stocked with wood, but no flames crackled in the hearth since the temperature had remained steady at seventy degrees. The glow of the candles threw dancing shadows on the walls at each end of the mantel. Harry occupied an armchair and puffed on a Camel cigarette, forming circles every time he exhaled. They spun upward, disintegrating into shapeless clouds. Nellie sat in the rocking chair facing him, knitting a pair of wool socks, the needles softly clinking together in the silence. Usually she rocked with slow movements. Tonight she was stiffer than a dried codfish.

"Joe will be thirteen next month," Harry said. He listened to the steady click of Nellie's needles. "Old enough to fish on the Grand Banks."

"That so," Nellie remarked, her eyes riveted on her task. *Click click. Click click.*

Harry blew out a circle of smoke and followed its rise to the ceiling. "Captain Ike's agreed to take him on."

The clicking stopped. Nellie's eyes locked on the needles in her lap.

Harry reached up to stub out his cigarette in a saucer on the mantel. "I've been thinking real hard about our talk today," he said.

Nellie's eyes went to her husband. "What are you telling me?"

"I already signed up with Captain Ike, and when I commits to something I have to see it to the end. Wouldn't be right to back out at the last minute. You made a heap of sense. This is my last trip. As for Joe, he's gonna have to find a job ashore."

The wooden rocker squeaked softly as Nellie relaxed and leaned back. "Thanks be to the Lord," she said. "While you're gone, I'll have a chin wag with Mr. Burke. I like him better than Mr. Young."

"No you won't. I can get a job without a woman butting in on my account. Anyway, time enough for that when I return."

Nellie resumed her knitting. She hummed "All Around the Circle" and rocked to the beat, smiling inwardly. She'd pay him no heed and would visit the plant owners as soon as the fishing schooner pulled out of the harbour.

His mother's horse-shaped clock struck nine. Harry yawned and stretched his arms high overhead. "Time for bed."

"You go on," Nellie said. "I want to finish the band on this sock."

Harry scratched the light stubble on his face. "Joe ain't gonna be too happy. He's some excited about fishing alongside his pa. Let's keep this between ourselves for the time being."

Nellie gently squeezed his arm as he passed her. "Thank you." Her boy would stay ashore.

Chapter 1

NELLIE WENT OUTSIDE TO the five-foot pile of junks stacked against the side of the house. A small group of pigeons pecked at the stale bread crumbs she'd thrown out to them through the window. A line of smoke drifted up from the chimneys around the harbour. Even though the sun peeked over the horizon, the morning was chilly. The temperature had dipped to zero overnight. Nellie shivered as she gathered an armful of wood and hurried inside. She scrunched up some old sheets of newspapers from under the sink, lifted off the damper, and stuffed them into the stove. She pulled a box of matches out of her apron pocket and scraped one along the stove. The match flared and she quickly ignited the papers. Flames sprouted up and she threw in a handful of splits.

The back door opened and a young girl Bessie's age swooped in. "Mrs. Myles. I—"

"Marie!"

A man's voice called from outside, cutting off the child. "You don't barge into someone else's house without even knocking."

Marie stopped in her tracks and grinned at Nellie.

Nellie winked at her. "Never you mind," she said, filling the brass kettle from the water bucket Joe had replenished the night before. "You're as good as family." Nellie put the frying pan on the stove as the man came through the door. *Wish I could say the same for you,* she thought, sparing Captain Ike a fleeting glance. Tall and brawny, with a bushy, black beard, Ike Jones reminded her of a mad pirate perched for an attack. Heavy, black eyebrows all but concealed his eyes, and Nellie often wondered what he was hiding.

"Sorry to stop by so early," Ike said.

Nellie sliced a bun of homemade bread. "Never mind that. I'm out of bed before the birds wake up." She cracked a few eggs, added Carnation milk and chunks of ham, and whipped the mixture with a fork.

Ike towered over his daughter, his big hands on her shoulders. "Marie couldn't wait to show you and Bessie her new purchase."

For the first time, Nellie saw the brown paper package tied up with white string that Marie hugged to her chest. She continued preparing breakfast. "Bessie's still in bed," she said, and put a dab of bacon fat in the frying pan. "Sit down. I'll fix you both a cuppa tea and something to eat." The melted fat bubbled and Nellie poured in the beaten eggs. The batter wobbled and popped as it transformed into an oversized omelette. Not many people made omelettes, but Nellie had learned about them from someone who cooked for a merchant family in St. John's. As a treat for Harry and the youngsters in the days before he shipped out, she always charged a bit of bacon and ham to her account at the shop.

"That's good of you," Captain Ike said. "Never had time to eat, with Marie rushing out of the house like it was ablaze."

Marie laid the package on the table and pulled out a chair next to her father. "Mrs. Myles, do you think Bessie will be out of bed soon?" Her fingers played with the knot in the twine.

"She had the Old Hag about a hooded man and was afraid to go back to sleep for hours," Nellie said. "She's good for a while yet."

Marie's forehead crinkled. "Old Hag?"

"The Old Hag is what we call an awful, horrible, waking nightmare," Nellie explained, "where someone or something is after you and you can't move. In her dream, Bessie was with you on the wharf when dark clouds turned the day as dark as night. A black-hooded figure appeared and walked toward you. Bessie went numb all over. She couldn't even cry out for help."

Marie quivered and rubbed her bare arms. "I hope I never have one of those."

"Angel," Ike said to his daughter, "since Bessie's asleep, show Mrs. Myles what's in the package."

Nellie scooped up the omelette, cut out two portions, and put the rest in the oven to keep warm. She set two plates on the table while Marie untied the knot and opened the paper, one fold at a time.

Marie lifted out the most exquisite porcelain doll Nellie had ever seen. Straight black hair fell to its waist and a straw skirt went just past the knees. The feet were bare. A wreath of white, red, and purple flowers she couldn't name encircled the head. A larger wreath hung around the neck and down the front. Nellie gasped and covered her mouth with both hands. "What a beautiful creature," she said.

Marie ran her hand the length of the doll's dark hair. "Her name's Leila and she comes from a place called Hawaii. Pa said that's in the Pacific Ocean. This is how the women dress when they dance. I ordered her for you."

Nellie's eyes opened wide. "For me!"

"I wanted an extra-special present for your birthday tomorrow."

Nellie blushed and reached for the doll. "I don't need a present. Celebrating birthdays is for children."

"You take care of my daughter when I'm away fishing and this is a thank-you," the captain said. "She's very happy here."

"You pay me for that. Besides, Marie helps me and Bessie with chores around the house."

"I loves you and Bessie," Marie said. "Oh," she added, as if she'd forgotten a very important detail, "I likes Mr. Myles and the boys, too."

Nellie placed the porcelain doll on the shelf with the other dolls. She picked up the teapot with a cloth and poured the steaming liquid into two cups. The captain sipped his black, but Marie added Carnation milk to hers. Nellie went back to the stove. "You all ready for the fishing trip, Captain Ike?" she said.

"Yes. We leave in two days' time."

"Have all your supplies, then?"

"Most of them."

"Making any stops along the way?"

"St. Pierre."

Nellie wiped sweaty palms on her apron. "Why is that?"

The captain turned to face her. "I always go to St. Pierre before I head to the Grand Banks," he said.

"But you have all your supplies." Nellie's heart galloped, but she forged ahead. "Trouble starts when the men drink in the *Hôtel de France*. My pa always said that booze and brawling goes hand in hand. And that French captain . . ."

Ike sprang to his feet. "Time to go, Marie."

"Pa, I ain't finished eating and I ain't seen Bessie yet."

Nellie crossed the floor in two strides. "Marie, take your tea and toast to Bessie's room," she said in a calm voice. "It's time she was up."

When Marie was out of sight, the captain continued. "Fishing is a man's business. It's nothing for a woman to bother her head about."

Nellie looked at him sideways. "Man's business?"

"Mrs. Myles, I've been going to St. Pierre since I became the skipper of the *Marion*. I don't plan to change that."

Nellie cracked open more eggs. "Finish your breakfast, Captain. Harry will be down in a minute."

The captain remained standing. "I have a lot to do today, so I'll need to drop Marie off early at the convent."

The frying pan sizzled. "School doesn't start for another hour, Captain. She can go with Bessie and the boys, if you like."

"Good day, then," he said as he tapped the rim of his hat. He closed the door behind him.

"Talking to Clive Pope would get better results," Nellie mumbled to herself. "He's deafer than a tree stump."

Joe, her older boy, came into the kitchen, rubbing the sleep out of his eyes. "Stupid girls," he muttered. "All they do is giggle over stuff not worth thinking about."

Sam, a year younger, trailed behind his brother. "Bessie and Marie woke us up with their blabbering."

Nellie smiled at her sons. Both were blond and blue-eyed like Harry. Soon they'd be as tall and muscular as him. "Good," she said. "Now you won't be late for school. That'll please Mother Patrick."

Joe groaned. "Do we have to go, Ma? Why cram our heads with book learning? Who cares about when Josh Cabot discovered Newfoundland?" He looked at his brother. "Right, Sam?"

Sam shrugged. "I enjoys arithmetic." He pronounced the word slowly, carefully. "Finds it some easy. Mother Patrick says I have potential. She said that means I'm smart and can do whatever I puts me mind to."

Nellie laid their breakfast on the table. The children each cut off a thick slice of bread, covered it with Good Luck margarine, and dug into their omelettes.

"School finishes for me this year," Joe said, his mouth packed with food. "I'll be thirteen in three weeks. Then I'm off fishing with Pa. Can't wait."

Nellie stood with her hands on her hips. "What is it you can't wait for? Getting up before sunrise to bait the trawls over a mile and a half long, with more than eight hundred hooks? Or maybe hauling in the trawls with your bare hands when the floater kegs are full with codfish, then starting the whole thing over again? Or losing two fingers, like Earle Fiander? Or getting your leg tangled up and torn to shreds like poor Frank Fewer?"

Joe stared wide-eyed at his mother.

"Or might it be cleaning and salting the fish before you go to bed," she concluded.

Sam looked at his brother. "You can get lost if there's a storm or fog," he said.

Joe glared at him. "You knows schooners has a bell and foghorn to guide the men out in the dories," he snapped.

Nellie folded her arms across her chest. "That, my son, doesn't guarantee you'll make it back."

"I . . ."

"Don't talk with your mouth full," Nellie said, giving Joe a soft slap on the back of the head. "Fishing isn't all there is. You could be a doctor, or a merchant like the Burke brothers. School learning got them far. They own plenty of businesses around here and are mighty rich."

"Your ma's right," Harry said, joining his boys at the table for breakfast. "The Burke family and Mr. Young ship goods all over Newfoundland and to the rest of the world. They don't have to suffer the hardships us fishermen face on the Banks."

Sam drained his tea. "The nuns say the same thing."

Nellie pursed her lips. "I like the Presentation Sisters. They know what they're talking about."

Joe pulled a face. "Don't care. I'm still going fishing."

"No more jacking about fishing," Nellie said. "For today, my son, it's school for you."

WHEN HARRY AND NELLIE were finally alone, Harry leaned back in his chair and stretched out his legs. "We'll talk Joe 'round," he assured her. "That was a nice birthday present Marie got ya. Real thoughtful."

"She most likely takes after her mother," Nellie said, and began to clear the table. Harry helped her, as he did whenever he was at home. With the dishes dried, he went to the shed. Nellie swept the floor, made the beds, and made a pan of bread. By the time she covered the dough to rise, it was mid-morning. She wrapped up the fruitcake she had baked two days ago for Mother Patrick, threw a shawl around her shoulders, and set off for the convent. The sun beamed down on her, yet the wind off the harbour chilled her to the bone. She pulled the shawl tighter around her shoulders and, taking a deep breath, climbed the steep slope leading to the convent. Nellie never failed to admire the exotic variety of trees that surrounded the building like a majestic lion's mane.

Mother Patrick waved from the doorway. The nun hailed from Ireland, and although old enough to be her mother, Nellie considered her a good friend and confidante. They spent many hours talking about everything from religion to cooking.

"Now, what could you have wrapped up all nice and neat tucked under your arm like that?" the mother superior asked. The shape gave it away and she licked her lips at the thought it might be one of Nellie's famous fruitcakes.

Nellie handed over the package without a word.

"Come inside," the elderly nun said. "Visit for a spell."

Nellie followed her down a long corridor to a large room. Mother Patrick sat behind a narrow table loaded with school books on one side and a stack of scribblers on the other. Nellie sat in one of four chairs tucked under the table and looked at the pictures of various saints hung around the room. She'd been here many times and experienced a sense of peace from the serene faces staring down at her.

Today she felt nothing.

Mother Patrick peered over the top of the wire glasses perched on the tip of her nose. "You look as happy as a chicken about to have its head chopped off," she said. "What's the matter?"

Nellie cracked a smile which didn't reach her eyes.

Mother Patrick folded her age-spotted hands on the table in front of her. "You've spoken to Harry about your concerns?"

Nellie flicked a strand of hair away from her face. "Yes. He agreed that this is going to be his last trip."

The nun's eyebrows disappeared under her wimple, the white, starched material allowing only the eyes, cheeks, and chin to show. "Then why aren't you rejoicing?"

Nellie wrung her hands. "I know I'm being foolish as an odd sock."

"Holy Mary, Mother of God," Mother Patrick gasped, as recognition dawned on her face. "You still have that unsettled feeling, don't you? Does Harry know?"

"He does," Nellie said, and related her conversations with both Harry and Ike Jones. "What can I do?" she sighed when she had finished. "Harry is signed up and can't pull out now. We all know what Ike Jones is like."

Mother Patrick's kind eyes shimmered. "Well, my child. Perhaps a little of the Irish good luck and plenty of prayer will work everything out."

Chapter 2

HARRY WENT TO THE church and paused to look at the cemetery that held generations of fishermen and their families. His gaze came to rest on his parents' headstones, their deaths dated a year apart. The wind picked up and ruffled his hair, so he took his salt and pepper cap from underneath his arm and slapped it on his head. A hacking cough made him turn around.

Sid Davies walked through the gate. He held a bunch of daisies. "Putting fresh ones on my little Rosie's grave before I ships out tomorrow," he said.

Frank Fewer limped alongside him and exchanged a knowing look with Harry. "Thought I'd keep him company."

Rosie was Sid's youngest child and had died of consumption a year earlier while he was on the Grand Banks.

"See you at the schooner, then," Harry replied. He left the cemetery and continued past the convent and down the hill to his brother's place. The smell of freshly baked homemade bread made Harry's stomach rumble. Mrs. Annie Cluett came out with a bucket, her dress sleeves rolled up past her elbows. Widowed at twenty with no children, she'd helped Uncle Joe look after Harry and his brother Tom when their father died. The bucket swayed with each step she took down the clay path. The frothy water sloshed back and forth.

"Morning to ya, Harry," Annie said. She squinted into the sun and shaded her eyes with a hand.

"Morning, Annie."

"Lovely weather we're having."

"Couldn't ask for better. Is Tom around?"

Annie tossed the dirty water into the grass along the side of the road. Some of the grey liquid sprayed back on her shoes. "He's in the shed behind the flake."

Harry tapped a finger against his hat. "Thanks, Annie."

"Stop in for a mug-up before you leave," she said, turning back to the house.

The door to the shed was open. "How's the baby?" Harry teased, holding back a grin. Tom, twenty-six, with red hair and a face smothered in freckles, looked sixteen. Tall and too lanky, according to Annie. She never stopped trying to fatten him up. He munched on one of the six tea buns she'd insisted he take to the shed.

"Very funny." Tom lifted down a bag of coarse salt from a shelf. "Something the matter?"

Harry pulled off his hat. "Came by for a chat. That's all."

Tom opened the bag of salt and scooped out a handful. A piece flicked up and hit the three-inch scar on his right jaw, a recent souvenir from the last time he had shipped out with Ike Jones. Tom rubbed a finger over the slightly swollen, reddened skin. "Still smarts awful bad," he said. "Annie was mad enough to row to St. Pierre to have a word with the man who sliced me face open."

Harry chuckled despite himself. "How could I forget?" Annie weighed two hundred pounds, stood nearly six foot, and was a match for any man. She had proven it on more than one occasion. "That was some tongue banging she gave Mr. Young when he wouldn't hire you at the fish factory. He thought you were too puny for the work."

Tom laughed. "Never saw a man change his mind so fast."

"Maybe you shoulda stayed put in the factory."

"Nah. Cooking is what I knows best and what I likes best."

"Nellie has a bad feeling about this trip," Harry blurted out.

The brightness faded from Tom's eyes. "B'y," he said, "wasn't expecting to hear that." Nellie's bad feelings were well accepted as fact in St. Jacques.

Harry sighed. "I promised her to stay on land after this trip."

Tom's mouth opened wide with surprise. "You're pulling my leg, b'y."

Harry shoved his hands deep into his pockets. "I hates to end up drowned young like Pa. You were a tyke crawling on the floor."

"That's a fisherman's life," Tom said, stating a fact everyone understood and accepted.

"I don't want Nellie left to raise our youngsters on her own."

Tom nodded. "That's the way of it."

"We were lucky Uncle Joe took us in." Harry smiled at the memory of the bachelor, who was set in his ways but proved to be a great stand-in father.

"Right," Tom said. "A great old-timer. Told the best yarns I ever heard in me life." The shed door swayed in the soft breeze as a quiet settled over the two men. Tom rubbed the fresh scar once more. "We needs to persuade the men to keep away from the *Hôtel de France*."

"Nellie will appreciate that."

"I have something to tell ya . . ." Tom said, ". . . between us." He laid down the half-eaten tea bun. "This is my last trip, too."

"That's a right shock," Harry said.

"You knows how Dr. Fitzgerald and his missus brags about my cooking all over the peninsula? The last time I took Annie to St. John's for some shopping, he suggested I look for a job as a cook. He gave me a real good reference, seeing as he's acquainted with lots of people there." Tom smiled. "I found me a job as a cook in a fancy hotel. Maybe someday I'll open my own eating place."

Harry shook Tom's hand. "Good on ya."

"Annie says she'll miss me but is right pleased I'll be off the ocean. As soon as I gets back, I'm packing my trunk for St. John's."

NELLIE HURRIED HOME FROM the convent to fix dinner and wasn't surprised to find that Harry was out. She made a conscious effort to close her mind to negative thoughts as she donned an apron, lit the stove, cut a loaf of bread, and set the table. She popped open a new jar of homemade raspberry jam, which would be emptied before dinner finished. A fresh boiler of chicken soup simmered on the stove next to the pot of tea. At the sound of the children's voices, she ladled bubbling soup into four bowls.

Joe charged through the door ahead of the others and ran to the table. "What a boring day," he said, stuffing a piece of bread into his mouth. "Sister Thérèse made us repeat the same French words over and over and over. She said we had to get the accent right."

Marie, who came to Nellie's for dinner on school days, sat across from Joe. "Pa buys me a bag of Bull's Eyes every time I gets a good mark on a French test," she said.

"That's dumb," Joe said. "What's so darn special about French?"

Marie showed no sign the comment had upset her. "Pa's happy whenever I does good in any subject. But he gets some silly about my French."

"I likes writing stories," Bessie said. "Mother Patrick told the class I got heaps of imagination."

Joe turned up his nose. "She wants us to learn 'proper' grammar," he said, quoting the nun's Irish accent to perfection. He poked Marie in the side. "Then we'll talk uppity like your pa." She made a face at him.

Sam smothered a slice of bread with jam. "I'm gonna be an accountant."

Joe slurped his soup. "You're gonna be a fisherman like me and Pa."

Nellie stirred the boiler. "Stop yakking and eat your food," she said, and glanced out the window. Harry stood on the wharf, staring out over the water. Fog swirled around him. She pushed the curtain aside to get a better view and shouted, "What are you doing down there when dinner's on the table?"

"Ma, is the tea steeped?"

Nellie dragged her eyes from the wharf back to Sam. "Help yourself," she said, and turned back to the window. Harry was gone. The fog was gone. She darted her eyes in every direction. "Where'd he go?"

"Who you talking to?" Bessie said.

"Your pa was on the wharf a second ago, and . . ." Nellie's voice trailed off as the door opened and Harry stepped in, holding a dozen raisin tea buns.

"These are from Annie," he said, placing them on the table. "Right out of the oven."

"Harry, were you just down by the wharf?" Nellie said quietly.

"No, love." He took off his light jacket and hung it on a hook by the door. "It's sweltering out. I'll eat later. There's a bit of work needs finishing in the shed."

Nellie's legs felt a little weak and she leaned against the stove.

"Ma," said Sam. "You all right?"

Nellie brushed away imaginary crumbs from the front of her apron. "Never been better in all my life."

Joe soaked up the last bit of soup with buttered bread. Nellie refilled his bowl. "Gee, Ma, you're awful white."

"It's true," Bessie said. "You looks like you had the Old Hag."

Nellie waved the comment away. "Finish dinner and get off to school." She sighed with relief when the door closed behind the youngsters.

Harry came in as she was clearing away the dishes. "I had some interesting chat with Tom," he said.

Nellie laid two bowls of soup on the table. "You sure you weren't down by the wharf a little while ago?" she asked again.

Harry spooned soup into his mouth. "I was with Tom all morning."

Nellie's heart flip-flopped. "With the fog and all, I figured it had to be you." She struggled to keep her voice level.

"Fog? The sun's been splitting the rocks all day."

Nellie wrapped cold fingers around the hot bowl. "It was there one second, then gone the next. You know how the land chews up the fog," she said. She continued to grasp the bowl.

"Aren't you hungry, love?"

"I ate with the children," Nellie lied, and poured the soup back into the pot. "Thought I had room for more. My eyes are bigger than my stomach." She took a deep breath to slow her heart. "What's this about Tom?"

Harry recounted the conversation.

"I bet Uncle Joe's singing praises up there," Nellie said. "Near broke his heart when you and Tom ignored his darn good advice and chose to go fishing."

Harry sighed, long and deep. "I wish he was here so we could tell him."

Nellie put her arms around his shoulders and kissed the top of his head. "He knows," she whispered.

There was a tap at the door. "That's what I like to see," a strong yet gentle voice said.

A smile creased the corners of Nellie's mouth. "Good day to ya," she said. "Would you like a bite to eat before you check Harry out?" Dr. Conrad Fitzgerald, an Englishman, and a gentleman by her standards, was the only doctor on the Burin Peninsula. At seventy-three, he looked as young and as nimble as a man in his forties.

The doctor laid his bag on the table. "Thank you for the kind offer, Nellie, but Harry's my first stop. I want to get to all the men before the day is out."

Nellie watched him listen to Harry's heart and sound out his lungs, free of charge. He made it a point to give all crews the once-over before they embarked on a long fishing trip.

"Sid Davies still got an awful cough," Harry said.

"I told him he mustn't go fishing for at least another week." Dr. Fitzgerald shook his head. "You fishermen don't have the good sense to take care of yourselves."

"We don't fish, we don't eat," Harry said.

The doctor returned the medical instruments to the black bag. "Is that fruitcake I smell?" he said, a twinkle in his eye.

"I see you've been to the convent," Nellie said. She'd told Mother Patrick she had baked a cake for Dr. Fitzgerald's wife.

"Indeed I have. My wife is pacing the floor in anticipation of my return home." He leaned in and whispered in Nellie's ear. "Even with your recipe, Hattie's attempts to reproduce your exquisite cake are dismal failures." He tapped the side of his nose. "Of course, the dear lady need never know I said that."

"I'm going to the shop once the dishes are done," Nellie said. "I'll take the cake to your house on the way."

"Right-o, Nellie. That's very kind of you. I'm on my way to Belleoram and I want to get back before dark."

Nellie glanced out the window. "The fog's hanging outside the harbour like a witch's cloak. How will you know where to steer that two-masted schooner of yours all alone?"

"Should have a man to help ya," Harry said. "It ain't safe going alone."

The doctor chuckled. "Now don't you two start on me. Mrs. Fitzgerald lectures me about the same thing every day. And I tell her every time, a boat is the fastest and most convenient way to get to all the communities in Fortune Bay. Snowstorms and windy seas haven't prevented me from attending to my patients."

NELLIE CARRIED A CLOTH bag containing only a fruitcake, the wide strap slung over one shoulder. Her shawl hung loosely around her shoulders, as the day had warmed up. She looked toward Burke's Cove and saw the *Marion*. The poles sticking up reminded her of a skeleton, naked without their white sails, like bones stripped of skin. A knot twisted in her stomach. Schooners had been a familiar sight all her life, yet she'd never remembered them that way before. The stench of dead fish drifted across the water as the men loaded the ship with capelin. *Little fish to catch big fish.* The idea seemed ironic to her, yet she couldn't explain why.

The jingle of a bell over a door broke Nellie's concentration. She'd reached Young's General Store without realizing it.

"Good day," Ned Noseworthy said, and sniffed, a habit repeated at the end of every sentence since he'd broken his nose as a boy.

Dave LaCroix came out behind him. "I'm stocking up on Bull's Eyes," he said, sucking on the hard candy made from molasses and brown sugar.

"Ned, how's Frances doing?" Nellie said.

"Dr. Fitzgerald says she might not have to go to the sanatorium in St. John's after all. My missus is some happy she can stay home."

"That's good news. Tell Frances I'll be 'round to see her in a day or so."

"Will do."

Dave tipped his hat to Nellie and ambled down the street with Ned.

Annie Cluett stepped out of Young's store as Ned said his farewell. "Ned's a fine man," she said, "but his constant sniffing drives me nuts. Don't know how Frances stands it."

"Harry says the men don't mind."

"That's because he's too busy fishing to talk." Annie looked toward Burke's Cove, where the *Marion* rocked on the gentle waves. A shadow fell across her face.

"Tommy and Harry leave tomorrow." Annie seemed to be talking to herself. Her husband, Robert, died in a blizzard at twenty-one years old, trapped on an ice floe while seal hunting. His shipmates found him three days later, frozen stiff, clutching Annie's picture to his chest. Annie blinked and turned back to Nellie. "Them boys'll make it back. Don't you worry none."

"That goes for you, too," Nellie said.

Annie's dark eyes watered, yet no tears fell. "I loves your man and Tommy like they were me own."

Nellie reached for her hand. "You're the only mother poor Tommy ever knew."

Annie cleared her throat. "You heard the good news about Tommy?" she said.

Nellie grinned. "Harry said it's supposed to be a secret."

Annie smiled. "I'm tickled down to my toes that Harry's finally come to his senses, too."

Chapter 3

NELLIE WATCHED HARRY SLEEP. She was tempted to wake him, to plead one last time for him to stay home. Her hand caressed his cheek, the contact softer than a feather's touch. He stirred but didn't wake. The nights were cold for late spring and Nellie pulled the cotton quilts up to her chin. Harry rolled over onto his back. The lines grooved into his forehead and the toughened, windblown skin, telltale signs that marked every fishermen, were already etched on Harry's face.

Something scratched against the window. Nellie got out of bed to check it out. A branch from the hundred-year-old maple tree next to the house swept across the glass. Reflected on the harbour water, the full moon looked like a giant snowball floating on the surface. Nellie shivered. The cold ate its way deep inside her.

"Love, why aren't you in bed?" Harry leaned on an elbow.

"You know I can't sleep before you head out to sea."

Harry lifted the quilts. "You look frozen. Come back to bed."

Nellie didn't move. "Is Ike Jones a rum-runner?"

"Not as far as I know. Why are you asking?"

"Maybe he gypped the French captain and that's why there's so much bad blood between them."

"Captain Ike never smuggled rum or anything else the times I sailed with him. Haven't heard any rumours of that sort, either."

A scream shattered the peaceful night.

Harry sprang from bed and rushed out of the room.

Joe and Sam were at the door to their room when their parents ran by. "What's wrong?" Sam asked. "Is Bessie okay?"

"She's likely having the Old Hag again," Nellie said.

All four hurried to Bessie's room. She moaned, the sound muffled, like someone was holding a hand over her mouth. Her chest heaved and her nightdress was soaked in sweat. Moonlight splayed across her face, giving her a ghostly pallor.

"Dr. Fitzgerald said not to startle her awake," Nellie said.

Harry quietly approached the bed and gently stroked his daughter's hand. "Sweetie," he whispered, so softly no one else heard him. "It's Pa." Bessie's chest continued to heave. Harry sat on the bed. "It's okay, sweetie. Pa's here."

Bessie's eyes shot open and she bolted into her father's arms. "Pa . . . I . . . I was awful scared." Her breath came in short gasps.

Harry rocked his daughter like he used to when she had the colic. "You had a bad dream. It's over now."

Bessie sobbed into his chest. "The . . . hooded man . . . again."

Harry stroked her thick curls. "He ain't real, Bessie. He can't hurt you."

Bessie gulped to catch her breath. Her voice broke into a hiccup. "Marie was with me on the wharf. We were making a French flag for school."

"Don't dwell on it, sweetie," Harry said.

"The man touched my shoulder this time and . . ." Bessie tightened her grip on her father. "It made me cold all over. I . . . I saw his eyes . . . They were green in the middle . . . and blood red around the edges," she said between hiccups.

Harry looked down at Bessie as tears cascaded down her face, like water over a falls. He kissed her forehead. "Try to put it out of your head."

Bessie could not be consoled. "He grabbed Marie and dragged her to the edge of the wharf," she continued. "I tried to run for help . . . but my feet wouldn't move."

Harry lifted his daughter off the bed. "The Old Hag won't trouble you any more tonight," he said. "You'll sleep with your ma and me."

Bessie clung to her father, her arms wound tightly around his neck as he carried her down the hall. Joe and Sam went back to bed.

Bessie was nestled close to Harry when Nellie got in bed. "Think about Marie's birthday party next week and all the fun you'll have," Harry said.

Bessie clasped her hands under her cheek. "Mr. Jones said he's gonna have a clown. Ma's gonna bake a chocolate cake."

"The best one ever," Nellie said.

"Pa, do you like catching fish on the Grand Banks?"

"It's back-breaking work," Harry said. "Why?"

"Joe told Marie it was heaps of fun. I told her that ain't true."

"You're right about that, sweetie."

"He'll be gone a lot like you are," she said and hiccupped.

Nellie saw the sad look in her husband's eyes. "Bessie, love," she said, "the silly Old Hag's got you upset."

Bessie nestled between her parents and relaxed.

"She's settled back into a quiet sleep," Harry whispered over his daughter's head after a while. "Her poor little heart was hammering."

NELLIE LAY AWAKE ALL night and watched the stars dim as night turned into day. Dressed by sunrise, she checked one more time to make sure Bessie was sleeping soundly and went downstairs.

Nellie followed her usual morning routine. She brought in wood for the stove, brewed tea, and started breakfast. She whipped up some pancakes, Bessie's favourite meal. The first batch was browning in the pan when Harry sidled up to the bowl, dipped his finger in, and popped a blob of pancake mix into his mouth.

She rapped his knuckles with a spoon. "Save some for the rest of us."

"I put Bessie back in her own bed," Harry said. "She didn't wake. Mother Patrick's right. Our little girl has a wild imagination that works overtime."

The back door opened and Tom walked in. "Howdy, folks," he said. He held a tiny parcel out to Nellie. "Happy birthday."

"At least one of the Myles brothers remembered it," she said with mock annoyance.

Harry left the kitchen and was back before Nellie could ask where he was going. "Here you go, love," he said, and produced a box wrapped in fancy, flowered paper.

Nellie opened the box, taking special care not to tear the paper. Her eyes feasted on a white lace shawl. Her mouth formed a perfect "O." "It's gorgeous."

"You didn't think I saw you admire it in the magazine at the shop, did ya? Mrs. Young helped me with the order."

Tom gestured to his gift on the table. Inside, Nellie found a silver angel with glittering white wings and a silver halo. "Annie picked out a brooch to match the shawl," Tom said.

"Annie sure has good taste. I love it."

"Stay for breakfast," Harry said. "It'll give the youngsters a chance to see you before we go."

"Can't. Annie's cooking a load of eggs and bacon. She'll think I'm sick if I don't finish them off."

Nellie kissed Tom on the cheek. He blushed and scurried away with a nod to Harry.

Breakfast was like any other. Bessie, recovered from the ordeal the night before, dived into the pancakes. Sam ate without saying much. Joe complained about school.

Bessie finished first and grabbed her school books from the chair by the door. "I'll miss ya, Pa." She said the same words every time he went fishing. "I loves you with my whole heart."

"Me too," Harry said.

Sam picked up his books. "So long, Pa."

Joe glared at his books. "I wishes I was going fishing with ya."

Nellie pointed to the door. "Go," she said, "or you'll be late again."

Harry piled dishes into the pan. "He'll come 'round to our way of thinking, don't worry."

Nellie frowned. "I finished knitting four pairs of socks and packed them with your three pairs of long johns."

"We'll only be gone a week or so, love."

Nellie added soap to the dishwater. “It’s best to be prepared.” A plate slipped from her hands into the soapy water. She turned to Harry. “I’m relying on you to keep Ike Jones clear of that French captain.”

Harry looked at her, his blue eyes bright, serious. “Have I ever let you down before?”

Nellie smiled and washed the last of the dishes.

THE *MARION*, A BLACK schooner anchored at Burke’s Cove across the harbour from St. Jacques, possessed seven two-man dories. Harry’s dorymate whenever he sailed on the *Marion* was Fred McEvoy, a seasoned fisherman the same age as Tom. The two men smoked cigarettes while they waited for the rest of the crew. “How’s Dottie?” Harry said.

“The baby’s not coming for a month or more,” Fred replied.

“We’ll be back in plenty of time. Women likes their men around for the first one.”

“Don’t want no trouble on this trip,” Fred said. He swung and twisted his arm back and forth. “It’s a bit stiff yet. A broken arm don’t help a fisherman none.”

Harry puffed out a cloud of smoke. “We’ll have to keep an eye to old Ike.” The captain had just turned forty.

Frank Fewer limped toward Harry and Tom, Sid Davies at his side.

“How’s the cough, Sid?” Harry asked.

“Dr. Fitzgerald gave me a tongue banging . . .” Sid began. He coughed, his voice raspy . . . “for not staying home.”

Frank massaged his thigh. “Aches awful today. Bad weather’s on the way.” There wasn’t a cloud in the sky, but Harry had never known Frank’s leg to be mistaken. “By the way, Harry, you dropped this in the graveyard yesterday.”

Frank held out a small, wooden seal sculpture that fit neatly into his hand. Harry’s father had whittled it from the branch of a maple tree on his final trip home from fishing. The flippers were outstretched when he first got it, but the right one had cracked off during a soccer game when he was a boy. Uncle Joe had varnished it after that and advised his nephew to leave the fragile sculpture in his room. Harry refused and continued to carry it with him at all times. He rubbed a thumb along the broken edge, now smooth with time. Twenty-five years later, he treasured the object as much as he had as a boy.

"Thanks," Harry said. "It must've dropped out of my pocket when I pulled my cap out."

"Glad I found it for ya." Every crew member understood the sculpture's significance for Harry.

More of the crew began to arrive. The single men had their mothers fretting over them while the married men were accompanied by their wives, some carrying infants and towing toddlers.

Harry stubbed out a cigarette butt with his heel. He saw Ned Noseworthy saunter over to Clive Pope, his dory partner. "Clive, my son. Been here long?" He sniffed.

Clive looked at him with raised eyebrows. "You knows darn well my son's name is Ben."

Ned shouted into Clive's ear. "I asked if *you've* been here long." *Sniff.*

Harry chuckled and lit up another cigarette.

"Look," Fred McEvoy said. "Simon Whelan and his new missus are here. She don't look too happy about his leaving four days after the wedding."

Harry looked at the curly-haired youth. "Can't say as I blames her."

"Speak up, will ya?" Clive's voice carried over the crowd.

Harry smoked two more cigarettes before Tom showed up with Fred's wife. He helped her around a stack of lobster crates. She held a hand to the small of her back.

Fred was glad to see her, but he was concerned. "Dottie, you shouldn't have walked all the way here. Are you all right?"

She rubbed her ripening baby bulge. "Everything's fine. I wanted to see you off."

Annie and Nellie came up behind Dottie. "Don't fret, b'y," Annie said. "We'll make sure your missus gets home in one piece."

"Thanks, Mrs. Cluett. I appreciate that."

Harry clapped a hand on Fred's shoulder. "Every man's nervous about the first baby."

The rest of the fishermen arrived. Sixteen crew in all. Family members clustered around their men to say goodbye and to wish them a good catch. Nellie listened to the hum of voices. There was no excitement or fear. This was a job dating back centuries, a job which every man and woman was resigned to accept. An outburst of laughter close by drew Nellie's attention back to the small gathering. She smiled.

Annie held Harry's face in her big hands. "You listen good to me, Harry Myles. I'm depending on you to watch out for yourself and your baby brother." Tom turned redder than a ripe tomato and lowered his head. "You hear me?" Annie continued. Harry, his head trapped in a vice grip and his jaw locked tight, managed to blink, which Annie accepted as a yes. "Good," she said, slobbering his cheek with kisses.

Harry massaged his jaw when Annie released him. Fred nudged him in the ribs. "I wouldn't want to get on the wrong side of her," he whispered.

Annie moved to Tom. "Tommy, my son, listen to Harry and stay out of trouble." Tom stood still and endured a kiss on both cheeks. Without another word, Annie took Dottie's hand and marched away.

"Bye, Fred," Dottie called with a wave.

Ike Jones appeared on the *Marion*'s deck. A dark cloud rolled over the sun. Nellie stared at the captain. *The only good thing about his going is having Marie stay with us.*

"Have to go, love," Harry said.

Nellie's stomach churned. "Please stay safe." She hugged him close.

"Love, you're shaking like fish on dry land. I promise you'll see me soon." He gently pulled away. "Don't worry."

Nellie grabbed his arm and pressed her mother's crystal rosary beads into his hand. "Keep these close to you until you're back with me."

Harry put the beads in his pocket. "I will, love. Right next to Pa's seal." He gave her one last smile and hurried to get aboard ship.

"See ya, Nellie," Tom said, and followed his brother.

As each man boarded the schooner, family members drifted away until Nellie was alone on the wharf. She'd seen Harry off countless times before and had left before he was off the wharf. Today, her heart wouldn't allow her to budge. The sails unfurled one by one, turning the skeleton ship into a majestic Arabian sheik dressed in his finest robes. *Such beauty,* she thought. *Wealth for a few, food for many, and death for the unsuspecting.*

The wind slapped at the sails as they billowed out. The ship creaked and groaned, unhappy with being disturbed, as she made her way from the dock. Clouds swarmed across the sky and Nellie felt the heat leave her skin.

She saw Captain Ike at the wheel and knew he was bellowing out orders to the men. The *Marion* picked up speed and sailed across the harbour for the open seas. Nellie opened her mouth to call out to Harry, but hesitated. "It's too late," she murmured to the wind. "He'll never hear me now."

"Such a graceful lady," Mother Patrick said. She stood beside Nellie, gazing at the *Marion*.

Nellie jumped.

"Didn't mean to startle you, child."

The *Marion* sped around the bend and out of sight.

Nellie sighed and looked at the nun. "I best get home and get dinner on the table."

"I thought you'd like some company on the walk back."

"Thank you," Nellie said. Arm in arm, the two women started toward St. Jacques.

Chapter 4

HARRY YAWNED, THREW OFF his blankets, and sat on the edge of the bunk. His toes bunched up on the cold, wooden floor. Tom's bunk was empty, he had gotten up an hour earlier to fix breakfast. Harry looked toward the galley in the after part of the forecastle and saw his brother shovel coal into the stove. A rail surrounded the stove to keep pots and kettles from rolling onto the floor in rough weather. The smell of freshly baked bread drifted through the forecastle and woke the men as effectively as a church bell.

"Homemade bread," Ned Noseworthy said. "What a treat!" *Sniff.*

"Right," Tom called out. "I hope you all appreciates my extra hard work. There's plenty of hard bread if you don't." Bags of hard bread were stored aboard schooners to replace normal bread if they ran short of flour.

The crew hopped out of their bunks and dressed quickly.

Fred walked into the galley. "Hope there's time for seconds before we dock," he said.

"What's that about your socks?" Clive Pope said, following him to the galley.

The men devoured every egg, every slice of bacon, and several loaves of bread.

Simon Whelan nibbled at his food. Clive tousled his thick locks. "You'll be home with your young bride soon enough, lad," he shouted.

Simon blushed. "I ain't got me sea legs yet, that's all," he said, and lowered his head. The crew had just finished when the helmsman called out that the French island of St. Pierre was in sight. Harry hurried up on deck and looked for the *Fleur de Lys,* the French beam trawler. Ships from the United States, France, and Newfoundland crowded the port.

"She's there," Tom said, coming to stand beside his brother, "anchored next to the *Sherman*." The *Sherman* was also owned by the Burke family.

"Our luck's run out," Harry groaned. "We're gonna have to anchor next to the trawler."

Captain Ike walked out of his cabin and went up to the wheel. "I'll take over, Mr. McCarthy," he said to the helmsman.

"What's the matter?" Gordy said, moving away from the wheel.

Ike's gaze stayed fixed on the trawler, and every man's eyes were on the captain. "Nothing at all."

"Why's everyone gaping at the captain?" Mick Drake asked.

Harry turned to Mick, who was his own age but whose hair had turned white in his early thirties, earning him a nickname. "Whitey, the captain never docks the ship."

Tom rubbed his scar. "Why is he doing it now?"

The *Marion* neared the side of the French trawler. A handful of men gathered next to Harry and Tom. "We're cutting awful close," Ned remarked. *Sniff.*

"Lord dying Jesus," Fred said, "we're gonna hit the trawler!"

Every man aboard the *Marion* held his breath. The schooner glided in, aft of the trawler.

"Maybe we'll make it," Tom said.

Clive whacked him on the arm. "This ain't the time to be thinking about baking."

A sound like crumbling bricks surged through the air. Mick gawked at Fred, his face the same colour as his hair. "We scraped the steel side of the trawler! Did he do it on purpose?"

Fred ran a hand over his forehead as if he were in pain. "The captain never made a mistake like that before."

Harry gritted his teeth. "Why'd he do a fool thing like that? Ike's well able to dock this schooner with his feet if he wanted." He looked up at the wheel and caught Ike and Pierre Maurice, the captain of the French trawler, staring at each other. Ike's expression was unreadable, but Maurice's eyes had narrowed to slits.

The trawler's crew rushed to the side of their ship. "*Vous êtes fou,* idiot!" a blond-haired man yelled at Ike.

A boy not much older than Harry's son Joe shook his fists. "Imbecile!" he shouted. Others joined in the insults and made rude gestures at the *Marion*'s crew.

"You don't need to understand French to know they're shouting insults at us," Dave LaCroix said, chewing down on a Bull's Eye.

"Shut your traps!" Gordy McCarthy shouted back.

"Yeah!" Billy Evans yelled. "Don't stick your fingers up at us." He slapped his backside. "Kiss that."

Tom glared at the seventeen-year-old. "Young as you are, Billy, I didn't think you were that stupid."

"Want another go at us?" Gordy McCarthy flung across the deck, his freckled nose flaring. "We pounded the shit out of you bunch last time."

"Take it easy, men," Captain Ike called out. After a bout of muttering and side glances at the trawler's crew, the schoonermen settled down.

"What happened?" Harry asked the captain as he headed for his cabin.

"My hand slipped on the wheel," Ike said without looking at him.

HARRY, TOM, AND FRED lazed on their bunks after supper. The other men sat at the tables playing cards. Sid Davies coughed deep in his chest. "Don't know what Captain Ike was thinking today," he said when he caught his breath.

"It was an accident," Fred replied. "The captain is not stun enough to start another row on purpose."

"Sure he would," Gordy said. "We licked the scrawny Frenchies real good last time. He figures we'll do it again."

"Nothing's stopping me for going for a swally later," Dave La-

Croix said, stuffing a candy into his mouth. "I needs a bit of relaxation."

Ned leaned his elbows on the wooden table. *Sniff.* "Where's Captain Ike been hiding all day?"

Frank Fewer limped back to his bunk. "He ain't stirred outside his cabin. Sent me and young Billy Evans ashore for some supplies."

"Guaranteed he'll be at the *Hôtel de France* tonight," Earle Fiander said. "He never misses." Harry watched him deal the cards with his three-fingered right hand and remembered Nellie's speech to Joe concerning the hazards of fishing on the Grand Banks.

"I have my doubts," Dave said, crunching on another candy. "He's riled up Captain Maurice something fierce this time."

Gordy McCarthy's freckled face turned toward the bunks. "Are you fellas going ashore later?"

"I'm warning ya," Tom said, "if trouble starts I'm staying clear of it."

"Me too," Simon Whelan said. "Lilly will have my head if I gets hurt."

Billy Evans ran the ace of hearts into Earle. "Ma said your mother-in-law warned you about getting drunk on this trip."

Earle wacked Billy over the head with his hat. "That there was s'posed to be a secret."

"Some secret," Mick said with a wink at the men. "She woke up every soul in Boxey warning you."

Earle beat the ace of hearts with the jack and hauled in the cards with his three-pronged hand. "Shut your trap, Whitey Drake. I have a few dandy yarns to report on you after your trip to St. John's last month."

Mick slapped Billy over the head. "Earle's right. You don't spill secrets."

Everyone in the forecastle laughed.

When the round of one hundred and twenties ended, Billy Evans threw down his cards. "Time to get spruced up for a night out."

The men hummed and whistled while they got ready. Harry ran a comb through his mass of blond curls. Captain Ike always went ashore with the men, but he wasn't on deck when they came up. A light glowed from under his cabin door.

"Guess he's staying put for the night," Harry said, relief evident in his voice.

The sun had set by the time they reached the *Hôtel de France*. The bar was crowded with men from all the other ships, and a steady blend of French and English words bounced around the room. Regular customers whenever they were in St. Pierre, the *Marion*'s crew were served their usual black rum and water. Harry spotted several men from the beam trawler at a corner table. They stopped in mid-conversation and stared at the *Marion*'s crew. Harry felt the hairs on his neck bristle.

"Who you looking at?" Gordy called across the bar.

"Ignore them," Harry said. "We ain't here for no fight." He sneaked a glance at the corner table. "We did scrape their ship, whether it was an accident or not."

"That's right," Tom said, eyeing the bald man who'd pulled a knife on him the trip before. "Another swally or two and I'm out of here."

Cigarette smoke formed a haze in the room as the night wore on. "Don't understand why the French captain ain't here," Fred said. "Captain Ike neither. Right puzzling, that is."

The door opened. Harry tensed up.

The new arrival nodded at their table. "Night, lads," a fisherman from the schooner *Sherman* said and joined his mates at the bar.

A string of laughter broke out at the beam trawler's table. A black-haired man at the head of the table raised his hands and placed them on an imaginary steering wheel. With an exaggerated expression, he mimicked the sound of a ship docking. The room grew quiet. Harry looked around. The trawler's table had a captive audience. The "incident" had travelled from ship to ship faster than a bullet. The imaginary *Marion* pulled alongside the imaginary trawler with a noise that closely imitated a long, drawn-out scrape. The French crew split their sides with laughter and pointed toward the *Marion*'s table.

"Who do them arseholes think they are?" Gordy said. He slammed down his glass and pushed back his chair.

Harry grabbed his arm. "Leave them be. Fighting ain't gonna prove anything."

The French trawlermen continued to jeer.

"Besides," Tom said, "this ain't got nothing to do with us. Captain Ike docked the ship, not you."

"He's our skipper," Gordy said, and pulled free of Harry's grip.

Earle grabbed Gordy by the collar of his coat and pulled him close. "I ain't ever run from a fight," he said, "but I ain't ever been the cause of one, neither."

Frank planked a hand on the helmsman's shoulder. "You got that, Freckles?"

Gordy grumbled and gulped down the last of his drink.

By midnight, neither Captain Ike nor Captain Maurice had shown up. Harry downed his drink. "Boys, I'm off to the ship," he said.

"Me too," Tom said. "I have to be up before you lot."

Fred strolled out with the brothers. "I wonder why Captain Maurice wasn't in the hotel?"

"He's likely home with his family," Tom said.

The three men turned down a side street, a shortcut to the wharf. Harry came to a full stop. "Do you hear that?" he asked.

"What?" Tom and Fred said at the same time.

"Sounds like a brawl." Harry pointed to an attached house at the end of the street. "There's two men. Hold on! That looks like Captain Ike."

"I can't make out who's in the doorway," Tom said, and took a step closer.

Harry hauled him back. "It's Captain Maurice. Must be his house. What's Ike doing there?"

"Cantankerous old fool," Tom said. "He can't leave well enough alone."

Captain Maurice shouted at Ike and shoved him off the front step. Ike stumbled back, lost his balance, and landed on his backside. The French captain babbled on in French, then laughed out loud. Ike scrambled to his feet and grabbed Captain Maurice by the sweater, nearly lifting the much smaller man off his feet. Ike spat out something in French, twisting Maurice's sweater by the neck until he gagged.

"First I knew Ike could *parlez* French," Tom said. "Did you fellas know?" Harry and Fred shrugged.

Captain Maurice punched Ike in the stomach and he doubled over in a fit of coughing. His hat fell off and landed in a patch of mud.

"The captain needs help," Fred said. "What should we do?"

"It's one on one," Tom said. "That's a fair fight in my book."

Ike recovered and landed a blow on Captain Maurice's jaw. The older man toppled back into the closed door. He growled like a wounded animal, yelled at Ike, then stormed inside. The wooden house shook when he slammed the door.

Ike straightened his ruffled jacket, snatched up his hat from the ground, and plunked it on his head. Harry, Tom, and Fred ducked into a doorway to avoid being seen when their captain looked up and down the street.

"Fred, your sister-in-law's from here. What did they say?" Tom said.

"Eloise gave up trying to teach me and Seth the French lingo ages ago." Fred scratched his chin. "One thing stuck in me head, though. Eloise says it every time Seth comes home loaded. Her hands start waving a mile a minute." He chuckled. "Not to mention her tongue."

Tom tapped him on the shoulder. "Are you gonna tell us what he said?"

Fred's expression became solemn. "'*Je vais vous tuer.*' I'll kill you."

Nellie's bad feeling thundered through Harry's head. "Good thing we're pulling out at dawn," he said.

"Eloise gave me a letter for her parents. They'll want me to stay the night. I'll see you boys at first light," said Fred.

Harry and Tom continued on their way. "Ike really hates Maurice," Tom said. "First he scrapes the trawler on purpose, then he shows up at his house. What's it all about?"

A nerve ticked in Harry's jaw. "Nellie was right to worry. Ike's got no damn right to drag the whole crew into his dirty affairs. I've half a mind to quit right now."

"You won't abandon the crew," Tom said. "Us Myles men keeps our word."

The door to the captain's cabin was slightly ajar when they went aboard. Ike was writing at his desk by candlelight. "Hope he's not planning on causing more trouble," Harry said.

The brothers undressed in the dark and climbed into their bunks. Almost immediately, Tom's snores resonated throughout the room. Harry reached for his jacket and took out Nellie's rosary beads. "Night, love," he said, and lay them next to the seal sculpture under his pillow.

Harry smelled pipe smoke and looked down at Skit Kettle's bunk.

"Didn't mean to wake ya," Skit said. He puffed out a cloud of smoke that reminded Harry of pine trees. "Ike left an hour after you fellas. How'd it go?"

"He never showed up at the hotel." Harry didn't mention the fight at Maurice's house.

Skit lay down his pipe. "I've sailed with many a captain in my forty years on the sea. Never met a man so hell-bent on trouble as Ike." He hauled the blankets up to his chin and looked across at the sleeping men. "The Hodders stayed in because they weren't in no mood for a brawl." John and Henry Hodder, first cousins, had worked under Ike many times before and knew his moods.

Harry closed his eyes and had just dozed off when shouts from the dock roused him. He recognized Mick Drake's voice. "You Frenchies couldn't beat your way out of a paper bag!"

"Whitey, shut up or . . ." A cough cut off the voice.

"We have enough trouble with the *Fleur de Lys* without you adding to it," Clive growled.

"A bunch of old maids fights better than ye!" Gordy McCarthy laughed.

Harry put his hands behind his head. "Will Gordy ever learn to keep his trap shut?" he muttered under his breath. Minutes later, a crowd of drunken men staggered into the sleeping quarters. Tom, now fully awake, shot up in bed. Dave LaCroix and Gordy Evans had bloody noses. Most of the others sported grazed knuckles. Mick Drake massaged his jaw.

"What happened?" Harry asked, although he already knew the answer.

"We had a free-for-all with the French crew," Gordy boasted. "They never shut their mouths about what Captain Ike did, so we shut their mouths for them."

"We gave 'em a right beating, too," Billy Evans said.

Harry sighed. Had he been so reckless at this boy's age?

"That'll show them not to mess with us," Simon Whelan said. Blood oozed from a gash on his forehead.

Tom looked sideways at him. "Your new missus might not agree."

Simon blushed.

John Hodder rolled over. "Time some of you men grew up."

"I agree," Henry Hodder said, his eyes on Gordy.

Groans and moans escaped the crew as they crawled into their bunks.

THEY WOKE AT THE usual time, although they were much slower in getting out of bed than the previous morning. Ike ate with the men, joking and acting like nothing had happened the night before. Harry, Tom, and Fred gave each other a look but said nothing.

Ike rose from the table. "Hoist the sails," he said, and went up to his cabin.

The men set about the task. Harry listened to the creaking of the ship as the sails opened out. The anchor chain churned, grating as it lifted the anchor from the bottom of the harbour.

Gordy stood at the steering wheel. "Ready to set sail," he called out.

Harry turned to go below deck when he saw Ike leave his cabin with a musket. He stood motionless while Ike raised the gun and fired it across the bow of the *Fleur de Lys*, where Captain Maurice stood talking with a crewmate. The French captain looked toward the sound just as the shot flew inches from his face and slammed into the door of the captain's cabin, a foot above his head. Fishermen from both ships gaped at Ike.

Harry crossed the deck. "Captain, why?"

"I've sent Captain Maurice a message. One he needs to carefully consider." Ike turned and went back to his cabin.

The *Marion*'s men murmured among themselves, shock stamped on every face. No one replied to the threats and curses from the crew of the *Fleur de Lys*.

Fred hurried over to Harry. "B'y, that was some show of defiance," he said.

Harry looked toward the captain's cabin. "One I hopes we don't live to regret."

GORDY STEERED THE SCHOONER away from the port and the sounds of growls and catcalls from the French trawler. It wasn't until St. Pierre was a faint shadow that Harry felt the tension drain out of his body. An eerie silence descended on the men as they baited the trawls.

Tom came up from below deck. A cool wind snaked around his neck and down his back. He buttoned his jacket and turned up the collar.

The wind whipped at Harry's hat. He looked up at the sky. Black clouds gathered in the distance. "A bad storm's brewing," he said. As if Mother Nature had heard the prediction, the dark clouds rumbled closer. Lightning bolts flared and seemed to reach down to the *Marion*. A *tap, tap* sounded as raindrop after raindrop spattered onto the deck, until it grew into a torrent that pounded the boards and bit into the skin.

Tom blew on his hands to warm them. "I'd love to be lazing at home by my fireplace with a hot toddy."

"Steady as she goes," Ike roared over the wind. Thunder boomed into the air like a discharged cannon. White specks floated on the horizon. "Icebergs ahead."

"That's all we needs," Harry muttered.

The ship lilted. Harry and Tom grabbed hold of the rail. A wave soaked the two men. The schooner heaved, swaying from side to side as it beared down on the icebergs.

Gordy gripped the steering wheel. "Captain, them bergs are awful big." One, the size of a horse and cart, walloped the side of the schooner. She rattled from stem to stern. The wheel slipped through Gordy's hands and spun around until it was almost a blur. The men below lost their footing. Arms flailing, they slid like slippery fish over the wet boards, groping for anything to hang onto. Gordy and Ike grabbed the wheel and steadied the schooner. She edged forward, chunks of ice chomping at her.

"All hands okay?" Ike shouted down.

"A-okay," Dave LaCroix yelled after a quick inspection around the ship.

"Captain, there's too many bergs," Gordy roared, his hands and arms strained. "We needs to drop sails and wait out the storm." His hat had blown off and his red hair was plastered to his head.

A wave slopped over Ike and sent him crashing to the deck. Gordy held the wheel tight with cold, stiff fingers. "Captain, you okay?"

Ike struggled to his feet, swaying with the roll of the ship. "Never mind about me."

Gordy swerved to avoid an iceberg as big as a house. "That bastard near did us in!" he bellowed.

Sid Davies peered over the side through rain that stabbed at his eyes like tips of daggers. A dark shadow sliced through the rough sea. "Is that a ship?" He coughed out yellow mucus.

Harry spit salty water out of his mouth. "Don't see any sails. Could be a trawler."

"It's closing in mighty fast," Skit said. "Hope it's not a German warship." Another wave sunk the *Marion* low in the water, followed by two bigger ones. Icebergs packed around the schooner. Billy stumbled into Harry and clung to the rail, his face ashen.

"Nothing to fret over," Harry said. "We've tackled worse conditions than this before."

Lightning flashed. Thunder boomed. The mystery ship slipped closer. *Please let it be a friendly one*, Harry thought.

Billy licked his lips. "I ain't ever sailed in weather this bad."

Harry gripped the young man's shoulder in a display of confidence. "You'll be all right."

"Skit," Tom screamed. "Watch out!" A sail snapped and fell across the deck. The tail end knocked Skit on the side of the head. The pipe dangled from the corner of his mouth as he dropped to his knees.

Harry spun around to see Tom reach for the injured man, but he was yanked off his feet by a rush of water. Before Harry could react, another sail crumpled like a piece of paper over Ron and John Hodder. A scream rang out.

Mick Drake hauled Skit to his feet. "All hands to the dories," he yelled.

Earle Fiander pulled Ron from under a sail. "Too late for that," he said.

Harry heard a boom, then a deafening groan like steel buckling, as he and Billy were thrown forward. Nellie's rosary beads tumbled from his pocket and washed into the ocean on a wave.

Chapter 5

JOE, SAM, BESSIE, AND Marie chewed on egg sandwiches. "Pa's been gone for eight days now," Marie said. "I misses him."

Nellie poured tea for each of the children. "He'll be home soon," she said with a forced smile.

"I misses my pa, too," Bessie said.

Nellie put the kettle back on the stove. The weather had grown cold and wet the day after the *Marion* departed. Today the temperature had dropped to forty-five degrees. She looked out the window, an unbreakable habit, before stepping away from the stove. Patches of fog lined the entrance to the harbour. Halfway across, a dory bobbed on the rough waves. Dr. Fitzgerald cast a fishing line into the water, and Nellie knew that a genuine smile would be softening his features. He enjoyed outdoor life, particularly fishing and yachting. Age hadn't interfered with either. The fog suddenly thickened and swallowed up the dory, partially concealing the doctor from view. Nellie wasn't worried.

Not until the whistle of a steamer sounded across the harbour.

A steamship cleared the rocks and entered the harbour on a direct course for the doctor. Shrouded in a thin fog, his boat blended in with the grey water. The doctor seemed oblivious to anything but his pipe and fishing line, the latter of which dangled over the side of the dory. The steamer chugged closer. Nellie's heart thumped. "Holy Mary Mother of God!" she cried out. "It's gonna ram him."

The words were barely out when the steamer slammed into the

front of the dory. Wood shattered and the doctor was lost from sight. "Joe, Sam," Nellie said. "Come with me. A steamer's run over Dr. Fitzgerald." Bessie and Marie followed them to the wharf, running all out. Joe jumped in a dory. Sam untied it, scurried in, and grabbed the oars.

Dr. Fitzgerald, a strong swimmer, yet burdened with warm clothing and rubber boats, struggled to stay afloat. His head sank below the surface. Bessie and Marie screamed. Nellie held her breath until he resurfaced.

"We're coming," Sam yelled, and pushed off. He rowed as fast as he could. "Hold on!"

"Bessie," Nellie said. "Go get a blanket." Bessie bounded up to the house and was back before her brother had rowed a few feet.

The steamer's captain lowered a lifeboat. It splashed down close to the dory's wreckage. Shards of wood floated around the doctor. "Not likely," he said, ignoring the rescue craft.

"Are you crazy?" a voice boomed through a horn from the steamer's deck. "Get in the dinghy."

"I have no intention of being rescued by you lot," Dr. Fitzgerald shouted back.

Sam pulled up next to him. "Hang on," he said, and steadied the boat while Joe helped the doctor out of the water.

"Thank you, young man," Dr. Fitzgerald said, sitting on the seat next to Joe. "For a moment there I thought my Maker was ready to take me."

Sam swung the dory around and headed back to shore. "Why didn't you get in the steamer's dinghy?" he asked, a little breathless. Sweat covered his brow.

Dr. Fitzgerald's white hair stuck to his forehead. He pushed it away. "I refuse to be beholden to the very people who ran me over."

Joe gaped at him. "You'd rather drown than let them help you?"

"It's a matter of pride, boy." He laid a firm hand on Joe's arm. "I'm glad you and Sam showed up in the nick of time."

Dr. Fitzgerald climbed onto the wharf without assistance. Nellie heard his teeth chatter and wrapped a blanket around him. "Best get you warmed up before you catch your death."

His lips had a blue tinge to them. "My dear madam," he said with a wink, "physicians never get sick."

"My dear doctor," Nellie returned, "there's always a first time for everything." She shooed the children off to school and led the dripping man up the hill. She hung his clothes to dry by the fireplace and gave him a scalding hot cup of tea while she filled a bowl to the brim with soup.

The doctor sipped the tea after adding three spoonfuls of sugar and a hint of milk. "That hit the spot," he said. The steam condensed on his nose.

Nellie sat down at the table, drumming her fingers and staring into space.

The doctor looked at her for a long moment. "Want to tell me what's bothering you?"

Nellie's eyes watered. "I feel in my heart that my Harry isn't coming home ever again."

Dr. Fitzgerald patted her hand. "Now, now, my dear. Don't think like that. They're supposed to be out for at least a week."

"Before Harry left, I saw him on—"

The back door flew open and smacked against the wall. "Doctor," Joe said with urgency, "come to the convent quick. Dottie McEvoy is having her baby."

"Goodness. She's a bit early. Run to my house for my medical bag and bring it to the convent," he said, whipping off the blanket.

Nellie accompanied the doctor, surprised he could maintain such a rapid pace.

Dottie lay on the bed in Mother Patrick's bedroom. Annie Cluett wiped her face with a wet cloth. The nun sat on the other side uttering words of encouragement. "Everyone out of the room except Annie," Dr. Fitzgerald said as Joe ran in with the medical bag.

Nellie and Mother Patrick paced up and down the hall outside the door. "Dottie brought me raisin tea buns," the nun said. "We were having such a lovely chat. The next thing I knew, there was water all around her feet."

Dottie cried out, long and shrill.

"Oh Sacred Heart," Mother Patrick said, and blessed herself.

Dottie screamed.

"Gentle Mother of God!" Annie's voice reached into the hallway. "I don't believe this."

Nellie sprang to her feet and knocked on the door. "Are Dottie and the baby all right?"

There was a moment's pause before Annie answered. "Come in and see for yourself."

DOTTIE LAY BACK AGAINST a stack of pillows. She held a newborn in the crook of each arm.

"Twins," Nellie laughed. "Fred's in for some surprise."

"Not to mention me," Dottie said, exhaustion written all over her face. Her cheeks were red and her hair was plastered to her head. Nellie thought she had never looked so pretty or so healthy.

Dr. Fitzgerald dried his hands on a towel. "As far as I can tell, they're identical."

"I can't wait for Fred to see his sons," Dottie said, her eyes glued to her babies.

Annie wiped Dottie's forehead. "You three are staying with me until Fred gets back." The new mother opened her mouth to object, but Annie held up a hand to silence her. "Listen to me, missy. Your ma was me best friend. She'd want me to look after her girl."

Dottie's eyelids fluttered. "Thanks, Annie. I'm too tired to argue. Oh no," she cried out suddenly. "Fred only made one crib! It's not big enough for two babies."

"Never you mind," Annie said. "We'll make do. In the meantime, I'll get some men to fetch your crib. Nellie will help get you and the babies settled in my house."

"I got a crib," Nellie said. "Joe and Sam will bring it over after school."

Dottie sighed and kissed each sleeping baby's cheek. "It'd be perfect if Fred was here."

*

DAYS PASSED WITH ANNIE catering to Dottie and the twins, only allowing the new mother to tend to her babies. "I'm all right," Dottie insisted on more than one occasion. "Let me help with the cooking and cleaning."

Annie brushed the protests away every time. "It takes time to get your strength back."

A week later, Dottie, Nellie, and Mother Patrick sat with Annie in her kitchen with a mug of tea and a slice of gingerbread. Dottie bit her nails. "Our menfolk should've been back long ago," she said. "Why haven't they returned?"

Annie picked at a piece of gingerbread. "All fishing vessels should carry one of them Marconi wireless. That way we'd know why the *Marion* is late."

Mother Patrick voiced out loud what the other women wouldn't—or couldn't—say. "Do you think she's run into trouble?"

Dottie and Annie stared at the nun. Nellie hung her head. A baby's cry broke the strained silence. "Fred's coming home," Dottie said. "He ain't even seen his children yet." Another wail came, and she ran from the room.

Nellie leaned into the table, her face ashen. "I didn't want to say anything in front of her. Our men won't ever see home again," she said in a raspy voice.

Annie squeezed her hand. "Love, that's not a proper way to think."

Mother Patrick laid down her mug and folded her arms beneath the broad sleeves of her nun's habit. "Child, why would you say such a terrible thing, let alone think it?"

Nellie placed her palms down on the table. "I saw a token."

Annie stiffened. "Who was it?" she whispered.

Nellie told them about the time she'd seen an apparition of Harry in a maze of fog on the wharf one morning, when he'd been at Tom's house. "I had a bad feeling all along. I told Harry and begged him to stay home."

Mother Patrick blessed herself and murmured a short prayer.

Annie went whiter than sugar. "Everyone knows a token means

death," she said. "I refuse to accept that about our Tommy and Harry." Footsteps sounded on the stairs. "Dottie's coming." Annie lowered her voice. "Best she doesn't hear about your token."

Mother Patrick stood up as Dottie came in. "I have a class to teach in twenty minutes." She cracked what could be considered either a smile or a frown. "History. Joe's favourite."

"I'll go with you," Nellie said. "I have to get supper ready."

WHEN THEY REACHED THE convent door, she parted from the nun and continued down the hill. A black schooner was anchoring in Burke's Cove. "The *Marion*!" Nellie cried, and sprinted toward the wharf at the foot of her house. In a heartbeat she untied a dory. She rowed halfway across the harbour, when her smile died. The fishermen on deck weren't the *Marion*'s crew. Nellie's shoulders stooped and her movements slowed. She pulled into the wharf and watched wives, children, and parents greet their returning loved ones. Nellie knew them all, either personally or by sight.

Simon Nugent, a forty-year-old fisherman who'd just disembarked from the black schooner, ambled over to Nellie. "Mrs. Myles, What are you doing here?" he asked.

"Simon, have you seen the *Marion* in your travels?"

The man's eyebrows drew together. "Isn't she back?"

"No," Nellie said. "There's been no word either."

Simon hauled off his cap. "She cleared the channel buoys at St. Pierre and sailed with the rising sun, due east for the Grand Banks. We were on our way into St. Pierre."

"When was that?"

Simon thought a moment. "Near on two weeks ago. When we reached the Banks the next day, she wasn't there."

"You didn't pass her on the way?"

"Never laid eyes on her after St. Pierre."

"Where could she be?" Nellie said, more to herself than to Simon. She rowed back home. Tears stained her cheeks.

Chapter 6

THE SUN ROSE OVER Fortune Bay in mid-July with still no word from the *Marion*.

"Dinner might be late today," Nellie said to the children at breakfast. "The Burke brothers are having a meeting at the church to tell us about their investigation into the *Marion*'s disappearance."

"Annie told us they travelled to St. Pierre themselves," Joe said.

"Ma," Bessie said softly. She held Marie's hand under the table. "Maybe they found Captain Ike, Pa, and all the others."

Sam threw down his fork. It clanged against his plate. "Pa's dead," he said. "They're all dead." He scraped his chair back from the table and ran out the door.

A lump formed in Nellie's throat. "We have to keep praying there'll be good news. Now finish your breakfast." She went to the door. Sam stood on the wharf, looking toward the harbour entrance. He'd done the same every morning for a month.

Nellie walked down the hill and stood next to him. "Sam, I don't want to give you any false hope. I believe your pa and Uncle Tommy are . . . dead." Sam didn't speak, didn't move. Nellie put her arm around his shoulder. "Bessie and Marie are going to need you to be strong for them."

"I will, Ma. I promise."

Together they climbed up the path to the house. *A fisherman's youngsters have to suffer unfair hardships,* Nellie thought. She sighed wearily when she saw that Joe, Bessie, and Marie hadn't touched their food. Sam gobbled the rest of his cold scrambled eggs and the others followed his lead.

"Me and Sam are going to the nun's field to help them make hay," Joe said.

"Sister Thérèse wants to teach me and Marie how to milk a cow today," Bessie said.

Nellie smiled. "That's some exciting. You've been waiting a long time for that."

Bessie shrugged. "S'pose so."

Things will get better with time, Nellie wanted to say, but the words wouldn't form on her lips, and the children left for the convent. She washed the dishes and swept the floor before the walk to the church, which seemed longer and more tiresome than usual.

SHE SLIPPED INTO THE front pew with Dottie, Annie, and Mother Patrick. Sister Thérèse was watching the twins at the convent. The church soon filled with the *Marion*'s family members and concerned people from neighbouring communities.

Denis and Jon Burke, local merchants, sat behind a table the priest had placed up front. Denis cleared his throat for attention and the murmurs subsided. "We questioned Captain Maurice and all the men from the *Fleur de Lys,*" he began. The French trawler was known to everyone in the church. "Eyewitnesses agreed with their story. Ike Jones scraped the steel side of the trawler when he docked the *Marion* at St. Pierre. People around were of the opinion it was a deliberate act." Denis paused to drink some water.

Jon took over. "That night at the *Hôtel de France,* the French crew taunted our men about the incident until a brawl broke out. Fred McEvoy and Harry and Tom Myles had already left by then. Captain Maurice and Ike never showed up at the hotel. The local authorities launched their own investigation and found nothing suspicious."

"Where was Captain Maurice?" Nellie asked.

"The French captain said he was at home. His housekeeper was at the house of a friend, so she couldn't confirm that. However, no one saw him that night. The next morning, before leaving St. Pierre, Ike fired a musket over the trawler's bow."

"The stun bastard," a man at the back said.

"Why'd he do a fool thing like that?" another man growled.

Jon continued. "Denis and myself have offered a handsome reward for any information concerning the *Marion*. There have been no takers so far."

Dottie stood up. "Our husbands didn't melt into the air," she said in a trembling voice. "They have to be somewhere."

"We were offered a possible explanation for the loss," Denis said. He stopped and looked at all the people crowding the church.

"Well, out with it," Annie said.

"It's wartime. German U-boats have sunk Grand Banks schooners with their deck guns."

"Baloney," Simon Nugent said. "I was on one of them schooners that got sunk. We used our dories as lifeboats and were picked up in no time by another schooner. The men on the *Marion* have vanished like they never existed."

"There were also reports of icebergs and storms on the Banks last month. Perhaps the *Marion* met her fate in a natural disaster," Denis continued.

"That's too easy an answer," Nellie said. There were other schooners in the area. "Why is it only the *Marion* that's lost?"

"We've done everything possible to locate the *Marion*," Denis said.

Annie waved a hand at the brothers. "It ain't enough."

"We'll keep the offer of a reward open," Jon said. "We're terribly sorry."

The last light of hope for the *Marion*'s safe return was stubbed out by a few words, extinguished like a candle blown out on a dark, moonless night. Men stared at their feet. Mothers and wives wept.

Nellie's expression hardened. "Seventeen souls vanished from the face of the earth, just like that. I can't—I won't!—accept it was an accident of nature."

Annie's eyes lost their lustre. Her body seemed to shrink in on itself. "My sweet Harry and Tommy, gone forever," she mumbled.

"No!" Dottie cried out. "It's not fair! Fred didn't see his sons yet." She beat her fists on the wooden pew in front of her. "It's not fair!"

Mother Patrick folded Dottie into her arms. "There, there, child. You must be strong for the babies."

Denis and Jon Burke walked down the aisle and out the church doors. No one paid any attention to them leaving.

Nellie took hold of Annie's shoulders and shook her. "Take Dottie home. She's all the twins have now."

Annie snapped out of her daze at the mention of the children. "The wee ones," she said softly. "They needs their ma."

Mother Patrick handed Dottie over to Annie's care. Everyone else departed, some with their heads low, some with red and swollen eyes, others with blank stares. Nellie sat alone in the pew, staring at the altar where she'd been married fifteen years earlier. How could she let go of Harry when there wasn't even a body to say goodbye to?

DRY-EYED, SHE WENT OUT to the cemetery and sought out Uncle Joe's grave. "Harry and Tom are with you," she said. "I know you'll look after them."

Mother Patrick opened the squeaky gate and walked to Nellie, who now stood facing Harry's parents' grave. "I saw you from my office," she said.

Nellie kept her eyes trained on the headstone. "Harry died the same age as his father." She felt a heaviness in her chest. "At least there was a body to bury." Still the tears didn't flow. "Uncle Joe told me Harry and Tom's mother couldn't get past the grief. Pneumonia took her a year later."

Mother Patrick shook her head. "A tragedy for everyone."

"Harry was ten, like Bessie is now. Tom was a baby. I always thought she was selfish to give up on her youngsters. I should not have judged her so hard." A balmy breeze lifted Nellie's fine hair out of her eyes. She looked at Mother Patrick. "I must find out the truth."

"The Burkes have tried."

"I want to go to St. Pierre to speak with the French captain myself. He did something." Nellie placed a hand over her heart. "I know it deep in here."

Chapter 7

THE EARLY MORNING SUN poured through Nellie's open kitchen window. Sweat dribbled down her back as she turned over French toast browning in homemade butter. There wasn't even enough of a breeze to flutter the curtains.

Bessie pushed away her plate, three-quarters of her French toast left untouched. "Ma, is Pa coming home?" she asked. Joe, Sam, and Marie all turned to Nellie. She looked at each face, hungry for the answer to the question neither of them had dared ask before.

Nellie's heart thumped so loud she was certain the youngsters could hear it. Her first instinct was to assure the children that they shouldn't give up on Harry, that he, Tom, and Captain Jones would arrive any day. She took a deep breath and pushed the frying pan to the back of the stove.

"It's best you learn the truth from me," she said, and laid out, one by one, the results of the Burke brothers' investigation. "The *Marion* is gone. The men are gone with her."

"No," Sam said. "We can't give up on them."

A lump formed in Nellie's throat. "I know it sounds awful, but there's no point in hoping for the impossible."

Marie clutched Nellie's arm. "Pa wouldn't leave us alone." She burst into tears. "He can't be gone forever. It won't ever be the same without him."

Sam glared at Joe. "See what fishing does," he snapped. "It's no good."

Joe lowered his head. "It's how we makes our living," he mumbled.

"We got to pull together," Nellie said, "not be angry at each other."

The children picked at their food, the usual chit-chat left somewhere in the past. "If you're not hungry," Nellie said softly, "get up from the table."

Bessie and Marie went to their room. Joe went outside to chop wood. Sam made for the wharf and dangled his legs over the edge, his eyes on a point somewhere beyond the harbour.

Nellie couldn't find the strength to get up from the table.

"How are you today?" Mother Patrick said from the doorway. She glanced at the plates of partially eaten food.

"I promised the youngsters last night I'd make French toast." Nellie fingered Sam's plate. "Couldn't disappoint them." She turned heavy eyes to Mother Patrick. "I told them the *Marion*'s gone for good."

The nun looked out the door at Joe and Sam. "The poor lads. Harry was a good father and a marvellous influence on them. Which is why I'm here. Nellie, are you still determined to go to St. Pierre?"

Nellie threw the napkin she had gripped with clenched fingers all morning onto the table. "I won't give up until I find out what happened." She rubbed her temples. "Tom was going to quit after this trip. He'd gotten a cooking job in St. John's."

"Another example of life's little injustices," Mother Patrick said. "Hattie Fitzgerald told me this morning that Charlie Whittle over in Boxey died of consumption yesterday. He was only seventeen."

Nellie's jaw tightened. "Shelly Fewer was shipped off to the sanatorium last month. If the sea doesn't get you, consumption will."

Mother Patrick took the dishtowel from the stove's oven handle and fanned herself. "This heat is unbearable. A drop of water wouldn't go astray." She drained a large glass in one extended gulp. "Nellie, if your mind's made up about going to St. Pierre, I'll assist you."

"I've a little money put aside," Nellie said.

"Nonsense, you'll need that for the children. I've made arrangements for transportation and a place for us to stay while we're in St. Pierre."

Nellie was afraid to believe she'd heard correctly. "We?"

"Yes, child. I'm as anxious as you to discover what fate befell those men. Eloise, Fred McEvoy's sister-in-law, hails from St. Pierre, as you know. Her parents will be happy to put you up. Old Steve Marsh volunteered to bring us to St. Pierre and pick us up for free." Mother Patrick put her hands on the table. "He's not satisfied with the results of the Burke investigation either."

"Where will you stay?"

"Father Jean-Claude is a good friend as well as St. Pierre's resident priest. He speaks perfect English and can act as our interpreter."

Nellie's face clouded over. "I can't go without Bessie and Marie. They're scared enough without me leaving for a couple days."

"Not a problem. When would you like to go?"

"Tomorrow if possible. I'll talk to Annie about the boys staying with her."

"It's a good possibility this French captain might be out to sea."

"I'll take my chances."

"We'll meet Steve Marsh at Burke's Cove tomorrow morning at nine. See you then." Mother Patrick got up to leave.

"I'll walk with you. I want to talk to Annie right away."

Nellie found her dozing in the rocking chair by the living room fireplace. She gently touched Annie's shoulder. Her eyes fluttered open. "You don't nap during the day," Nellie said.

"Dottie's in her room with the twins. She cried all night long. I had to tend to the darling babes."

Nellie knelt beside the woman she considered her children's grandmother. "Are you all right?"

"I can keep going as long as someone needs me. That's the only thing worth any salt."

"Me and the youngsters will always need and love you."

*

AT PRECISELY NINE O'CLOCK the next morning, Mother Patrick arrived at Burke's Cove. The sky was heavy with black, lumpy clouds threatening rain. Fog gathered across the harbour entrance like a grey stone barrier. Steve took the nun's small suitcase and helped her down from the wharf. Nellie, Bessie, and Marie were seated inside the boat.

"Not a good day for travelling on the ocean," Mother Patrick said.

"I've gone in weather way worse than this," Steve said. "It's a long run. Try to get comfy."

The boat eased away from the wharf, then steered toward the open sea. A large sack in the corner fell open. Nellie noticed a homemade wool sock protrude from the hole where the tie strings had loosened. "I see Mrs. Marsh has been busy knitting," she said. "You're not thinking of smuggling certain goods back to St. Jacques, are you?"

"Trading is more like it," Steve said. "We've run low on the cooking basics. A hundred pounds of sugar costs three dollars in St. Pierre."

Nellie almost gagged. "It's more than three times that at home."

"Got that right," Steve said.

"Are you sure you won't be trading for cigarettes or rum? They're a lot cheaper as well."

Steve hauled off his hat and held it over his heart. "I gives my word of honour, missus. I'm bringing back sugar and molasses." He slapped the hat back on his head. "This time."

Nellie leaned close to Mother Patrick. "Generations of Steve's family have smuggled rum, tobacco, sugar, molasses, flour, and other goods for family and friends, not for profit. It's as much a way of life as fishing is."

"Isn't that risky?" Mother Patrick said. "What happens if someone gets caught by the Newfoundland Rangers who patrol the area?"

"That depends," Steve called out. "Some customs officers make us pay duty charges on the goods. Others take the stuff for themselves."

The boat cleared the harbour and they entered a world of shadowy mist. The dampness seeped under Nellie's skin. She shivered and hauled a blanket across her shoulders. Marie and Bessie played alleys on the floor. Mother Patrick's bright red complexion became a pale shade of green.

"We Irish folk turn this lovely colour on water." She looked at Nellie with a weak smile.

Nellie handed her a dry slice of bread. "I brought this along to settle the girls' stomachs in case they got seasick."

The nun chewed the offering gratefully. "I have a note from Eloise to her parents explaining why we've come to St. Pierre. I suggest we meet Father Jean-Claude first. He'll introduce us to the family."

The boat slashed through the water, swaying like a toddler learning to walk. The wind whipped up waves that slopped into the boat.

"Oh my," Mother Patrick wailed, and hung over the side. She was even greener when she turned back to Nellie. Her face was soaked with ocean spray.

"You should've told me you get so seasick," Nellie said. "This is too much for you."

The nun held a hand over her mouth. "Nonsense. Once we touch land, I'll be myself in no—" She spun around and lunged for the side yet again.

THE BOAT DOCKED AT St. Pierre mid-afternoon. Steve escorted his four passengers to the church rectory. "I'll pick you up in two days," he said.

"We'll be waiting," Nellie said. "Don't forget about your trading."

Steve grinned.

Mother Patrick was about to knock on the rectory door when it opened. "*Ma mère Patrick*," a priest said. "*Quelle belle surprise!*"

"*Bonjour, mon père,*" Mother Patrick said in flat French and pointed to Nellie and the children. "*Nous avons besoin de votre aide.*"

"*Bien sure. Entrez donc.*" The priest smiled and stepped aside for them to enter.

Marie's face beamed. "Mother Patrick said we need his help and the priest said to come in."

Father Jean-Claude reminded Nellie of a grizzly bear. He stood well over six feet tall, with shoulders like a Japanese wrestler she'd seen in a magazine at Young's General Store. A head of busy black hair and a beard to his chest, along with black robes, completed the illusion.

Once the luggage was deposited in the front hall, everyone congregated in the den. A tiny, white-haired woman brought in tea and croissants topped with cream and melted chocolate. The children dug into the treats. "*Eh bien,*" Father Jean-Claude began. "*Ma chère mère Patrick*. You hate to travel by boat. There must be a grave reason for your presence here."

"Indeed there is. This is Nellie and her daughter Bessie. Her husband, Harry, and his brother Tom were on the *Marion*."

The priest's eyes softened. "Madame, I am terribly sorry for your loss. *Quelle tragédie.*"

Mother Patrick gently touched Marie's arm. "This child is Marie Jones, the captain's daughter. Her mother died many years ago."

"*Pauvre enfant*," the priest said. "Poor child," he repeated in English.

Marie held Bessie's hand. "*Nos pères nous manquent*," she said quietly. A tear slid to the tip of her nose.

Father Jean-Claude smiled at the girls. "Of course you miss your fathers." His eyes lingered on Marie. "You speak French almost as well as a native. Was your mother from St. Pierre?"

"I don't remember her."

"Marie has a good ear for languages," Mother Patrick said. "We never met her mother, nor do we know where she came from."

The priest's gaze wandered back to Marie. "Have you been here before, *mon enfant*?"

"No, Father."

Father Jean-Claude opened his mouth to speak, when the housekeeper came in to remove the dishes.

"Father," Nellie said. "I appreciate any help you can give me. I need to find out exactly what happened to the *Marion*."

Mother Patrick licked cream from the corner of her mouth.

"Nellie and the girls are staying with the Lavier family. Where do they live?"

"Just around the corner," the priest said. "Come with me."

THE LAVIERS GREETED BESSIE and Marie with hugs after they read their daughter's letter. Marie's limited French was sufficient to make herself understood. Nellie put her bags in the bedroom and returned to the rectory to the sound of Louisa, the Laviers' youngest daughter, babbling in French to Marie and Bessie.

"We eat," Father Jean-Claude said. "Then we begin with our questions about the *Marion*."

Nellie tried to finish the delicious lamb chop and sweet peas but only managed the occasional bite. She finally gave up and drank a mouthful of red wine. "Goodness gracious. It takes your breath away."

"I enjoy a good French wine," Father Jean-Claude said.

Nellie folded her napkin and laid it on her plate. "Father, do you know anything about Captain Maurice?"

The middle-aged priest hesitated. "*Le capitaine* is not an easy man to get to know since his wife's death." He sipped wine and savoured the taste. "I came to St. Pierre from France as a young curate. Maurice, his wife, and baby girl travelled on the same ship."

"He'd visited France?" Mother Patrick said.

"*Non.* He is from Marseilles. Mme. Maurice was born and raised in St. Pierre and wished to return. *Le capitaine* adored his wife. *Alors,* they moved here."

Nellie rested her elbows on the table. "I'm surprised he was so considerate of his wife's feelings."

"Two years later she died from an illness you call consumption. Maurice grieved very badly and devoted himself to their daughter, Chantal. He gave her whatever she desired. Sent her to the finest school in Paris." Father Jean-Claude sighed. "His daughter was the centre of his life. Not a good thing for Chantal, I think."

"Why not?"

"When Chantal was twenty, she went to St. John's on a shopping trip, where she met a man. Maurice forbade her to see him ever again." Father Jean-Claude threw his hands up in the air for emphasis. "*Le vrai amour, c'est pour toujours.*"

Annie looked at Mother Patrick with a perplexed look.

"Something about love," the nun said.

Father Jean-Claude laughed softly. "True love is forever. Chantal ran away and married the man. I never saw her again."

"What did the captain do?" Nellie said.

"There was nothing for him to do. He felt betrayed by his daughter."

"Do you have any idea why he and Captain Jones were always at each other's throats?"

The priest shrugged. "Bitterness intensifies when we embrace it. Who knows what it leads to?"

"I want to talk to him," Nellie said.

"Maybe we should speak to the people who were present on the dock when the *Marion* left before we approach *le capitaine* Maurice. I hate to say it, but he is not a pleasant man."

Nellie's spirits rose. "It's possible they saw or heard something."

"*Eh bien,*" Father Jean-Claude said. "We finish our meal, then go to see these people."

THE EARLY EVENING SUN beamed down on the trio walking toward the dock. Nellie and Mother Patrick stood off to the side while Father Jean-Claude talked to a small group of dock workers unloading a ship from France. Nellie listened to the men's responses, in foreign, lilting tones that sounded almost musical. She paid particular attention to their facial expressions and hand gestures, a universal language.

Mother Patrick murmured in Nellie's ear. "The French speak like they have to get everything said in five seconds. I can't catch a single word."

"*Merci bien,*" Father Jean-Claude said with a nod and turned to the women.

"You found out something," Nellie said. "I could tell."

"*Oui, madame.*" Sweat beaded on the priest's forehead. "It is very hot. Let us go to the *Hôtel de France* for a cool drink."

They each ordered a glass of orange juice. Nellie spoke first. "Father Jean-Claude, what did the men say?"

"None of them were surprised to hear the *Marion* never arrived home in Fortune Bay."

"Why do you mean?" Mother Patrick asked, the glass nearly slipping from her hand.

Father Jean-Claude waited a moment before he answered. "When the *Marion* was leaving port, *le capitaine* Maurice shouted at Ike Jones that he would pay for everything he did. Maurice vowed Jones would never see his daughter again."

Nellie somehow managed to keep back her tears. "Was there anything else?"

"The French trawler followed the *Marion* to sea a few hours later. She was not due to leave for another four days." Father Jean-Claude looked from Mother Patrick to Nellie. "The trawler returned a day later with a badly damaged stern."

Mother Patrick blessed herself. Nellie went cold all over.

"Maurice said the ship collided with an iron channel marker."

"The Burkes didn't mention that," Nellie said. She sounded winded.

"*Le gendarme,* our police, found the iron marker. They took pictures that proved the dents and paint on the trawler were caused by the marker."

"Did the police question why he left port so early?" Nellie said.

"I dine with the police captain tonight and will speak to him about it."

Nellie rubbed both hands over her face. "I've left Bessie and Marie alone long enough for one day."

Father Jean-Claude downed the last of his juice. "Tomorrow we go to see *le capitaine* Maurice."

*

NELLIE LAY IN BED with Bessie on one side and Marie on the other. She'd never spent a night away from her sons and ached to see them, to touch them. Her eyes closed and Harry's handsome face filled the dark void. *Why didn't you stay home like I wanted?* Nellie stuffed part of the blanket in her mouth to strangle a sob.

The night dragged on. Bessie moaned so often Nellie was tempted to wake her.

Marie never stirred. Nellie watched the slow rise and fall of her chest. *Poor little mite*, she thought. *Ike was a brute, but he loved you. No matter what comes to light about him, I'll make sure you remember that.* She turned to Bessie and kissed her forehead. *I'll protect you both from the truth.*

The first rays of light streamed in through the window just as Nellie drifted off to sleep. A soft tap on the door woke her. Bessie and Marie were gone.

"Mme. Myles." Mrs. Lavier's head poked around the bedroom door. "*Le petit dejeuner . . .* breakfast *est prêt.*"

Nellie sat up. She wasn't in the mood to eat but didn't want to be rude. "*Merci.*"

Father Jean-Claude and Mother Patrick were seated at the table with the children, munching on a breakfast of cheese croissants and tea when Nellie came down. She itched to ask the priest what information the police had told him, yet decided to wait until the youngsters were out of hearing range. Father Jean-Claude conversed with the Laviers while Nellie ate.

After breakfast, Marie and Bessie accompanied the adults to Maurice's house. They walked with Mother Patrick while Nellie and Father Jean-Claude stayed several steps behind. She heard Marie say good morning in French to every passerby.

"I can tell that you and your daughter love Marie very much," the priest said.

"She's like a sister to Bessie." Nellie lowered her voice. "You spoke to the police captain?"

"*Oui. Le capitaine* Maurice left port early because his cargo of salt fish was ready."

"Where was he going?"

"Barbados, to exchange the fish for salt and molasses. The accident with the marker forced him to return to St. Pierre for repairs."

Nellie frowned. "Was it unusual for him to leave days earlier?"

"Not at all."

Father Jean-Claude turned a corner and indicated the last house on the street. "That is the residence of *le capitaine* Maurice."

"Bessie, Marie," Nellie said, "wait here with Mother Patrick while me and Father Jean-Claude chat with the captain."

"Mme. Myles," the priest said, "I must warn you again. Maurice is a difficult man to deal with at the best of times. The police and the Burke brothers grilled him about the *Marion*. He may not talk to you."

Nellie squared her shoulders. "That's all right. It's really important I see his face."

Father Jean-Claude knocked on the black, wooden door. It creaked open to reveal a grey-haired, elderly woman.

"Bonjour, Mme. Dubois. Je suis ici pour voir le capitaine Maurice."

"*Bonjour, mon père. Entrez,*" Mme. Dubois said, her expression one of pure delight. She brought them down a narrow hallway carpeted in dark red and showed them into a room surrounded with wall-to-wall bookshelves. She indicated two armchairs facing a desk. "*Asseyez-vous.*"

"*Le capitaine* is well read," the priest remarked, browsing through the books. "He speaks several languages, including English."

"Puis-je vous aider?"

Nellie turned to see a short, wiry man in his early sixties, clean-shaven, his dark hair peppered with grey and neatly combed. Nellie had never seen a more gentle-looking man. *The devil wears many disguises,* she thought.

"Mme. Myles is the wife of Harry Myles, a fisherman lost on the *Marion*," Father Jean-Claude said in English.

Maurice turned to Nellie, the soft edges around his mouth and eyes suddenly replaced by harsh lines. "I am not responsible for the disappearance of the *Marion*," he said in a monotone. "I have been harassed enough."

"What did you and Ike Jones argue about?"

"Ike Jones is not worth my time or effort to discuss. He takes pleasure in destroying people's lives."

The tone of voice, more than the words, pricked at Nellie's skin like ice chips. "How did he destroy your life?" she asked.

"I refuse to respond to any more of your questions. *Allez-vous en.* Please leave my home." The French captain escorted them out of the room. He barely glanced at Nellie when she passed him on the way out the front door.

Outside, Bessie stared at Maurice, her body rigid, her breathing ragged. Mother Patrick pressed her hands lightly on Bessie's shoulders. "There's nothing to be afraid of."

The captain's deep green eyes flared. "Do not bother me again! I have had enough of—" His voice died abruptly as his gaze swept over the group toward the children standing side by side. He mumbled something in French to Marie.

The tall, burly priest gaped at the door even after the captain had shut the door.

Marie threw her arms around Nellie's waist. "I'm scared of him."

"Me too," Bessie sniffed. "I want to get away from here."

Mother Patrick turned Bessie around to face her. "Don't let the captain upset you," she said. "Some people are so unhappy they want everyone else to feel the same way."

Father Jean-Claude came out of his trance. "*Mes petites enfants*," he said, addressing Bessie and Marie. "I have a marvellous idea. We have a wonderful chocolate shop and a bakery with all kinds of croissants that are baked fresh every day. I would like to treat all of you to these delights."

Bessie's and Marie's frowns slipped away like smoke through an open window. Father Jean-Claude took each child's hand. "Which will we visit first? The chocolate or pastry shop?"

"The chocolate shop," the girls said as one.

*

THEY ALL MUNCHED ON French chocolate and ate croissants taken directly from the oven. As they left the pastry shop, Bessie stopped and stared into the distance, squinting against the sun. "Those are really small stone houses," she said.

Father Jean-Claude looked at Mother Patrick as if seeking advice. "Tell them," she said.

"That . . . that is the cemetery," the priest said. "We follow the custom of France. We bury our people in crypts where you can look inside."

Bessie gazed up at the priest. "We couldn't bury Pa."

"It's almost suppertime," Nellie said, a slight tremor in her voice. "We'd better get you and Marie back to the Laviers' house."

Louisa Lavier was waiting outside. She hugged Marie and Bessie like they'd been gone for years.

"Father Jean-Claude, what did Maurice say to the children?" Mother Patrick asked when she and Nellie relaxed in the priest's den.

"*Le capitaine*'s anger is like an open sore that has been left untreated."

Nellie sighed. "He drains the life from you."

Mother Patrick shook her head. "Shocking but true."

Nellie slowly got to her feet. "I'll see you both in the morning." Father Jean-Claude walked the short distance with her.

Marie was asleep when Nellie stepped into the bedroom. Bessie lay on her back, wide awake.

"You should be snoozing, young lady."

Tears slid down Bessie's face onto the bedsheet. "I'm scared of the French captain."

Nellie consoled her daughter. "He won't hurt you. I promise."

Bessie flung her arms around her mother's neck. "He's the hooded man in my dream."

"That's impossible, sweetie."

"He has the same eyes."

"A lot of people have green eyes." Nellie laid her daughter back on the pillow. "The captain's are bloodshot; that's why they're red."

"Ma, don't leave me alone."

Nellie kissed her cheek. “I promise to never leave you.”

Bessie’s eyelids drooped as drowsiness swept over her. “He is the hooded man,” she mumbled. “You’ll see.”

Chapter 8

A FARAWAY NOISE ROUSED Annie from a restless sleep. She leaned on her elbows and waited. A baby's cry sounded and turned into a howl as another tiny voice added its hungry wail. Annie got out of bed and hurried to Dottie's room. Two cribs stood together at the foot of the bed. The infants had kicked off their blankets, their faces red from crying. As if oblivious to the twins' plea for milk, Dottie sat on a chair and stared out the window.

"Your babes are hungry," Annie said softly.

Dottie gave them a fleeting glance and turned back to the window. "I have no milk."

"You ain't tried to breastfeed."

Sam stumbled up the hallway and peered through half-open eyes into the room. "What's wrong?"

"The darlings are starving," Annie said. "Go warm up the milk like I showed ya."

The babies howled louder, and Sam darted down the hall.

"Go ahead, Dottie," Annie yelled over the noise. "Stare out the window at whatever is more important than your youngsters. I have better things to do." She picked up Fred Jr. and rocked him. "These babes are lucky Mother Patrick has cows and gave you milk. She hasn't charged you a penny either."

Dottie continued to sit and gape out the window, looking like a rag doll, her limbs limp, her hair a tangled mess stuck to her face.

For the second night in a row, Sam helped feed the twins and change nappies. At first he'd grumbled that it was women's work. "Your old Uncle Joe changed more than one nappy in his day," Annie had said with a broad smile. "So did your pa."

Sam put Robert back in his crib. "The boys will crucify me if they finds this out."

"I'll have a word with Joe," Annie promised. "He'll answer to me if he blabs."

Sam grinned. "Maybe next time he can change the nappies."

Annie patted Sam's back. "You've been a grand help. Now go back to bed."

"Thank you," Dottie mumbled, without turning from the window.

"You nibbles at your food," Annie said with quiet patience.

"I feel like throwing up when I tries to eat," Dottie said.

"You mopes around all day long, pitying yourself, leaving the care of your youngsters to me and Sam. They deserve mother's milk and your attention."

"Don't be mad at me," Dottie whimpered. "My heart is broken that Fred will never see his sons."

"I'm not angry, but you must come to your senses. What would Fred say if he knew you was ignoring his little ones?"

MOTHER PATRICK AND FATHER Jean-Claude sat in the priest's den, enjoying tea and custard-filled pastries. Mother Patrick sank back into the oversized armchair, the teacup resting on a saucer in her lap. She put her fingertips together under her chin. "Father, how long have we known each other?"

"Since I arrived in North America. I cannot believe it's been over thirty years."

"And we know each other well?" She stared at the priest as if assessing him.

The priest raised an eyebrow. "Of course."

"Very well. Why didn't you tell Nellie everything about Captain Maurice?"

Father Jean-Claude's eyes opened wide. "I told her all that I know."

Mother Patrick placed her cup and saucer on a side table. "What did Maurice say to Bessie and Marie?"

"Unspeakable, foul names."

"Jean-Claude, you cringed at what Maurice said. You've lived among hardy fishermen for most of your adult life. A few foul words wouldn't have affected you like that. What did he say?" she insisted.

Father Jean-Claude ran a hand through his scruffy hair.

Mother Patrick moved to the edge of the armchair. "Did he threaten Marie because she's Ike Jones's daughter?"

"Not exactly."

"Now what's that supposed to mean?"

The priest hesitated. "Give me time to consider the best course of action for Nellie and Marie."

"What he said was that awful?"

"Even I did not comprehend to what degree bitterness has warped Maurice's heart." He reached across and touched Mother Patrick's hand. "Will you say nothing to Mme. Myles for the present?"

"You have my word."

"Shall we call it a night? You have a long boat ride tomorrow." Father Jean-Claude grinned. "But of course it is common knowledge you love to travel by sea."

Mother Patrick slept on and off during the night, ate very little breakfast, and arrived at the port at eight-thirty. Steve Marsh greeted her with a warm smile. Nellie and the children came twenty minutes later and they all set out under a blue sky and calm seas. The pale nun stayed glued to the side of the boat and chewed so much dry bread she gagged. She scrambled onto the wharf at Burke's Cove as soon as Steve pulled in. Once the bags were collected, the women and children hitched a ride in a horse and cart to St. Jacques. With a weary wave, Mother Patrick disembarked at the convent. Nellie and the children continued on to Annie's house.

Annie was stirring a big boiler on the stove when they arrived.

"Hope you're hungry," she said. "I made pea soup with extra dumplings. Joe and Sam already ate."

Nellie noticed the dark circles under her eyes and the exhausted edge to her voice. "Hope the boys weren't too much for you."

"To be honest, I would've been lost without them."

Marie and Bessie lapped up the soup. "Go feed the chickens," Annie said after they each devoured a second bowl. "I wants a quiet chat with Nellie."

"You look ready to drop on your feet," Nellie said.

"I ain't had a proper night's sleep since you left." Annie rubbed her eyes with her fingertips. "Dottie's acting like the babes aren't there. It breaks my heart to see her so miserable."

As if on cue, Dottie came into the kitchen; her eyes were red and swollen, her shoulders slumped.

"Nellie, did you find out who killed my Fred?" Her voice was raspy, as if she had a sore throat. Tears spilled down her face. "He never got to see his babies." She lowered her head in her hands. "It's not fair."

"Truer words were never spoken," Annie said. "Sadly, it's the way of a fisherman's wife."

Nellie led the new mother to the table. "There's no denying you've suffered like the rest of us. But you've been blessed with two precious gifts from heaven."

Dottie wiped her nose with the back of her hand. "I ain't got nothing. My parents are dead. Fred's dead. He was some excited about being a father. His babies will never know him."

Annie shook Dottie none too gently. "Don't be flying in the face of God. I was a year younger than you, and childless, when my man died in a blizzard, frozen like a chunk of ice. Listen good to me, girlie. Enough of this nonsense. Thank the Lord you have Fred's youngsters, the best part of him."

Dottie bawled even louder and ran from the kitchen.

Annie stared toward the hallway. "I wasn't trying to be hard on her," she said.

"I understand," Nellie said. "Dottie must put the babies before her grief. I have to do the same for Harry's sake, for his youngsters' sake." She sighed. "Harry lived through the pain of losing his own father too soon."

Annie dropped her chin into her hands. "Are you any closer to the truth about the *Marion*?"

Nellie told Annie all she'd learned, with emphasis on the trawler's damaged stern spotted the day after she'd chased the *Marion*. "I'm going straight to the Burkes this minute to ask why they left that bit out."

"I'd love to give that crowd a piece of my mind," Annie said.

"Tell the youngsters to be home before dark." Nellie hopped off the chair and walked with a determined step down the hill. The Burke's Rooms, a large building where supplies were kept, came into sight against the glittering water. Attached to it was the family home and business office.

Denis was reading papers when Nellie threw open the door. It whacked against the wall and the glass at the top rattled. Denis jumped off his chair. "Mrs. Myles! What brings you here at this late hour?"

Nellie marched to his desk. "Why didn't you tell us about the stern of Captain Maurice's trawler being damaged by a so-called iron marker?"

"Ah," Denis said, "I see you had a fruitful visit to St. Pierre."

"You're damn right. How dare you keep the truth from us! Our menfolk were murdered and you covered it up."

"Hold on one minute, Mrs. Myles. That is a very serious accusation."

Nellie slapped her hand on the desktop. "Why did you lie to us?"

Denis Burke's face flushed to the tips of his ears. "I'll explain, only if you calm down and hear me out."

Nellie plunked down into a chair. "All right."

"Your reaction is the reason me and Jon decided to keep the trawler's accident a secret. You've assumed the trawler scuttled the *Marion*. I presume you're aware the French *gendarme* proved the trawler did collide with a marker. We didn't want the community to ignore the facts and hear what they wanted . . . as you did. Which proves my point." Denis got up, came around the desk, and stood in front of Nellie. "You're well aware that we offered a very handsome reward for any information. Not one person approached us. No one could resist that much money if they knew something."

Anger burned inside Nellie, rising like lava ready to erupt from a volcano. She sprang to her feet, her face inches from Denis. "You high and mighty merchants have more money than a thousand fishermen could ever hope to earn in their lifetimes." She wagged a finger under his nose. "Why didn't you equip the *Marion* with a Marconi wireless, instead of wasting money on a 'very handsome reward' that's too late to do any good?"

"Really, Mrs. Myles. That's not—"

"Spare me your selfish excuses."

Nellie stormed from the room and slammed the door. She didn't hear the glass shatter and crash to the floor. Nor did she or anyone else in Fortune Bay ever learn of the incident. Outside, Nellie breathed deeply to quiet the drumming in her chest. She topped the hill, swinging her arms furiously.

"Merchants," she grumbled. "Think they can do what they want."

Images of Tom and Harry crowded her head: soft-spoken Tom, a proud, loving uncle and godfather to Joe; Harry in the brown suit he'd saved for months to buy for their wedding. Nellie gritted her teeth to fight through the wave of grief threatening to crush her.

A WEEK LATER, RAIN splashed against the church's stained glass windows and pounded on the roof like horses' hooves. With all hope for the *Marion*'s return gone, the priest held a service to say a final farewell to the crew. All four Burke brothers sat in the front pew, their wives and children seated with them. Denis Burke glanced at Nellie with a half-hearted smile. She looked away. The families of the *Marion*'s crew were spread out among the many residents who had come from surrounding communities to offer their sympathies. Seventeen tragic deaths at one time impacted the lives of all the families along the coast.

Dottie wore a black dress, which had once fit her to perfection but now hung loose. A black shawl draped over her back as she leaned against Annie. The dark clothes accentuated the chalk-white pallor of her once rosy complexion. Mother Patrick had volunteered herself and Sister Thérèse to watch over the twins.

Every face turned to the priest as he climbed the steps to the pulpit. Children who normally squirmed and grumbled remained motionless, the almost imperceptible rise and fall of their chests the only indication they were alive. There was no low murmur of voices to quiet down when Father Curran began his talk.

"This is a sad, tragic time for all Newfoundlanders. So many decent, God-fearing men taken without warning."

Stolen is more like it, Nellie thought. *Cheated out of a life they deserved.* The priest's voice droned on. All she heard was a jumble of meaningless words until a familiar name penetrated the haze.

"Fred McEvoy. Never had the good fortune to know he'd been blessed with twin sons."

Dottie sobbed into her handkerchief.

"Frank Fewer." Another widow wept, surrounded by her five teenaged children. "The best carpenter in Fortune Bay, despite his gammy leg."

Nellie realized the names of the crew were being called out.

"Gordon McCarthy. Never got the chance to drive a train like he always wanted." A child cried, and a mother's soothing voice tried to calm him.

Every name pierced Nellie's heart.

"Beloved brothers, Harry and Tom Myles, who lent a hand whenever needed." Father Curran smiled down at Annie Cluett. "The lads couldn't have had a finer mother figure."

"Captain Ike Jones. Doted on his motherless little girl." Bessie hugged Marie.

"Billy Evans. Far too much life left to live." His mother bawled out loud and Father Curran paused long enough for Mrs. Evans to compose herself.

"Cousins John and Ron Hodder. Big men with even bigger hearts. Avoided trouble whenever possible.

"Ned Noseworthy. I never saw another human being smile so often." Six children, aged three to eight, sat between their mother and grandparents directly in front of Nellie.

"I'd give years off my life to hear his sniff," Nellie heard his widow sob into her handkerchief.

"Dave LaCroix. Young's store couldn't keep up with all the Bull's Eyes he ate." Mrs. LaCroix smiled through her tears. "Ate more than his ten youngsters put together.

"Skit Kettle. Loved his pipe and was more at home on the sea than on land." Mrs. Kettle nodded in agreement.

"Clive Pope." His seven children filled a pew. "A humble man of few words." The priest gave a wistful look. "Guess that's due to the fact he couldn't hear much." Soft chuckles rippled through the church. Even Mrs. Pope cracked a smile.

"Mick Drake, known as Whitey to his friends. Signed on with the *Marion* at the last minute. Took care of his three little sisters as well as his own children.

"Sid Davies. Sickness couldn't keep him down. Worked in the lobster cannery, as well as fished on the Banks, to help out his widowed brother's family.

"Earle Fiander. Who among us has never had his three-fingered hand poked in our face while he regaled us with one of his sea adventures?

"Simon Whelan. Just begun his married life." Alice, his bride, scrambled out of the pew and dashed to the double doors.

Father Curran's deep voice boomed around the church as he concluded his roll call. "They will live on in our hearts and minds." His eyes roamed over every face. "Let us pray that some day we'll come to terms with this tragedy and find peace." The priest blessed the congregation and left the pulpit. He stood at the double doors and greeted people as they filed past him.

The pews emptied one by one. Nellie listened to the tread of footsteps on wood. Slow. Heavy. Defeated. She knelt down to pray, only half-aware of the sun's shadow creeping down the aisle.

Annie entered the church and softly walked to the middle pew. "It's time to go, Nellie. Dottie and the youngsters are waiting for you at the convent."

Nellie's head shot up. "What?" She looked around the deserted church. The candles on the altar had burned down to the quick.

"Father Curran finished an hour ago."

"Annie, I won't find peace until we know for certain what happened to our menfolk."

"Come along," Annie said, and helped Nellie to her feet. They made their way to the convent.

"I INSIST YOU STAY for tea and rhubarb pie," Mother Patrick said when Nellie declined the invitation. "The twins are asleep and the youngsters are busy shelving books in the library." She pulled the white cloth off the pies. "Picked the rhubarb myself."

"Guy Hays is getting hitched this afternoon," Annie said.

Mother Patrick cut the pie. "I don't recall anyone by that name in St. Jacques."

"He's from Belleoram."

"That's the Anglican community," Mother Patrick said. "Why's he getting married in the Catholic church?"

"His mother's from St. Pierre, so all the children were raised Catholic." Annie ran her fingers around the rim of the china cup Mother Patrick used for guests. "Guy's real name is Guillaume. He's . . . was Tommy's best friend. Spent as much time at Old Joe's house as he did in Belleoram."

Nellie produced a crooked smile. "He speaks French like he was raised in St. Pierre. He tried to teach it to Tom."

"Right," Annie said. "Tommy felt silly trying to speak a foreign language he didn't need."

Nellie shook one leg, which had fallen asleep with the circulation cut off. "I forgot all about the wedding. Tom was supposed to stand up for Guy."

"His brother's stepping in," Annie said. "Guy stopped by last night to make sure I'll be at the reception in Belleoram. He said it'd be like having a bit of Tommy there."

Nellie patted Annie's hand. "What a lovely thought. You should go."

Dottie drank a cup of tea and dug into a hefty chunk of pie. Mother Patrick smiled at her. "What a lovely surprise to see you eat with such heartiness."

"The service really knocked the fact into my head that Fred's gone. My boys needs me to look after them, and to think about their future, like Annie's been preaching all along."

"I'll help you out," Annie said.

"I can't depend on handouts for the rest of my life." Dottie looked at Nellie. "We're widows with youngsters. We have no choice but to find a way to feed our families."

Nellie squeezed her eyes shut as the statement bore into her brain. "Of course," she said. "I've been so angry about what happened."

Dottie picked pie crumbs from her lap. "I ain't got no intention of marrying again just to put food on the table like some poor widows are forced to do."

"Joe Myles saved me from that fate," Annie said. "He paid me to help look after two darling boys."

A slight smile curved Nellie's lip. "Everyone thought you'd marry Uncle Joe."

"There wasn't any room left in me heart for married love. My Robert filled it up too much."

"Fred's brother, Seth, has his own family to look out for," Dottie said. "It's time to think seriously about my next step."

Mother Patrick poured more tea. "There's another problem to consider." All the women stared at her. "Marie. What's to become of the poor child?"

"That's not a problem," Nellie said. "She'll live with me. She and Bessie are closer than sisters. Even Joe and Sam consider her one of the family."

"I hate to say this," Mother Patrick said. "You're a widow with three mouths to feed. How will you cope with a fourth?"

Robert woke up and began to fidget. Dottie reached for him. "Maybe Marie has relatives who'll take her in," she said. Robert stuck a thumb in his mouth and fell back to sleep.

"No," Nellie said. "Marie won't be happy with strangers." She caressed Robert's cheek. "For the first time in my life I don't know what to do."

Annie looked at her. "You'll find the answer. Strong women always do."

Chapter 9

NELLIE PUT SUPPER ON the table. Fish and brewis, smothered in grease, with extra large chunks of scruncheons. She sighed inwardly. Harry liked the fatback fried like that. Annie had dropped off a coconut cream pie, the only sweet Harry ate. *Old habits are hard to break,* Nellie thought as she called to the youngsters.

Joe said grace, taking over the practice from his father. "Ma, how are we gonna pay for food and the other stuff we need?" he asked when they began to eat.

"We're good for a while," Nellie said. She'd wondered when the subject would arise. "Don't give it another thought."

Sam lowered his head and glanced sideways at his brother. Joe made eye contact with him, then quickly looked away.

"What's going on between you two?" Nellie said.

Joe stuffed his mouth with food. "Nothing."

"Tell me what the stares are about," she said.

Sam kept his head down. "Joe, Ma has a right to know."

"One of you tell me," Nellie said in a sharper tone than she'd intended.

Joe looked at her. Nellie saw a faint glimmer of the boy he had been when Harry was alive. She shivered. "Pa's gone," he said. "It's my job to support the family now. I was thirteen two weeks ago, old enough to fish on the Banks. I've signed up on the *Sherman*. She leaves tomorrow."

"Don't go," Bessie cried out. "You won't come back, like Pa and Uncle Tommy!"

Marie's deep green eyes swelled with tears. "And like my pa, too."

Joe sat up tall. "I made up my mind. Pa would want me to take care of the family."

Nellie's mouth went dry. "I'm proud you want to look after us, but you could do it by working at one of the fish plants or the lobster cannery."

"No, Ma. I wants to go fishing like Pa."

"I know nothing I say will stop you from going." Nellie stabbed a lump of brewis with her fork. "So there's no use wasting my time."

Sam raised his head for the first time. "Joe is doing what he can to help out. Don't be mad at him. I'd go too, if I was old enough."

Nellie fought back tears. "Eat before your supper gets cold."

Her sons had been forced to become men before their time. Dottie's anguished cry echoed in her head: *It's not fair.* Nellie attacked another lump of brewis. Fairness had nothing to do with a fisherman's lot in life, or that of his family. The meal progressed in silence. Nellie wondered if the carefree chatter would ever return. Bessie left her plate half-full. No one touched the coconut cream pie.

"I'm gonna cut wood for the stove," Joe said.

"I'll help," Sam said, following him outside.

Nellie threw down her fork. "Bessie, Marie, wash the dishes. I have an errand to run." She grabbed a shawl from the hook on the door and left without another word.

DENIS BURKE WAS ONCE again sifting through papers when Nellie barged into his office.

"Mrs. Myles . . ."

"I have something to say," Nellie said, cutting him off. "Have you any notion about how the widows of the *Marion* are struggling to survive, with no money?" She stomped to his desk. "Do you even care?"

"We—"

"Anyone claim the 'handsome reward' yet?"

Denis blinked. "Ah . . . no."

"Put it to good use, then. Give it to the widows and orphans."

Denis's jaw dropped. "That isn't how business is done," he said finally.

Nellie placed her hands on the desk and leaned toward him. "Seventeen strong, hardy men disappeared on your schooner under very mysterious circumstances. It's the least you could do."

Denis moved back in his chair. "Really, Mrs. Myles. I've never heard the likes before."

"I thought so. You merchants pay a pittance to fishermen for all their hard work catching and salting the fish. You own the general store where we buy your goods, so you get back all the money anyways."

"You make that sound like a crime. Mrs. Myles, my family has suffered in this as well. We've lost a schooner. Can you even imagine the amount of money it takes to build or buy another one? I won't bore you with the considerable profits we're out of as a result of the *Marion*." Denis waved a sheet full of figures in front of Nellie's face. "If we merchants don't make money, then we can't supply our general stores or keep the fish factories open. What would the community do without those?"

Nellie slapped the paper out of Denis's hand. "The only reason you started an investigation weeks after the schooner didn't return was because of pressure from the grieving families." Red blotches flushed Nellie's cheeks. "Don't take me for a fool about the so-called handsome reward. If anybody had information about the *Marion*, they would have come forward in the beginning, reward or no. You and your family knew that." Nellie paused to catch her breath. "Don't sit in your fancy chair in your big office and tell me a load of bull about profit and loss. Money means nothing when human beings are involved."

"Mrs. Myles, please be reasonable. My brothers and I understand the community's grief."

"What a pile of shit! You have to experience grief first-hand to truly understand it. Who did you lose on the *Marion*?" Nellie glared at the man. "Don't compare your loss of profit to this community's loss of men." She turned and stormed out of the office. This time she didn't touch the door. Her shawl hung off one shoulder as she left the building and headed for the convent.

Mother Patrick answered Nellie's pounding on the door.

"What are you in such a state about?" she asked. "You look like you're ready to take on the world."

"Just the Burkes," Nellie said, and related her visit to their office. "It was like talking to a chicken. All they do is squawk and say nothing."

Mother Patrick laughed. "My dear Nellie, that's how it is. The Burkes are no worse than any other merchant family. Although, to give them their due, at times they are better."

Nellie folded her arms across her chest. "I don't want to talk about them any more. Joe announced at supper he's going fishing on the Banks tomorrow. He says we need the money."

"I'm sorry to hear that. But he was determined to go anyway."

"If I stand in his way, he'll be more stubborn to go. That's why I'll pack his bag like I did for Harry." Nellie's voice quivered. "It's been near two months and I still can't believe he's dead."

"The worst part about the whole affair," Mother Patrick said, "is not knowing what happened."

"No, the worst part is not being able to prove what we suspect. Maybe someday one of the French crew will find a backbone and tell the truth."

"Don't hold your breath, Nellie."

Nellie took her leave, muttering to herself about greedy merchants. Joe was still chopping wood and she stopped to watch him.

"I wants to make sure you have enough while I'm gone," he said, swinging the axe down on a log.

The logs shattered. *Like my heart*, Nellie thought. "That's right good of you," she said. "I'll get your bag ready."

Joe split another log. "Ma, I'm sorry I upset ya."

"I understand. Just take care of yourself. That's all I want." Nellie brushed past her son into the house so he wouldn't see her tears.

Marie sat in the armchair by the fireplace reading *Alice in Wonderland*. The convent contained a substantial library to which the community had access.

"Where's Bessie?" Nellie asked.

"Lying down. She's got a sore throat and is shivery all over."

Nellie found Bessie wrapped up in a quilt. "My throat," Bessie began, but a fit of coughing choked off her words.

Nellie felt her flushed cheeks. "You're a little warm. I'll get some water and molasses to ease the burning in your throat."

"Ma, will Joe come home again?"

"God willing," Nellie uttered, the only thing she could bring herself to say.

She tucked Bessie under the covers and placed a glass of water by her bedside, then began to prepare Joe's bag, trying not to think about the last one she'd packed for Harry. The memory pushed through to the surface and, breathless, she dropped to the edge of the bed. Bessie coughed, a loud and congested hack. Nellie took a deep breath and said under her breath, "You don't have time to pity yourself, Nellie Myles. There are youngsters to look after."

Bessie held up an empty water jug. "I'm thirsty," she croaked.

Nellie helped Bessie undress, then brought up more water and a jar of molasses. Bessie began to cry, tears rolling down her flushed cheeks. "Ma, nothing will ever be the same without Pa."

"I know, sweetie," Nellie said, using Harry's pet name for his daughter.

JOE HAD TO BE up extra early, so the entire household went to bed at eight. Each time Bessie coughed, Nellie went to check on her. The noise didn't wake Marie. As the stars faded into pinpoints against the brightening sky, Nellie finally fell asleep. Her eyes flickered open when the sun shone across the room and danced on her hair. The smell of cooking filled the room.

Joe smiled at her when she came into the kitchen. "I got up early and lit the stove," he said. Porridge bubbled in a pot. "Started breakfast, too."

"And put out the dishes as well," Nellie said, her eyes moving to the table. She took over the breakfast duties and stirred the porridge. "Everyone's a bit nervous their first time out on the Banks."

"I'm excited, too."

"I can see that," Nellie said, resolved to stifle all traces of worry. "Call the others down. They won't want to miss seeing you off."

Joe's face shone like a lighthouse beacon. "Thanks, Ma," he said, and bounded out of the kitchen.

At the table, Bessie played with her food. She sneaked glances at Joe, yet said nothing. Nellie wanted her to stay home, but Bessie insisted on seeing her brother to the schooner. Yesterday Annie said she'd stay home to help Dottie, yet Nellie knew the real reason had more to do with not wanting to watch Joe sail away.

"Don't worry about me, Ma," Joe said at the dock. "I'll be home in two weeks."

Nellie smiled. "God keep you safe."

Bessie hugged her brother until he had to pry her arms from around his neck. "The days will pass so fast you won't know I'm gone."

The *Sherman* was out of sight before Nellie and the children turned away and headed back for St. Jacques. Bessie coughed in harsh, guttural barks. Her face burned bright red, her eyes watered, and she gagged as cough after cough choked her breath away.

"I'm all right," Bessie wheezed, before another bout of coughing racked her body.

Annie and Dr. Fitzgerald were waiting in the kitchen with Sam when Nellie, Bessie, and Marie got home. Before they went to see Joe off, Nellie had asked Sam to see if Dr. Fitzgerald could come see Bessie today.

"Get Bessie in bed," he said, the second he heard her cough. "Sam and Marie, stay down here."

Nellie had never heard Dr. Fitzgerald speak with such urgency before. She was startled when Bessie didn't resist going to bed.

The doctor looked down Bessie's throat and sounded out

her lungs. "Mrs. Myles, she needs plenty of fluids. Please fetch her some water." Bessie drank half a glass before heavy coughing stopped her.

Nellie smoothed the hair away from her daughter's damp forehead. "You'll feel better after a good rest."

Dr. Fitzgerald closed his black bag. "Drink as much of the water as you can," he said.

"What's wrong with her?" Nellie asked as soon as they were in the hallway.

"I think it's pneumonia."

Nellie fell back against the wall with relief. "I've been real scared it was consumption, especially since Charlie Whittle. I can't lose Bessie," she said quietly.

"Then we'll both make sure you don't." The doctor smiled reassuringly. "The good news is that only one lung is affected. She has a dry cough and a low-grade fever. Keep her warm and make sure she drinks plenty of water."

Nellie poked a strand of hair behind her ear. "She hardly touched her supper last night or her breakfast this morning."

"Give her soup. She needs to keep her strength up to fight off the infection." Dr. Fitzgerald closed his medical bag. "As a precaution, keep the youngsters away from her for a while."

"Marie can sleep with me."

"If Bessie gets worse, or if you're concerned for any reason, send for me no matter what time of day or night." He smiled again to reassure her. "Bessie's young and strong."

"I'll get back to Dottie and the twins," Annie said, and left with Dr. Fitzgerald.

Nellie closed Bessie's window and saw Annie and the doctor chatting. She thought nothing of it and rubbed warm goose grease on Bessie's chest, a remedy her mother swore by for chest ailments. Her daughter fell asleep and Nellie spent the day on a chair by her bedside, only taking time to prepare dinner and supper. Marie did the dishes so she could hurry back to Bessie. Near dawn, Bessie awoke, her nightgown and bedsheets soaked in sweat. She drifted back to sleep after Nellie put a fresh gown on her and changed the bed.

Dr. Fitzgerald dropped by when Nellie was making breakfast. “Her temperature’s the same,” he said. “Continue bedrest and fluids.”

Sam and Marie came into the kitchen seconds after the doctor left. “Is Bessie gonna be all right?” Sam asked.

Nellie put pancakes on the table. “She’s the same. Eat your breakfast while I bring her up some soup.”

Bessie coughed mucus into a handkerchief as Nellie entered the room. “Ma, my chest hurts.”

“That’s because you’re coughing so much,” Nellie said, laying the tray on Bessie’s lap. “I made some nice hot chicken soup for you.”

Bessie slurped one spoonful but couldn’t manage a second. “I’m not hungry, Ma,” she said, and sank back into the pillows.

Nellie placed the tray on the side table. “I’ll leave it here in case you get hungry later.”

THE CHILDREN WERE GONE, the table cleared, and the dishes washed when Nellie returned to the kitchen. A lump formed in her throat. She swallowed it away as Guy Hays knocked on the kitchen door.

“Guy,” Nellie said. “This is a surprise. Come in for a cuppa tea.”

Guy took off his salt and pepper hat. “Much obliged, Nellie,” he said.

She set two mugs on the table, along with a slice of coconut cream pie. She watched Guy put in three spoonfuls of sugar and enough Carnation milk to turn the tea white. He bit into the pie. “This has to be one of Annie’s.”

“Congratulations on your wedding. Annie told me it was lovely, and she was tickled to meet your mother’s parents. She was more than a bit relieved your mother could speak English.”

Guy half-smiled. “It wasn’t the same without Tommy there.” He pushed away the partially eaten pie. “Annie’s taking real good care of Fred’s twins. Ma says it’s a shame she never had her own.”

“That’s a fact,” Nellie said.

"Me and Chiselle got back from St. Pierre today."

"It was real nice that you got to have a bit of a honeymoon," Nellie said. "What brings you by?"

"We delivered a message to Mother Patrick from Father Jean-Claude. She told me about your visit to St. Pierre, and that's why I'm here."

"What do you mean?"

"François, a cousin on my mother's side, is part of Captain Maurice's crew. I had some interesting chat with him about the *Marion*."

Nellie's heart fluttered. "You found out something?"

"François said it spooked him the way Maurice hated Ike. Lots of men get beat up in a fight and don't go crazy like Maurice." Guy put his elbows on the table. "François wasn't on board the day the trawler set after the *Marion*. He says the crew have been mumbling about nothing else since then. Nothing was said out loud, but François thinks Captain Maurice scuttled the *Marion* and took off."

Nellie felt sick to her stomach. "If no one's said anything for sure, why does your cousin think that?"

"Captain Maurice could sail around the iron channel markers blindfolded. He even did it one time to show off. In all his years on the ocean, that was the first time he hit one."

"The French police said he struck the iron marker."

"I said the same to my cousin. He had a mighty good explanation."

"What?"

"Who's to say he didn't ram the *Marion* first, then hit the marker to cover the damage of what he'd done?"

"I was convinced he was guilty," Nellie said. "Yet somewhere inside me I wanted him to be innocent. I wanted Harry's and Tom's death to be an accident. That's easier to accept, to live with." She stared at her mug. "How could the crew let him get away with it?"

"Captain Maurice is a powerful and influential man in St. Pierre. He could put the men out of work if they went against him. They have to think of their families first."

"Can we prove any of this?"

"François only told me because we're related and because I was supposed to be on the *Marion* when she went missing. I was going fishing even though Dr. Fitzgerald said I wasn't well enough, with the flu. Tommy convinced me to hang on another week, said it wouldn't put me in the poorhouse." Guy's voice broke. "I'm alive because of my best friend."

"We owe it to Tom and all the others to find out the truth."

"If Captain Maurice scuttled the *Marion*, his crew won't own up to it. Not if they want to continue feeding their families."

"Then why tell me all this?"

"Because Mother Patrick told me you want to go back to St. Pierre to talk to the trawler's crew. But now you know as much as anyone, without putting yourself in harm's way."

Nellie heard Marie's voice drift in through the window. "Seventeen innocent men died because of one man's hatred for another. Marie has to be sheltered from the guilt and shame of that."

Chapter 10

DR. FITZGERALD FINISHED HIS exam of the twins. "Fred Jr. and Robert are two very healthy babies. Keep up the good work." He chuckled. "I'm sure Annie was delighted when you named one after her husband."

"She cried when I told her," Dottie said. "Annie's done so much for me. It's the only way I could think of to repay her in some small way."

"Where is Annie, by the way?"

"Gone to Nellie's house. She's really worried about Bessie."

Dr. Fitzgerald snapped his bag shut. "That's my next stop."

Robert started to cry. He quieted down as soon as Dottie picked him up. "It's been nearly two weeks since Bessie took sick, and she doesn't seem any better."

The doctor retrieved his hat from the dresser. "I'll drop by again in a few weeks."

Dottie laid Robert back in the crib. "I may not be here then."

"You're moving back home?"

"I'm leaving St. Jacques. I've got no money and no family, and I've certainly got no intention of marrying anyone just to feed my youngsters."

"You could work in one of the fish plants."

"Who'll look after my boys?"

"Annie's told me several times she'd love to do it."

"Annie's been an answer to my prayers so far, but I can't depend on her forever." Dottie blinked back tears. "She's on in years and not up to caring for two babes on her own."

"Yes, you have a point there. Maybe Fred's brother will help out."

Dottie shook her head. "Seth's got his own family." She wrung her hands. "The truth is, Dr. Fitzgerald, I wants to leave St. Jacques to get my youngsters away from fishing."

"Where will you go?"

"St. John's. Mother Patrick said the nuns will give me a room and help me with the twins until I gets myself settled with work." Dottie's tears flowed freely now. "There's no way my babies will end up like their pa, if I can help it."

"It won't be easy for a widow with two small children to find work."

"I'll scrub floors on my hands and knees for twenty hours a day if that's what it takes to rear Fred Jr. and Robert."

The doctor tugged on his right ear, a habit of his whenever he did serious thinking. "I'll write to some of my friends in St. John's. Perhaps one of them will find suitable work where you and the babies can live."

Dottie wiped her eyes with the sleeve of her dress. "Thank you, Dr. Fitzgerald. I really appreciates this."

BESSIE LAY AGAINST A pile of pillows Nellie had stacked at the headboard to ease her cough. Nellie peered down at her sleeping daughter, a female version of Harry.

"How's she today?" asked Dr. Fitzgerald.

Nellie spun around, startled.

"I didn't mean to frighten you," he said. "Annie asked me to come up."

"This is the first time she's slept in two days. The cough keeps her awake and gives her a pounding headache. She's whiter than chalk and has grown awful thin." Nellie dabbed the perspiration on Bessie's forehead with a cloth. "Look at the dark shadows under her eyes."

"Her recovery is rather slower than I'd like," Dr. Fitzgerald admitted.

"It's been almost two weeks. She still got a fever and—"

"Her fever's down some, a little," Dr. Fitzgerald interrupted, "and Annie said she has fewer night sweats."

Nellie took a deep breath. "I have to force her to eat. I know you don't want to tell me the truth about my little girl."

Dr. Fitzgerald stroked his chin. "I will admit that Bessie is showing all the symptoms of tuberculosis."

Nellie flinched. "Sam and Marie have been real upset since young Brian Whittle told them his brother Charlie was exactly like Bessie before he died."

"Nellie," Dr. Fitzgerald continued, "I'm still not convinced it isn't a bad bout of pneumonia."

"What are her odds if she does have consumption?"

The doctor touched Bessie's cheek with the back of his hand. "One in four survive."

Bessie coughed and opened her eyes. "Ma, is Joe home yet?"

"Anytime now, sweetie. Dr. Fitzgerald wants to check out your lungs again."

Bessie coughed each time she took a deep breath for the doctor. He tapped her on the nose after the examination. "Annie tells me you haven't eaten a thing for two days. What's that about?"

Bessie looked away. "I'm not hungry."

"What will Joe think when he comes home and finds you as thin as a sewing needle?"

"Pa didn't come home like he was supposed to. Joe won't either."

Nellie sat on the bed and held Bessie's hands. "Joe is coming home. He'll be some mad at you for not eating on his account."

Bessie threw her arms around Nellie's neck. "I misses Pa," she choked out, followed by a cough. Her rib cage dug into Nellie. "Why did Joe have to go away, too?"

Annie came into the room with a tray. "I made a batch of pancakes for my special girl." She laid the tray on the bed and her face broke into a wide smile. "In case anyone's interested, Joe's schooner just docked at Burke's Cove."

"I told you," Nellie said, and pointed to the pancakes. "Now eat."

Bessie tore off a huge chunk.

"Take small bites and chew slowly," Dr. Fitzgerald said. "You don't want a tummy ache."

"Doctor," Nellie said, "come to the kitchen for a slice of apple pie I baked this morning."

"I THINK BESSIE SHOULD recover nicely now that Joe's back," Dr. Fitzgerald said while Nellie poured tea for both of them. "She fretted about him not coming home and it delayed her recovery. The manner in which she lost her father would scare any child."

Nellie dropped into a chair. "What about the next time Joe leaves? Bessie will be haunted every time he's on the Banks."

"Indeed," Dr. Fitzgerald said softly. "She's been introduced to tragedy much too soon."

"All the families of the *Marion* crew have," Nellie said. "If it takes the rest of my life, I'm going to find out why Ike and the French captain hated each other."

The back door swung open and Joe came in. Nellie's heart jumped into her throat. *He's different*, she thought. His youthful happiness had dulled with Harry's disappearance, but now it seemed dead, burned out forever.

"Ma, how about a cuppa tea?" Even his voice seemed older, coarser.

"Sit yourself down," Nellie said.

Joe laid his duffle bag by the door. "It sure is good to be home."

"I've got other patients to see today," Dr. Fitzgerald said. "Joe, I'm pleased to see you back safe and sound."

The doctor was just out the door when Joe turned to Nellie. "Who's sick?"

"Bessie got pneumonia right after you shipped out. She's a lot better." Nellie passed Joe his tea. Her eyes lingered for a brief moment on the cut, bruised, and cracked hands that reached for the mug.

"Was it what you expected?" she asked quietly to hide her deepening sadness.

"Sorta."

Annie swooped into the kitchen. "You're a bright light on a foggy day," she said, hugging Joe to her. "Go up to Bessie's room. She's bursting at the seams to see you."

"She's been afraid you wouldn't come back," Nellie said.

When Joe poked his head around her bedroom door, Bessie's squeal echoed throughout the house. That night she ate supper with the family for the first time in two weeks.

"Back to bed," Nellie said, when Bessie tried to follow Joe and Sam out to the wharf after supper. Nellie watched her sons through the window. Both quiet. Both staring out to sea. The first stars had begun to sparkle when they returned. Sam went to bed and Joe joined Nellie in the living room.

"The house wasn't the same without you," Nellie said, knitting the heel of a sock by the glow of a candle.

"Before Pa left he had a long chat with me about fishing and my future," Joe said.

Nellie continued to knit. "He never said a word to me."

"Pa told me Uncle Joe had the same chat with him at my age. Tried to talk him out of fishing. Pa told me to finish school."

Nellie sighed. "Did he tell you that he and Uncle Tom had decided to leave fishing for good? Uncle Tom even got a job as a cook in St. John's."

Joe nodded and looked up at his parents' wedding portrait. "Pa was right. Fishing is some hard . . . and lonely. Bessie took sick because she was scared for me."

Nellie thought she saw tears in her son's eyes, yet she couldn't be sure in the faint lamplight.

"Maybe I should finish my book learning. I can work in the fish plant after school."

Nellie wanted to get up and dance a jig.

"If it's all right with you, Ma, that's what I'll do. Like Pa said, the Grand Banks ain't going nowhere."

Nellie's knitting needles clicked faster. "That's a good idea."

"Pa promised to give me his wooden seal on my first trip out. I kept thinking about it the whole time."

Nellie smiled. "He surely treasured that little sculpture."

"See ya in the morning, Ma."

Nellie heard herself hum as she finished the sock heel and was astounded by it. She truly believed she had forgotten how. She continued to hum on the way up the stairs but stopped abruptly and stared down the hall when she heard Joe and Sam talking.

"Joe, what made you tell Mom you changed your mind about fishing?"

"I was thinking of Bessie."

Nellie tiptoed past the boys' partially open door but stopped when Joe spoke again.

"I'm going back to the Banks once I finish school for good."

"But you said it was hard and lonely."

"Hard work don't matter none. I was lonely because I'm still missing Pa. He was supposed to be with me."

I'll change your mind, Nellie thought. *Mark my words.*

JOE SPENT THE NEXT two days with Bessie. Her fever returned to normal and she coughed less and less. The third day she went outside to play with Marie. They'd hardly gone through the door when Marie ran up the stone path and burst into the kitchen.

"Mrs. Myles," she said, her eyes wide and filled with tears.

"What's wrong?" Nellie asked, looking past Marie. "Is Bessie all right?"

Bessie appeared in the doorway and bent over, hands on her knees. "I'm all right, Ma," she said between gasps. "I tried to keep up with Marie."

"Dr. Fitzgerald warned you not to run for at least a week."

"Is it true?" Marie said. Her cheeks were flushed. "Have I gotta go live in an orphanage?"

"What? Who told you such nonsense?"

"Johnny Dunn and his friends said that's where all youngsters go when they got no relatives to look after them," Bessie said.

"Marie may not have any relatives, but she has us. People who love her like she was family."

Bessie looked at Marie. "See, I told ya. Those stupid boys don't know what they're yakking on about."

"Go play in the shed and don't pay any more heed to such nonsense," Nellie said. "I'll call you when dinner's ready."

The girls whizzed around Mother Patrick, who stood in the doorway. "I'm pleased to see Bessie back to herself."

Nellie smiled. "Joe's return worked a miracle."

Mother Patrick pulled a white envelope from her robe. "Sorry to say I'm the bearer of bad news concerning Marie. This arrived this morning from Montreal, Canada."

Nellie's fingers shook as she pulled out the letter. She read silently.

> *Mother Patrick:*
>
> *My name is Sheila Jones. Ike Jones was my brother. I have only just been informed of his passing and was quite shocked to learn he was the captain of a fishing schooner. As my niece's mother is also deceased, it is my duty to care for his child.*
>
> *My brother's lawyer, Mr. William Fleming of St. John's, gave me your name as a contact person in St. Jacques. I am busy at the moment so cannot come immediately, but I hope to arrive in your community by late September.*
>
> *Please advise the family where my niece is staying that she will live with me. Thank you in advance for your assistance.*
>
> *Sheila Jones*

Nellie threw the letter on the table. "Ike's sister seems as pleasant as a sack of rotted, spongy potatoes!"

"She does come across as somewhat stuffy."

"Cold-hearted, you mean. It sounds like she's making a business deal. She doesn't even say Marie's name." Nellie rubbed her forehead. "Most likely doesn't know her name."

Mother Patrick folded the letter and jammed it back into the envelope.

"What are we going to do?" Nellie said. "I can't let Marie go. She's scared to death of leaving us."

"We have time to figure something out."

Nellie paced across the floor. "I'll allow this Sheila Jones has never laid eyes on Marie before. Marie for sure has never mentioned her."

"As far as I'm aware, Ike never mentioned having a sister," Mother Patrick said. "Along with the letter, that tells me they weren't very close. I'll write Mr. Fleming. Maybe he can shed some light on this Sheila Jones."

Nellie's voice quivered. "Ask him if Marie can stay with me. Losing her would be like losing one of my own."

Mother Patrick tut-tutted. "This isn't the time for Marie to be torn away from people who love her and whom she's known for most of her life."

Nellie clenched her fists. "None of this would be happening if Ike and the French captain hadn't acted like spoiled youngsters. This mess makes me want to know even more."

"Sadly we may never learn the reason why," Mother Patrick said. Then, as an afterthought, she added, "What good would it do, anyway?"

Nellie was quick to answer. "Peace of mind."

"I'll write that letter as soon as I get back to the convent," Mother Patrick said, already halfway out the door.

There's got to be someone who knows what the two men fought about, Nellie thought. An idea sprang to mind. She grabbed her shawl and sprinted up the hill to talk to Eloise McEvoy.

NELLIE RAN INTO ELOISE as she was coming out of Young's General Store. "Mme. Myles," Eloise greeted her. "*Bonjour*. 'Ow are you?"

"Coping," she said. "Like all the other widows."

"*Quelle tragédie.*" Eloise sighed. "I feel so sad for everyone."

"I was on my way to your house to ask you a few questions, if you can spare the time," Nellie said.

"Of course. 'Ow can I help you?"

"Maybe you can tell me something about Captain Maurice."

"'E is a friend of my father, and my mother does not like 'im." Eloise turned up her nose. "She thinks 'e is rude and very nasty."

"What was the trouble between him and Ike Jones?"

"*Mon papa* does not know. But the first time Mr. Jones came to St. Pierre, 'e asked many people where *le capitaine* Maurice lived."

"Did Ike say why he was looking for him?"

"*Non. Le capitaine* Maurice refused to allow M. Jones into his home. Maybe *le père* Jean-Claude can tell you more."

Nellie smiled at the petite, dark-haired French woman. "I already talked with him. Thanks, Eloise. You've been a grand help."

"You are very welcome," Eloise said, and went on her way.

Nellie ran all the way to the convent. Sister Thérèse showed the panting woman into her superior's office.

Mother Patrick sat at her table, reviewing a new history textbook she would be using in the fall. "Sit down and catch your breath, Nellie. Then tell me who was chasing you."

"I talked to Eloise," Nellie blurted out. "It appears the feud between Ike and Maurice started before Ike moved to St. Jacques. Ike was so secretive about his life. He never talked about his wife to anyone, not even his own daughter."

Mother Patrick had a faraway look in her eyes.

Nellie collapsed into a chair. "Are you all right, Mother Patrick?"

"Of course."

"The only thing Marie knows is that she's named after her mother. Ike has kept quiet about his past life because he's hiding something awful." Nellie shivered. "I can feel it."

"Poor Marie," Mother Patrick said. "I'm afraid to think what might be in store for her."

"Me too," Nellie said. "I'll protect her no matter what it takes."

A bell rang out. "One o'clock. I must go on home and get dinner on the table."

The door closed behind Nellie. Mother Patrick pulled a piece of paper out of the desk drawer. On it was a single sentence neatly scribed in black ink. *Well, Jean-Claude, have you had enough time to consider the best course of action for Marie and Nellie?*

Mother Patrick sealed the note inside an envelope and set out for Burke's Cove.

"Mr. Marsh, see that Father Jean-Claude gets this," she said to the trader. "Wait for a reply."

Steve tipped his salt and pepper hat. "That I will, Mother Patrick. See you tomorrow." His boat chugged toward the ocean on its semi-weekly trip to St. Pierre.

Mother Patrick returned home to write to Ike Jones's lawyer, then delivered the letter to the post office herself. "How long will it take to reach St. John's?" she asked the postmaster, a tiny man with a bald head.

"Let me see. The supply ship came yesterday, so the next one isn't for another two weeks."

Mother Patrick tut-tutted. "I won't receive a reply for at least a month."

"Right," the postmaster said. "Sorry 'bout that."

Mother Patrick thanked the man and strolled back to the convent.

THE FOLLOWING AFTERNOON, MOTHER Patrick waited at Burke's Cove for Steve Marsh. He handed her a small square piece of paper that contained a brief note. *Come to St. Pierre.* "Did Father Jean-Claude say anything?"

"No. Just passed me that there paper and said to give it to you."

Mother Patrick crumpled up the paper and tossed it in the harbour. "You have a passenger for the day after tomorrow," she said.

"Sorry, Mother Patrick. I wasn't reckoning on any passengers this time. You'll have to wait until the next trip."

"It's a matter of utmost importance."

Steve grinned. "Didn't get enough of the sea air and rough waves the last time, eh?"

Mother Patrick groaned. "I wish that's all it was."

Steve rubbed the stubble on his chin and cocked an eyebrow. "All right, then. See you at nine the day after tomorrow."

Chapter 11

GREY CLOUDS HUNG LOW in the sky as Father Jean-Claude stepped out of the rectory. Fog surrounded the island when he reached the wharf, where Steve Marsh's boat bobbed on the lively waves. Mother Patrick's face was ashen and covered in sea spray when the priest helped her ashore. She grabbed onto a post for support the second her feet touched solid ground.

"You came alone," he said. "The mother house won't be pleased to hear their sisters are taking such chances."

"I won't tell if you won't," Mother Patrick said. "Besides, it wouldn't be Christian to subject anyone else to the tortures of the sea."

Father Jean-Claude looked for his friend's overnight bag. "I'm not staying the night," Mother Patrick said. "Mr. Marsh has some business to conclude and will come for me when he's done."

"Are you up for the short walk to the rectory?"

"My legs are still on the boat, but I'll give it a try anyway," she said, leaning on the priest.

"The mother house would not be pleased with this close contact either."

"You going to tell them?"

Father Jean-Claude threw back his head and laughed as they moved slowly down the road. The housekeeper had hot tea ready in the den. Mother Patrick sank into a big armchair and gulped down the steamy liquid. "Never thought I'd warm up again."

Father Jean-Claude offered her a strawberry pastry. "I have your favourite."

She took the sweet. "My stomach isn't quite in my throat anymore." She pinched off a flake. "You could've told me in a letter what Maurice said to the child. What's all the secrecy?"

The priest sat forward and whispered every word Maurice had spat at Marie. "Now you understand why I preferred not to put such information on paper."

"I . . . I don't know what to say," Mother Patrick said. "This is beyond anything I could have imagined."

Father Jean-Claude sat back in his chair. "I am truly sorry, *chère amie*. The decision, or should I say the burden, to reveal or not to reveal the truth is now in your hands."

Mother Patrick laid the pastry on her saucer. "I must pray for guidance."

"*Oui*," Father Jean-Claude said. "We will pray together."

Both bowed their heads. The housekeeper broke the silence a few minutes later when she came for the tea tray and leftover pastries.

A serene look softened Mother Patrick's face. "Prayer does work," she said. "I know what must be done."

"You are a little green around the gills, as you English say, *ma mère* Patrick. Maybe you should stay the night. M. Marsh can wait until the morning."

"I'd only spend the night worrying over how sick I'll be. Better to deal with it quickly."

The housekeeper poked her head in the door. "*Monsieur Marsh est içi pour la bonne soeur.*"

"Steve was quick," Mother Patrick said.

Father Jean-Claude accompanied his friend to the boat and wished her safe journey. "I am here if you need my help," he said. He smiled at Steve. "Take care of my good friend."

"Count on me, Father," he said, and started the engine.

Mother Patrick spotted cigarettes and rum stacked neatly at the back of the boat. "I see you're trading for smokes and swallies, as Nellie would say."

Steve covered the lot with a blanket. "My son's getting hitched. Can't have a proper wedding without a drop of the good stuff."

"Have you ever been caught?"

"No. My grandpa was once. It taught him to be more careful after that. That's why I'm bringing my stash to an island near Burke's Cove. I'll pick it up tonight." Steve looked at Mother Patrick. "I'm right sorry about the inconvenience, Mother Patrick. Especially since the sea don't agree with ya."

"It was my choice to come. Don't give it another thought."

She pulled a small bag of stale bread from her pocket. "This will suffice for the time being."

Steve chinwagged about his son's upcoming wedding and the new house near completion for the couple over in Boxey. "Terrible business, the *Marion*. The community's so small to begin with; they couldn't afford to lose any men."

The day remained sunny as the boat eased over the water. A patch of rocks appeared to the left. "Is that the island?" Mother Patrick asked.

"Right-o, Mother Patrick. Won't take me long to unload."

Mother Patrick disembarked with Steve. "Maybe I'll just stay here for the night," she said.

"Another thirty minutes and we're back at Burke's Cove. You'll hold out for that long."

Steve carried the last case of rum to a small cavern. Mother Patrick stared at the stacks of boxes spread over every available space. "Is this all yours?"

"No."

"Aren't you fishermen afraid someone will come along and steal it?"

"Hasn't happened yet."

The holy nun and the smuggler returned to the boat. "You missed something," she said, pointing to a carton of French cigarettes.

"What's that noise?" She turned around and saw a large boat chugging toward them. "Blessed Mother of God, it's the Rangers! You're in for it now, Steve Marsh."

The Rangers pulled alongside. Steve winked. "Not to worry, Mother Patrick."

"Steve Marsh!" a tall, thin man of thirty called down. "I'm coming aboard to . . ." His voice faded to a murmur at the sight of Mother Patrick sitting with her hands folded on her lap. The carton of cigarettes had somehow found a home under her long robes.

She looked up at the young man. "Why, if it isn't young Willy Burns. I haven't seen your mother since the family moved to St. John's. How is she?"

"Very well, Mother Patrick."

"Are you married, Willy?"

"Two years."

"Any children?"

"One on the way."

"Lovely. Your mother must be overjoyed."

"Mr. Burns," Steve said, "it's late. Might I be on me way?"

Willy glared at him. "Go ahead," he said, and signalled for the boat to move away. Mother Patrick wagged a finger under Steve's nose. "You were lucky I happened to be aboard the one time you're stopped by the Rangers."

Steve grinned. "I don't believe in luck, Mother Patrick. Do you?"

She couldn't help but grin as well. "You have quite the head on your shoulders, Mr. Marsh, and you use it well."

"As do you, Mother Patrick."

ALTHOUGH THE SEA WAS calm and shone like a polished mirror, Mother Patrick threw up twice on the return trip.

"A few more crossings will make you a hardy sailor," Steve said once they docked at Burke's Cove.

"And make me your smuggling partner," she added.

Sister Thérèse greeted her superior from a horse and cart, but Mother Patrick waved her on. "Go on ahead, Sister. I'll walk. I can't handle any more rocking motion. The good solid earth beneath my feet will do me a world of good."

"Begging your pardon, Mother Patrick," Steve said. "I'm going right by the convent. How about I walk with ya?"

"That would be very much appreciated." Mother Patrick linked her arm through his. "You can help keep me upright."

"My Lilah would fair faint to see me arm in arm with a nun."

"We're plain ordinary people, not supreme beings to be paced on pedestals," Mother Patrick said.

Steve laughed. "Try telling that to my missus." The convent came into view. "Here you go. Right to your door."

Dry toast and tea awaited the fatigued traveller in her bedroom. "This will help your stomach," Sister Thérèse said. The nun from France suffered from seasickness as well. A loud *thump, thump* on the front door called Sister Thérèse from the room.

Nellie barrelled into the bedroom and dragged the only chair to the side of the bed. "I just saw Steve Marsh on my way here. He told me you just got back from St. Pierre. Did you discover any news about the *Marion*?"

"No, nothing like that. Father Jean-Claude wanted to talk to me about a recent personal problem which greatly troubled him."

"Oh," Nellie said.

"I'm beginning to believe it's time to forget about all that for a while."

"I won't let it go," Nellie said. "I can't."

"I didn't mean forget about it forever. Don't you agree that for now we should put all our efforts into making sure Marie stays where she belongs?"

"Maybe Sheila Jones will put Marie's happiness first."

"There's more of a chance I'll never be seasick again."

THE NIGHTS COOLED OFF toward mid-August. Nellie lit the fireplace and sat in the rocker, staring at Harry's armchair. Her eyes wandered to the mantel. A package of opened Camel cigarettes lay at the far end. Harry had opened it the night before he set out on the *Marion*. Nellie couldn't bear to throw them out. She turned to her husband's boyish face in the wedding portrait. "Oh, Harry," she sighed, "were you alone or with Tom when the end came? Did you suffer?"

She closed her eyes and imagined how Harry would respond. *Never you mind, love. Taking good care of our youngsters is all that matters now.*

"I will, Harry," she whispered. "I promise." She rested her head on the back of the rocker. The heat from the fire grazed her face. Her lids grew heavy. "I'll just rest a spell," she murmured.

The clock ticked, the steady sound comforting, familiar. The fire burned down to embers.

"Ma, wake up." Sam was shaking her shoulder.

Nellie's eyes fluttered open. Daylight flooded the room. "Goodness me," she said. "I fell asleep." She stretched to loosen the knots in her back and neck muscles. "I'll get breakfast started."

Sam smiled, his sky-blue eyes bright. "Can't you smell anything?"

Nellie sniffed. "Bacon."

"Marie and Bessie wanted to surprise you."

Nellie wanted to hug her son but knew she'd embarrass him. "Indeed they have."

Joe came in from chopping wood the same instant that Sam and Nellie strolled into the kitchen.

"All of you, sit," Bessie said. "Me and Marie will serve the food."

Nellie watched the two girls portion out the bacon and scrambled eggs onto each plate, talking and giggling as they did. *Harry,* she thought, *you're missing the best years of your youngsters' lives.* Yet again, Dottie's words rang in her head. *It's not fair.*

The youngsters finished every scrap on their plates.

"That was gorgeous, scrumptious," Nellie said. "A grand treat."

"Me and Bessie will wash the dishes, too," Marie said.

"Since you two made breakfast, the boys will do them."

Sam's fork fell and clanged when it hit the floor. Joe's eyes bulged out of his head. "You're not serious. Right?"

Bessie giggled. "Don't be so silly, b'y. Ma is joshing."

Her daughter's laughter lifted Nellie's spirits. "After I do the dishes," she said, "we'll get the rest of Marie's clothes and the porcelain dolls from her house."

"I don't want to go there any more," Marie said, and ran outside with Bessie.

"We're off to Ned's Field," Joe said. "Father Curran's gonna show us how to play football proper. Did you know he was on a school team in Ireland?"

Nellie shook her head.

"After that we're going to the beach for a swim."

"Not me," Sam said. "I hates the sea, since it took Pa and Uncle Tom from us."

Nellie expected Joe to whip out a sarcastic remark. Instead, he slapped a hand on Sam's shoulder.

"Come on, little brother. Father Curran's waiting."

Nellie busied herself with the dishes and made the weekly batch of bread, putting aside enough dough for toutons. Finally out of molasses, she decided to visit the general store. Sam wouldn't touch the fried dough unless it was dripping with the brown, gooey sauce.

Denis Burke came out of the store as Nellie approached. He nodded briefly and hurried on his way. "Oh well," Nellie said under her breath, "maybe Joe won't work in the Burke's fish plant after all." She watched Denis go toward the Rooms. "There's always the Young's plant."

The general store was empty except for the clerk, Mr. Hodder, a big, quiet man like his son Ron and nephew John.

Nellie looked around the large store. Sweets, medicines, clothes, food, books, and household supplies lined the floor-to-ceiling shelves. Furniture lay haphazardly displayed on the shop floor. Nellie picked up a bottle of molasses from a shelf by the door.

"Good day, Nellie," Mr. Hodder said, skimming through a woman's clothing catalogue behind the counter. "How are you doing?" His son, Ron, had left behind a young widow and five small children.

"I'm doing my best to cope." Nellie laid coins for her purchase on the marble counter. "Like you and all the rest of the families."

"At least Susie has me and her brothers to help out moneywise. I'm ordering a fancy hat for her birthday." He paused. "But John's missus only has me."

"She's luckier than most of the widows."

Mr. Hodder slid Nellie's coins back to her. She opened her mouth to refuse his charity. "Please take it, Nellie. Harry and Tom repaired my barn more than once without taking a penny. Let me do this one small thing for them."

"Just this once, then. Thank you."

The bell over the door jangled and Ned Noseworthy's wife came in. She lived in Boxey, and Nellie hadn't seen her since the church service. She was thinner, paler. Nellie suddenly realized her own clothes didn't fit as snugly anymore either. The woman exchanged the same artificial smile as every other *Marion* widow, a smile that didn't quite make it to the eyes. *Grief destroys the body faster than any sickness*, Nellie thought. She said hello and left.

She made her way to Annie's house, which took her by Tom's place, once owned by Uncle Joe. The saltbox-style home looked forgotten, sad, as if it sensed the owner would never return. Nellie looked away. Previously unshed tears gushed to the surface.

Annie and Dottie puttered around in the kitchen, cleaning and cooking. Dottie wore a determined expression and Annie's lips were pressed together so tightly they were white.

"Anything the matter?" Nellie said.

"Not a thing," Dottie said. "Dr. Fitzgerald found me work with a Dr. and Mrs. Williams as housekeeper and cook in St. John's. I starts next week."

"It's too big of a step to take on your own," Annie said. "'Specially with two infants." She put the kettle on the stove. "Nellie, help me talk some sense into her."

Dottie took down three mugs from the cupboard. "Dr. Fitzgerald and his missus are taking me to St. John's to meet Dr. Williams. They wants to make sure everything goes all right."

"Aren't you worried about such a big change?" Nellie said.

"Dr. Williams is an old friend of Dr. Fitzgerald. He's retired and his wife has awful bad arthritis. She can't cook and clean anymore."

"What about the twins?"

"It's a live-in job and I can keep the twins with me. If it doesn't work out, I'm to write to Dr. Fitzgerald right away."

Nellie pulled out a chair. "Annie, you know Dr. Fitzgerald wouldn't pick out just anybody for Dottie."

"She should go by herself first, to see how she manages. What a sin to uproot newborns and cart them all the way to St. John's."

"I ain't going anywhere without my youngsters," Dottie said softly. "There's nothing here for me. I can start a new life in St. John's."

Annie dabbed at a tear with the corner of her apron. "Dottie, I'm an old woman. What if I never sees you or them precious angels again?"

"You and Nellie are family. I could never forget about either of you. Fred's brother, Seth, is gonna visit as often as he can, to keep in touch with his nephews. Come with him." Dottie looked at the clock over the sink. "The twins will wake up any minute now and start howling for their milk."

The young woman walked out of the kitchen.

"I'm some worried about her," Annie said.

"Dottie's stronger than we give her credit for," Nellie said.

Annie smoothed down the red and white checkered tablecloth. "Life's real hard sometimes. Especially when you're getting on in years like me."

"Marie doesn't want to go to her house ever again," Nellie said, changing the subject to break Annie's sombre reflections.

"Poor mite. It's not the same without her pa."

"Maybe I'll pick up some of her things myself. Ike gave me a spare key in case Marie needed anything while he was away."

"If Marie wanted any of her stuff, she would have said so by now."

"She's missing Ike, that's all. Every child loves to have familiar things around them."

"Leave well enough alone, Nellie. Marie is doing just fine."

"But—"

"Nellie," Annie interrupted. "Did you forget about Ike's sister? She might be bad enough to accuse us of stealing. Do you want to risk that?"

"It's only Marie's things."

"So wait until she asks to go."

*

NELLIE ESCAPED TO THE living room, as she'd done every night of her married life, once the youngsters were in bed. Harry's vacant armchair loomed as a constant reminder of the long, lonely evenings ahead. She looked at the wedding portrait. "Harry, I don't know how to help Annie." Her voice was a shade softer than a whisper. "All the heartache is getting the better of her. She's terribly upset about Dottie." The room grew dark as clouds drifted over the full moon. Nellie lit the candle on the table next to her and began to rock. The chair squeaked and groaned into the early hours of the morning. Nellie yawned yet didn't move, her eyes transfixed on Harry's portrait. She couldn't get used to going to bed without him.

"Ma, what's wrong?" Nellie hadn't heard Joe come down the stairs. "You goes to bed later and later every night."

Nellie turned misty eyes to her son.

"I misses Pa, too," he said.

Nellie eased herself out of the rocker. "You're a good son to worry about your mother." She ruffled his hair.

"Ma," Joe said when they reached his room. "Pa would want us to be happy, right?"

"That's the one thing I'm sure of."

Nellie lay in bed staring out at the water, thinking about how the *Marion*'s disappearance had forever changed the lives of so many. Annie was shaken, her tough outer surface cracked. She deserved someone to be strong for her. Youngsters struggled to cope without their fathers. Everywhere she went in the community, someone grieved. All because of one man. The conversation with Guy Hays suddenly came to mind. He believed the deaths of the *Marion*'s crew was a deliberate act of revenge that would never be proven. Nellie buried her head under the covers. For the first time since Harry's death, she cried herself to sleep.

Chapter 12

DOTTIE STOOD ON THE wharf with Mother Patrick, Annie, and Nellie. Her trunk, containing every possession she owned, was already loaded on board the supply boat. The only memento of Fred was the small knife he used for whittling, which she carried in her purse at all times. Dr. Fitzgerald and his wife had gone aboard earlier with the twins.

Annie hugged Dottie. The younger woman almost disappeared in her friend's embrace. "Are you sure this is what you wants to do?" Annie said.

Tears stained Dottie's cheeks when she drew back. "I'm awful scared," she said. "But I have to do this for my boys."

Annie patted Dottie's shoulder. "Don't fret, dearie, I understands."

Mother Patrick folded her arms. "There's nothing to worry about. Dr. Fitzgerald and his good lady will make sure you're settled and feeling good about your new home."

"That's right," Nellie piped in. "Your parents couldn't do any more if they were alive."

"You've all been so helpful and loving." Dottie's voice broke. "I'll miss all of ye."

Annie wiped away Dottie's tears. "Don't carry on like that. You're doing what any good, sensible mother would do for her youngsters."

"Thanks for everything. You all helped me get through Fred's loss."

Mother Patrick sniffed and pulled out a crisp white handkerchief. "Hay fever is such a bother," she said, rubbing her nose.

Annie wiped a tear from her own cheek. "The darn fever is catching."

"I best go before the boat takes off without me," Dottie said.

Annie took her hands. "Write the first chance you gets. We'll keep you up to date on all the happenings here."

"I'd really like that. No matter where I lives, this will always be my real home."

Nellie smiled. "Never forget, we're only a boat ride away."

Dottie gave Annie a final hug and hurried away. She waved from the dock.

Nellie turned to Annie and Mother Patrick. "Come to my house for a mug-up," she said. "A little pick-me-up is what we all need right now."

"Life goes around until we ends up where we started," Annie said as they walked. "I'm alone again in a big, empty house." She closed her eyes. "The older you are, the harder it is to deal with."

Nellie gave Annie's arm a squeeze. "You'll be too busy with the youngsters and making jam preserves from the buckets of blueberries they'll pick to even think about being alone. In no time you'll be begging for a little peace and quiet."

Annie looked sideways at Nellie. "Don't forget all the butter I'll have to churn, because that's the one chore you hates."

Mother Patrick screwed up her nose. "Milking cows is mine. Those cantankerous beasts don't like me for some inexplicable reason."

The women laughed and continued past the convent. Sister Thérèse opened the door. "Mother Patrick," she called. "A Sheila Jones is here to see you on a very urgent matter. She is in your office."

"What?" Nellie cried out. "She's not supposed to be here for another month."

"Come along, ladies," Mother Patrick said, scurrying to the convent.

*

SHEILA JONES SAT TALL in a chair with white gloved hands on her lap. She turned her head toward the door when Mother Patrick and her two companions walked in. "You are Mother Patrick, I presume," she said with a Canadian accent.

Nellie stared at the woman who planned to steal Marie away from her. She was at least sixty years old with grey hair tied back in a neat, tight bun at the nape of her neck. She wore a black dress with a stiff, white lace collar and a black coat. Her skin was pale. Her lips were almost as pale and seemed to fade into her face. She took in Nellie and Annie with a single, quick glance as if they were unimportant before focusing her attention on Mother Patrick. "I wish to speak to you in private."

Mother Patrick extended her hand to Sheila. "Good day to you."

Sheila's fingers lightly grazed the nun's hand. "It's been a long day. The boat ride to this . . ." She paused and flared her nose as if there was a bad smell in the room. ". . . to this quaint little settlement lasted forever."

"Yes, indeed," Mother Patrick said. "Our community is quite lovely. Must be a breath of fresh air compared to the stuffy, overcrowded city of Montreal."

Nellie smothered the urge to laugh.

Sheila stiffened and flicked an invisible object from her dress. "As I wrote in my letter, I'm here to pick up my niece."

"Of course," Mother Patrick said. "First I'd like to introduce two of my closest friends. Mrs. Anne Cluett."

Sheila gave a slight nod.

"Mrs. Nellie Myles. She's taking excellent care of Marie."

Sheila stood up. She was as tall as Annie and thinner than a stick of wood on a picket fence. "I'll take the child off your hands as soon as possible."

Nellie's heart thumped in her ears. She opened her mouth to speak, but Mother Patrick cut across her. "Before we get down to business, Mrs. Jones—"

"Miss Jones," Sheila interrupted.

Mother Patrick smiled. "My apologies, Miss Jones. Let me offer you something to eat."

"I've been informed that the supply boat doesn't return for another two weeks, and the train doesn't run this far," Sheila said. "Therefore, I have no choice but to remain. Where's the hotel?"

"You'll stay at the convent. That way we'll get to know each other much better."

Sister Thérèse entered the room. "Mother Patrick, tea is ready in the dining room as you requested," she said.

Egg and cheese sandwiches were laid out on white plates. Tea had been steeped in a matching white teapot. "I'd like to convey my sympathy for the sudden loss of your brother," Mother Patrick said.

Sheila chewed on the corner of a cheese sandwich. "At fifteen I met my brother for the first time. He was a mere infant. I never saw him again." She chewed her food and swallowed. "We have different mothers. Mine died when I was four. My father sent me to live with my mother's sister. I rarely saw him after that."

"How awful," Annie said.

"Not at all. My aunt raised me to be the person I am today."

"Like I said," Annie mumbled under her breath, "how awful."

Nellie rubbed sweaty palms on her knees. "Why are you willing to take care of Ike's child if you haven't seen each other for years?"

"It's quite simple," Sheila replied. "I was taught that duty and obligation must be upheld no matter how unpleasant or inconvenient."

"What about love?"

Sheila bit off another corner of her sandwich. "I don't see your point."

"Marie is happy and loved. Why take her away from that?"

Sheila raised an eyebrow. "My dear woman, what does love have to do with anything? Marie will learn to accept her new life with contentment. Just as I did." She cast a glance out the window. "Montreal has so much more to offer a young girl."

Annie's jaw tightened. "Like what, for instance?"

Sheila stared at her, the frown line between her eyes deepening. "Paved streets, sidewalks, theatres, museums, a proper education, reliable transportation. Need I say more?"

Annie folded her arms across her large bosom. "Mother Patrick and the nuns give the best schooling around."

Sheila looked at Mother Patrick. "No offence, Mother Patrick. I believe there's more to education than religious teachings."

The nun smiled. "I agree with you one hundred per cent."

Nellie saw Annie's lips press together and sprang to her feet. "Come on, Annie," she said. "It's almost suppertime. It's been a pleasure meeting you, Miss Jones."

Sheila gave an almost imperceptible nod. Nellie grabbed Annie by the arm and dragged her from the room.

"The nerve of that woman," Annie said once they were outside the convent, "coming here and acting like she's better than us. The old bat would ruin our sweet Marie." Annie paused to catch her breath. "She never even asked how the child was coping with Ike's death."

"Mother Patrick wrote Ike's lawyer in St. John's ages ago looking for advice about Marie," Nellie said. "He hasn't written back yet."

Annie flicked a strand of hair out of her eyes. "Townies are all alike. You can't depend on them." She sighed. "We can't put off any longer telling poor Marie about her lovely Auntie Sheila."

"Come home with me. You should be there when I break the bad tidings to the youngsters."

Joe was out chopping wood when they arrived.

"Where's Marie?" Annie asked him.

He split a round of wood in two. "They're playing alleys in the shed."

"Go get them. Your ma needs to talk to all of you right away. Don't worry, no one's been hurt," she added when Joe stared at her with frightened eyes.

Two buckets full of blueberries sat on the kitchen table. "Bessie and Marie picked those," Nellie said. "They can't wait for me to make tarts." She moved the buckets to the counter. "Why does everything have to be so complicated?"

Nellie, Annie, and Sam were seated in the living room when Joe came back with the girls. Marie flopped on the chesterfield next to

Nellie. "You wants to tell us something real important?"

Nellie's throat was dry. Her face felt frozen and she couldn't even give her a reassuring smile. "Marie, I have some news that concerns you," she said after a slight hesitation. "Your father's sister is in from Montreal to see you."

Bessie hugged Marie. "How exciting!"

"I don't have an aunt. Pa would have told me."

Sam shifted on the chesterfield. "She's here to take Marie away." He sounded old. Every head turned toward him.

"You're nuts," Joe said. "She wouldn't do that to Marie."

"I'm afraid Sam's right," Nellie said.

Marie's chest heaved. "I won't go with her."

Nellie smoothed down Marie's hair. "She's your real family. That should make you happy."

Marie shook her head over and over. "No! You're my real family. Please don't let her take me away."

Nellie's eyes pleaded with Annie for help.

"We all loves you," Annie said softly. "None of us wants you to go, but your aunt has the right to raise you."

"Please, please," Marie sobbed. "I don't want to go."

"If Marie leaves," Sam said, "we'll never see her again."

"Just like Pa," Joe added quietly.

The lump in Nellie's throat almost choked her. "Maybe if we tell Miss Jones how much we love Marie, she'll change her mind," she said.

SHEILA JONES PUSHED HER plate aside and cleaned the corners of her mouth with a white handkerchief from her pocket. "I didn't realize I was so hungry," she said, digging into a second slice of pie.

Mother Patrick stared at the woman over the rim of her cup. "May I ask when was the last time you spoke to your brother?"

"Ten years ago. He wrote to me about his marriage and the birth of his daughter."

"Do you know anything about his wife?"

"Only that she was from St. John's. I don't recall her name."

"How did Ike's lawyer know where to contact you?"

"Obviously Ike gave him my address. We may not be close, but we were brother and sister, after all." Sheila consumed the last crumb of pie. "I'd like to rest after the long trip."

"Of course," Mother Patrick said. "I had your luggage brought up to your room. Marie always stayed with the Myles family whenever Ike went to sea. It's her second home."

"She'll thrive in my care," Sheila said, and followed Mother Patrick down the hall and up the stairs.

"Marie adored her father. She needed love and stability to get through the heartbreak. The Myles family bestowed both in abundance." Mother Patrick turned to face Sheila. "I don't see how ripping her away from that will make her thrive."

Sheila's expression remained unreadable. "I will make it so."

Mother Patrick nodded to the door on the left. "This is your room. Have a good rest."

"I want to see my brother's house as soon as I wake."

"Mrs. Myles has a key and will be delighted to take you there," Mother Patrick said, and went downstairs, muttering to herself. She turned a corner and almost ran into Sister Thérèse.

"Mother Patrick, are you okay?"

"Forgive me, Sister. I didn't see you there. I'm going out for a while."

Her face was flushed when she barged into Nellie's kitchen a few minutes later.

"Miss Jones wants to see Ike's house after her nap," she said. "Any self-respecting aunt would prefer to meet her niece first."

Nellie peeled potatoes at the table. "I thinks she's more interested in how much money Ike has," she said.

"Ike's lawyer should've had the common decency to respond to my letter," the nun said. "I've never been so riled up in all my life. Heaven help me."

Nellie wiped her hands on her apron and put water in the kettle. "A hot cuppa tea is what you need."

"Lovely idea, child. My nerves are getting the better of me. A slice of fruitcake will surely revive me."

Mother Patrick devoured the sweet and left the house with half the cake wrapped in parchment paper.

Nellie peeled the last of the potatoes and put them in the boiler. Then she went outside to get an armful of wood for the stove. Marie sat alone on a stump.

"Mrs. Myles," she said. "I wants to go to my house."

"What brought that on?"

"There's something I wants to give Bessie." Marie dug her toe into the dirt. "I heard Mother Patrick tell you that Pa's sister wants to see the house. She might not let me . . ." She paused. "Can we go right now?"

Nellie quickly grabbed the key from the cupboard and, taking Marie's hand, hurried down the path. Ike's house stood on the crest of a hill overlooking a waterfall. A magnificent garden had once graced the front. The grass needed to be cut and weeds had begun to ravish the flowerbeds. *What will become of it now?* Nellie thought, inserting the key into the door. She glanced at Marie. *Especially if you're forced to leave.*

A large marble table stood in the centre of the front room. Dust had formed on the smooth surface and on a glass vase that held dry, withered carnations picked from the garden. Carpeted stairs wound up to reveal a wide hallway with three bedrooms on each side; a dining area lay straight ahead. The hallway to the right led to the living room, den, and kitchen. Nellie walked toward the den where, according to Marie, Ike had spent most of his time. A desk stood in front of a floor-to-ceiling window with royal blue curtains partially drawn. The sun peeked through, giving just enough light for them to inspect the room. Books adorned every shelf along three walls.

A wedding portrait hung over the mantel fireplace. The bride had blonde hair, pale skin, and a smile that made her blue eyes sparkle. "Ma was pretty," Marie said.

"You got Ike's hair colour, but you're the image of your mother," Nellie said. She looked at the captain. The smile he exuded from a clean-shaven face matched the glow of the woman's happiness. *Why didn't you ever talk about your wife?* she thought. *A child needs to know about her mother.*

"I miss Pa so much my heart hurts." Marie turned to Nellie. "Bessie's afraid she'll forget Mr. Myles."

Nellie's breath caught in her throat.

"I told her that won't happen," Marie said with a certainty that brought Nellie close to tears. "All we have to do is remember how they made us laugh."

Nellie smiled down at Marie. "What did you come to get?"

"It's in my bedroom."

Nellie followed her up the stairs to the second room on the right. Marie opened the door to reveal a space twice the size of the room she shared with Bessie. A large bed with a pink and ivory bedspread stood opposite a huge bay window with ivory lace curtains. One wall held shelves containing books and porcelain dolls. A white bureau and wardrobe occupied the wall next to the bed. Marie made straight for the night table and picked up a sterling silver jewellery box inlaid with speckles of gold. The letters M.J. were engraved on the cover. "Pa had it made for my last birthday."

"It's lovely," Nellie said.

She opened the drawer and took out an exact duplicate. B.M. was engraved on the cover. "This one's for Bessie." She put the jewellery box in a white tie string bag. "Only Bessie."

"Are you sure about this?" Nellie asked.

Marie hugged the box to her. "Yes. It's our secret."

Chapter 13

NELLIE WALKED IN THE back door and saw Bessie poke a fork into a bubbling pot. Marie hid the music box behind her back.

"I boiled the potatoes," Bessie said.

Marie backed toward the hallway. "Come upstairs, Bessie. I have a surprise for ya," she said, and raced out of the kitchen.

Nellie donned her apron. "Before you go, Bessie, get me a tin of bully beef from the pantry. We're having beef patties for supper. Where are Joe and Sam?"

"They're at the convent helping the Sisters milk the cows." Bessie started toward the door. "Ma, is that woman really gonna take Marie away?"

"Miss Jones is determined to get her way."

"Captain Jones would be mad at his sister because he liked Marie staying with us."

"Indeed he did," Nellie said. "We're not giving up on Marie."

Bessie's right about Ike, Nellie thought, and mashed the potatoes. She dumped in the beef to form patties, then placed them in the frying pan.

Joe and Sam bustled through the door, each with a rhubarb pie. "Mother Patrick sent these over," Sam said.

"Sit down," Nellie said. "Supper's about ready."

Marie and Bessie's footsteps sounded on the stairs. Neither one said a word, nor did their faces betray any excitement. Nellie hoped the music box would improve Bessie's spirits. Joe and Sam hardly spoke. Nellie wanted to scream, to cry out—anything to strangle the silence that was the new norm at mealtimes since the *Marion*'s disappearance. The silence cut deeper into Nellie's heart than the ache of loss.

Marie pushed her plate away after eating only two mouthfuls of food. "I'm not hungry."

"Me neither," Bessie said.

Nellie cut one of the rhubarb pies into four large pieces. "Not eating isn't gonna help anyone."

"I'm sorry," Marie muttered.

"School starts soon," Nellie said, in an effort to spark conversation.

"Right," Sam said. A hint of the child he once was sneaked into his voice. "I can't wait."

Bessie frowned. "I can, if Marie won't be there."

"The supply boat won't be back for another two weeks," Nellie said. "Make the most of our time together instead of moping around." She gave each child a slice of pie. "I'll tell Mother Patrick if you don't eat that."

Joe dug into his. "Not that. She'll preach on and on about the poor, starving youngsters of the world."

"And keep us at least an hour," Sam added.

"Go play while it's still light out," Nellie said, and filled the dishpan with water from the bucket.

"Nellie." She turned to find Mother Patrick and Sheila Jones in the doorway. "Are you too busy to take us to Ike's house now?" the nun said.

"Is Marie in?" Sheila Jones asked.

"She's in the shed with my youngsters. I'll get her."

"Don't bother her right now. I'd like to see my brother's house first."

Nellie felt the key in her pocket. She couldn't allow Sheila to know she'd been there, so she pretended to reach behind a cup in the cupboard.

Mother Patrick led the way down the path, Sheila by her side.

"The French island of St. Pierre is only twelve miles from the tip of the Burin peninsula," she said. "Sister Thérèse grew up there."

"How interesting," Sheila said, her eyes straight ahead. "Is the house much farther?"

"Up there," Nellie said, and pointed toward a hill. "The garden hasn't been tended to since June. Ike planted it himself."

"Didn't he hire a gardener to maintain the grounds?"

"No need for that," Mother Patrick said. "The man had quite the green thumb."

Nellie unlocked the door and Sheila whizzed past her. Her breath quickened. "I never dreamed the house would be this large and luxurious."

Nellie and Mother Patrick followed her from room to room. *She's like a vulture circling over a load of helpless baby chickens*, Nellie thought. *She can't decide what prey to snatch up first.*

Sheila glanced at the wedding portrait and concentrated on the brass candle holders on the mantel. In the den, her eyes glowed. "What an exquisite mahogany desk," she said, running her fingers along the edge. She opened the top drawer, withdrew all the papers, put them in her bag, then checked the bottom two drawers. "I'll look around upstairs." A broad smile widened across her face. Sheila inspected every item in every room, including Marie's night table.

Mother Patrick tapped her right foot, a habit all the children knew was a sign of agitation. "Material goods don't impress that one," she growled to Nellie.

"I've seen enough," Sheila said, and bounded down the stairs like a schoolgirl set free from a boring class.

The walk back to Nellie's house was brief and quiet. "I'll put the kettle on," Nellie said once they arrived back home.

"Good idea," Sheila said. "It's time I met my niece."

Nellie called Marie and Bessie in from the shed. Marie's light hair framed her face.

Sheila smiled at Bessie. "You have your mother's lovely hair."

Mother Patrick's foot tapped. "Actually, she has her father's lovely hair."

"This is my daughter, Bessie," Nellie said.

Sheila turned to Marie, ignoring Bessie. "Come here, child."

Marie shuffled closer, her hands clasped behind her back, her head low. "I wants to stay in Newfoundland," she said without looking up.

"You'll feel at home in Montreal in no time."

THE COASTAL BOAT ENTERED Burke's Cove as Sam walked with his brother toward the Rooms, the Burkes' warehouse. "Does Ma know you're doing this now?" he asked. They had just come back from the first day of school. "She wanted to talk to them first."

"I told her last night I was coming."

They stopped at a waist-high boulder not far from the Rooms. "Wait here, Sam," Joe said.

"Maybe I should go with you for moral support, like Mother Patrick is always talking about."

"I'll be all right." Joe continued on to the Rooms. He looked back at Sam before entering.

The office was to the left at the end of a short hallway. He walked slowly to the office and knocked twice.

"Come in," Denis Burke called.

Joe opened the door, his head high, his back straight. "I wants a job in the fish plant," he said.

Denis laid down his pen. "You get straight to the point like your mother." He folded his hands under his chin. "You even sound like her."

"Thanks for the compliment, sir."

Denis indicated the chair by the desk. "You're welcome, boy."

Joe remained standing. "I can work every day."

Denis sat back in his chair. "Where are you going to find time for school, fishing, and the plant?"

"I'm finishing school before heading back to the Banks. That's why I needs the work in the plant."

"Your mother made you give up fishing. She's quite a fearsome woman."

"Ma had nothing to do with it. Bessie came down with pneumonia worrying about me." Joe stared down at his hands. "Nothing's been the same without Pa."

"Does your mother know you're here?"

"Yes," Joe said, his voice strong. "She wished me good luck."

"Did she indeed," Denis asked gently.

"Ma wants me home in time for supper. Marie leaves tomorrow morning with her aunt on the coastal boat."

"I heard," Denis said. "You can start work at the fish plant tomorrow."

DENIS'S BROTHER JON CAME into the office as Joe went out. "What did he want?"

"I gave him a job at the plant."

"We have all the workers we need." Jon rummaged through the papers on the desk. "This is a business, not a charity."

Denis stared out the window. The dying sun threw shadows over his face.

"Well?" Jon said.

Denis glanced over his shoulder at his brother. "Well what?"

"I asked why you took on Joe Myles."

Denis turned back to the window. "Harry and Tom Myles were good, hard-working men." He shrugged. "It was the least I could do for them . . . and Nellie."

SAM JUMPED DOWN FROM the boulder when his brother came out of the warehouse. "I starts tomorrow," Joe said. "Ma will be glad."

They neared the hill to their house when Sam came to a full stop. He stared toward Burke's Cove, the colour draining from his face. The coastal supply boat bobbed on the gentle waves. "She's a day early."

Joe sprinted up to the house into an empty kitchen. "Ma, where are ya?"

Nellie was sitting in the rocking chair; Marie and Bessie were on the chesterfield holding hands. Marie's two bags of luggage took up the centre of the room. Sheila Jones lounged against the mantelpiece. "Please have Marie at the boat in one hour," she said.

Marie sprang to her feet and glared at Sheila. "I'm not going." Her chin quivered. "You can't make me."

"Don't use that tone of voice with me, young lady."

"Pa told me the Myleses would be my family if anything happened to him."

"Enough. We've been through this nonsense before. I'll see you at the boat." She turned on her heel and walked out of the room.

Marie flew into Nellie's arms. "I won't go," she bawled. "Please, please let me stay."

Bessie sobbed into one of Harry's handkerchiefs. "Ma, we have to help Marie."

Mother Patrick hurried into the room and fell into Harry's armchair. "My goodness. I'm too old for all this running about," she said, fanning herself with an envelope. She took a deep breath. "When I saw the coastal boat I literally ran to the post office to see if Ike's lawyer had written me back." She held out the envelope. "Here it is, Nellie. Mr. Fleming wants you to go to St. John's right away. All expenses paid."

"Why does he want to see me?" Nellie said over Bessie and Marie's squeals.

Mother Patrick gave the stern look every child recognized. "I'd like to know why he took his sweet time notifying you. Anyways, Ike left a will."

"I'd better get packed, then," Nellie said, and took off up the stairs.

"I'll tell Annie," Mother Patrick said. "She—

Annie appeared in the doorway. "Tell me what? I already knows the darn boat's here."

Nellie hurried back down with a half-closed travel bag. Pieces of clothing stuck out on one side.

"Don't worry none about the youngsters," Annie said. "This Mr.

Fleming might have a way to keep our Marie with us. You'll get a chance to see Dottie and the twins, too."

"Let's go," Mother Patrick said. "We don't want to be late for the boat."

Nellie wished she felt the certainty etched on Annie's face that everything would be all right. She caught Mother Patrick's eye and saw that the nun had her doubts as well.

Nellie began to feel confident about the future on the walk to Burke's Cove.

"Don't tell Miss Jones about the letter," Mother Patrick said. "One can never tell what a desperate woman will do."

"Here comes the old bat now," Annie said. "Poor Sister Thérèse is carrying her two suitcases.

Sheila eyed Nellie's bag. "Mrs. Myles is coming as well, Annie?"

"Of course," Annie said. "Seeing as how you're stealing Marie from us."

The wrinkles around Sheila's eyes deepened. "My good woman. I am doing what is best for my darling niece." She took Marie's arm and walked down to the boat.

"Nellie," Dr. Fitzgerald sang out, waving as he hurried toward her. "Thank goodness I caught you. Hattie and I had just arrived home when Steve Marsh came to tell me about poor Marie. She must be devastated."

Annie looked toward the boat. "Sheila Jones has no heart. Money's her main concern."

"Nellie," the doctor continued, "Mother Patrick told Steve that Ike's lawyer wants to see you."

"We're praying that means good news for Marie."

Dr. Fitzgerald pulled a piece of paper from his coat pocket. "This is Dottie's address. She's homesick but really likes St. John's. Dr. and Mrs. Williams dote on the twins."

Nellie kissed Bessie's forehead. "Sweetie, I promise you'll see Marie again."

Dr. Fitzgerald bid her farewell and left with Mother Patrick. Bessie clung to Annie like a drowning girl as her mother boarded the boat.

"Time to head home," Annie said, taking Bessie's hand. "A good supper is what we needs and deserves." Bessie waved to her mother and Marie one last time.

SHEILA SAT ON A bench shaded from the sun. "What are your plans for Ike's house?" Nellie asked when they cleared the harbour.

"I intend to sell it."

"Me and Pa loved our house," Marie said. "He said it would be mine forever."

Sheila's right eyebrow twitched. Nellie could see she wanted to tell Marie to shut up. "It's silly to let the house sit vacant when a family could enjoy its splendour." Sheila produced the smile that never quite brightened her face. "You'll come to think of Montreal as your home."

Marie's eyes welled with tears.

"I'll send you to the best boarding school, where you'll become a fine young lady."

Nellie gently pulled on Marie's arm. "Let's go find a nice spot to eat. I packed buttered tea buns and a gingerbread loaf." She looked at Sheila. "We'll see you later." Nellie sneaked a peek at Sheila as they walked away. The scowl on the woman's face brought a smile to Nellie's lips.

"Aunt Sheila don't like me," Marie said.

Nellie tightened her grip on Marie's hand. "Some people have an awful hard time letting out their feelings."

"I don't care one bit." Nellie was surprised by Marie's calmness. "I just have to keep remembering what Pa told me."

Nellie found a secluded spot far from Sheila's watchful eye and set out the food on a white napkin. "What did your pa tell you?"

"He'd tell me every time he went fishing that—"

"Nellie." A young woman's voice cut Marie off. "I didn't know you were on board." The pale, pretty face of Alice Whelan, another *Marion* widow, looked down at the seated pair.

"Join us for dinner. You look dead on your feet."

"Mother Patrick's face is the same colour as yours when she's seasick," Marie said.

"The sea never bothers me," Alice said quietly. "I'm in the family way."

"No one told me," Nellie said. "That's lovely."

"I didn't want anyone to know till I was sure." Alice put a hand to her belly. "A part of Simon will always be with me. Something to live for."

"I'm some delighted for you."

Alice accepted a slice of gingerbread. "Ma says this helps when you're queasy. Simon's sister wants me to stay with her in St. John's until I have the baby. I won't be so lonely with Dottie there." She sighed. "Poor Mrs. LaCroix's having some awful time trying to feed her ten youngsters."

"It's not easy at the best of times," Nellie said.

"I'd help if I was allowed," Marie said.

Alice gently pinched Marie's cheek. "I knows that, maid." She tore off a small portion of gingerbread loaf. "Mrs. LaCroix was delivered a surprise load of food from the general store."

"Well," Nellie said. "That was good of Mr. Young."

"Wasn't him." Alice cracked off more gingerbread cake. "Denis Burke paid and didn't want anyone to know. Mr. Hodder let it slip."

Nellie gasped. "Are you sure it was Denis Burke?"

"His brothers near had a fit when they found out." Alice leaned against the side of the boat. "He paid for my boat ticket, too. Pa was mad at first. He didn't want to be beholden to no merchant. Changed his mind, though, when Denis had a private word with him."

"I've heard it all now," Nellie said. "Maybe a guilty conscience can force a man to do the right thing."

Alice laid down her half-eaten piece of gingerbread. "I'm some scared, Nellie. Women shouldn't have to be so dependent on men for everything."

"Dottie felt the same way and did something about it."

"I haven't told my parents I'm staying in St. John's after the baby's born. I'll find work like Dottie. I refuses to marry just for support or spend the rest of my life cleaning fish in the factory." Alice shut her eyes tight. "I never wants to see another fish or fish flake as long as I lives."

"Joe starts in Burke's fish plant tomorrow," Nellie continued. "Sam'll do the same next year. That'll keep us going for a while." Her appetite had gone. "They'll both end up fishing on the Banks some day."

"Bessie will marry a fisherman," Alice said. "She'll worry if her man will go the way of her father."

Marie crammed her mouth with a tea bun. "Pa didn't want me to marry a fisherman," she said.

"Why was that?" Nellie asked when Marie remained quiet.

"He said I'd understand when I was older."

Alice turned away, but not before Nellie saw the look of anger on her face. An anger that matched her own. At least the old coot didn't come right out and say his daughter was too good to marry a lowly, uneducated fisherman. Nellie threw the remainder of the food back in her bag.

Alice stared back toward Sheila, who sat in the bow of the boat. "Marie, do you like your aunt?" she asked.

"She hardly ever speaks to me and doesn't care that I wants to stay here. I hates her."

"She talked to no one the whole time she was in St. Jacques."

"Mother Patrick said she hardly ever left the convent," Nellie said.

"She went to see the Burkes," Alice said. "My uncle brought fish to the Rooms and overheard her ask Jon if he wanted to buy Ike's house."

"She can't sell my house," Marie said. She gaped at Nellie. "Can she?"

"Sorry, angel. I know nothing about legal things." Nellie hadn't intended to call Marie by her father's nickname. "Your pa's lawyer will know."

"Jon Burke is real interested in the house," Alice said.

Marie grabbed hold of Nellie's arm. "Pa promised I'd never have to leave St. Jacques if I didn't want to." Her voice quivered. "Why did he lie to me?"

THE COASTAL BOAT PASSED through the Narrows into St. John's harbour. Nellie couldn't believe how appropriately the name fit. The Roman Catholic Cathedral was the first landmark along the sloping hillside to catch her eye. "St. John's is so big. It'd be some easy to get lost."

"What's that?" Marie said. She pointed to a brick building standing alone at the top of a hill across from the city.

"Cabot Tower," Nellie said.

"Oh! That's where Marconi sent the wireless message across the ocean to England. Mother Patrick told us all about it." Marie looked toward the shore. "Look at all the tall brick buildings!"

"That's Water Street," Alice said. "That's where all the stores are."

"Stores!" Marie's eyebrows almost disappeared into her hair. "There's more than one."

"Yes," Alice said. "My sister-in-law says you can buy whatever you wants."

Sheila gave no indication she was impressed with the oldest city in North America. "Probably thinks it's a hovel compared to gorgeous Montreal," Nellie muttered.

"What?" Alice said.

"Thinking out loud is all."

Once the passengers collected their luggage, they stood on the wharf and greeted loved ones. Alice's sister-in-law and husband arrived in a horse and cart. "We'll be here for two weeks at a hotel," Nellie said. "Maybe we could visit Dottie before the boat leaves."

Alice looked at her sister-in-law. "Can we do it tomorrow at nine?"

"No problem," the older woman said. "Are you ready to go?"

Sheila strode over to Nellie. "Marie will come with me now. Oh," she said looking over the child's head at the new arrival. "How nice to see you again, Mr. Fleming."

"How are you, Miss Jones?" He was a medium-built man with greying hair and moustache.

"Quite good, considering the long stay in St. Jacques and the very tiresome boat trip."

Mr. Fleming patted the top of Marie's head. "And this little girl has to be Ike's daughter. She's the image of her mother."

Marie tried to smile at him.

He extended a hand to Nellie. "I'm William Fleming. You are Mrs. Myles, I presume?"

"Yes."

The lawyer smiled for the first time. "It's a pleasure to meet you. Ike spoke very highly of you."

"I'd like to get down to business as soon as possible," said Sheila.

"Of course, Miss Jones. I've booked Mrs. Myles and Marie into a hotel. Once they're settled, we—"

"A hotel?" Sheila interrupted. Red blotches formed on her cheeks. "How can a fisherman's widow afford such a luxury?"

"I'm following my client's instructions," Mr. Fleming said in a level, lawyerly tone.

The blotches on Sheila's cheeks spread down her neck. "Why would my brother waste money in that manner?"

Mr. Fleming smiled at Nellie and Marie. "We'll discuss that in my office after you're checked in at the hotel. Please follow me, ladies." He picked up Marie's two suitcases.

"Surely you have transportation for us," Sheila said. "My cases are quite heavy."

"Indeed I do. A few steps and we're there." They walked the short distance to Water Street. Nellie's head buzzed with a flurry of questions.

Sheila dragged her cases and had to stop when one opened and clothes tumbled out. Marie giggled. Nellie rushed to help retrieve the clothes and hid a smile, noticing the many undergarments.

Marie jumped up and down on the street's smooth stone. "The nice flat rocks would be some good for skipping rope," she said excitedly. "Look at the train tracks!"

"The rock is called cobblestone," Mr. Fleming said. "The tracks are for the streetcar. It runs near the hotel. I thought you'd enjoy a run."

Marie clapped her hands. "I can't wait to tell Bessie."

"Your best friend," the lawyer said. "Ike filled me in on every aspect of his daughter's life," he added when Nellie shot him a questioning look.

Sheila's lips twitched, but she said nothing.

Marie sprang back when the streetcar arrived. "It's some big," she said.

The lawyer took her by the hand. "There's nothing to be afraid of," he said, and guided her up the steps. The streetcar began to move.

Marie jolted back into a seat. "That was fun," she giggled.

Sheila sat with Mr. Fleming and tried to question him in a low voice.

"As I stated earlier, Miss Jones, we'll discuss business in my office."

The car stopped, letting three people off. Two got on. "That store is called Parker and Monroe," Marie said, reading the sign over a door.

"A wonderful shoe shop," the lawyer said.

The streetcar slowed. Marie read another sign. "Bowring Brothers."

"It's my little girl's favourite store," Mr. Fleming said. "They have lovely dresses."

"I never saw so many people in my whole life," Marie said, gaping at the crowded sidewalk.

The streetcar rounded a slight bend and stopped beside an old hotel. "Here we are," Mr. Fleming said. He carried Marie's bags to the front door and came back for Sheila's.

"Mrs. Myles," Marie said. "It must be the tallest building in the world."

"My dear niece," Sheila said in a tone of voice Nellie felt sure the woman thought dripped with affection. "This is nothing compared to the buildings in Montreal."

The joy went out of Marie's face.

Mr. Fleming held the front door open. "After you, ladies."

Nellie studied the furniture in the lobby. "Marie, this is as pretty as your house."

Marie walked over to the lawyer, who was talking with an elderly man at the front desk. "Sir, why can't I live with Mrs. Myles in St. Jacques?"

Sheila hurried over. "Marie, dear. That's already been decided. You'll feel better when we're in Montreal."

Mr. Fleming handed Nellie a key. "Your luggage will be brought up to your room. Once Miss Jones is checked in, we'll go to my office."

"Wonderful," Sheila said. "The sooner the better."

"Miss Jones," Nellie said outside the hotel. "When are you taking . . ." She looked at Marie, but couldn't say her name. ". . . when are you going back to Montreal?"

Sheila rolled her eyes. "Not for another week. This island of yours is rather difficult to get to, and even more difficult to get away from."

"My office is at the other end of Water Street. We'll take the streetcar if there aren't any objections," Mr. Fleming said as the streetcar made its stop.

"I'd love to," Marie said, and hopped on without any assistance. They disembarked in front of a three-storey brick building and climbed the stairs to the second floor.

Deep green carpet ran the length of the corridor and into the lawyer's outer office. Summer landscapes hung around the room and a long cushioned bench hugged one wall. A woman in her early twenties smiled at the group from behind a desk.

"Miss Murphy, I don't want to be disturbed for the next hour," the lawyer instructed his receptionist.

"Yes, sir. The file you asked for is on your desk."

"Grand," Mr. Fleming said. He smiled at Marie. "Young lady, would you mind waiting here with Miss Murphy?"

The receptionist came around the desk. "Would you like a sweet treat?"

Marie rocked on her feet. “Do you have any Bull’s Eyes?”

Miss Murphy opened the top drawer of her desk and pulled out a paper bag filled with the candy.

Mr. Fleming opened the door to his office. “Miss Jones, Mrs. Myles, let us begin.”

Chapter 14

MR. FLEMING'S OFFICE WAS spacious with a large desk in front of a window that covered one wall from floor to ceiling. The sun blazed across the room to where several framed pictures of Signal Hill and the Narrows lined another wall. A blue velvet lounge chair in the far corner beckoned exhausted visitors to take refuge in its luscious material. The lawyer directed the women to cushioned wooden chairs in front of the desk. A family portrait adorned the wall to the right.

"Your wife and child are very pretty," Nellie commented.

"Thank you, Mrs. Myles. Joanie, my little girl, is ten."

"The same age as my Bessie and Marie."

Sheila fidgeted. "Yes, yes," she said. "Smart-looking family."

Mr. Fleming sat in a faded black leather chair, the back and seat worn thin from years of use. Nellie noticed a half-empty jar of Bull's Eyes on the corner of the desk. "I enjoy a sweet while I work," the lawyer said with a grin. "Keeps my brain sharp."

A shadow passed over Nellie's face. "Dave LaCroix loved them, too." The lawyer looked at her with a curious expression. "He was on the *Marion*," she said softly.

Mr. Fleming folded his hands on the desk. "I wish to extend my deepest condolences for the loss of your loved ones."

Nellie stared at his family portrait. "We have to carry on for our families."

"I agree," Sheila said. "Mr. Fleming, why is Mrs. Myles even here?"

The lawyer tapped a glossy file folder with a pen. "Mr. Ike Jones requested her presence for the reading of the will."

Sheila's back stiffened. "Very well. Let's hear it."

"Before I do, there are several questions I'd like to ask you concerning Ike's estate."

"I know nothing about my brother's affairs." Sheila waved a hand. "But I will comply to move matters along."

"Thank you, Miss Jones. What do you intend to do with the Jones home in St. Jacques?"

"Mr. Jon Burke, a merchant from the area, wishes to buy it."

A rush of sadness overwhelmed Nellie. Marie was to be thrown out of her home without the slightest consideration for her feelings.

"Jon Burke," the lawyer said. "I know him well."

"A fine gentleman with exquisite taste," Sheila said.

"That's only your opinion," Nellie blurted out. A hand flew to her mouth. "I'm sorry, Mr. Fleming. I didn't meant to interrupt." She thought she saw a hint of a smile on his face.

Sheila raised an eyebrow at Nellie.

Mr. Fleming continued. "Miss Jones, what are your plans concerning Marie?"

"She'll live with me in Montreal. There are several fine schools for girls where proper manners are a priority."

Nellie dug her fingers into her palms. "So you're gonna send her to a boarding school," she said.

"Is that correct, Miss Jones?" The lawyer asked, as if addressing a witness on the stand.

"Of course it isn't. Marie will stay with me and learn how to be a gracious young lady." She smiled. "I only want the best for my sweet niece."

Mr. Fleming gave Sheila an equally charming smile. "I should expect no less." He turned to Nellie. "Would you please bring Marie in?"

Marie was sitting with Miss Murphy on the bench in the reception area. She chewed a Bull's Eye candy while listening to the receptionist talk about all the fancy stores on Water Street. Nellie reached for Marie's hand. "Mr. Fleming wants to see you."

"I'd like a private chat with you, Marie," the lawyer said with a big grin when they walked in together. "That is, of course, if you don't mind."

Marie stuck close to Nellie. "It's all right," Nellie said. "I'll be in the next room."

The telltale red blotches sprouted on Sheila's cheeks like burned skin. "Mr. Fleming, what's this about?" she said.

"As I told to you earlier, I'm following Mr. Jones's instructions."

Sheila walked past Nellie. "Come along, Mrs. Myles." She closed the door with a heavy hand.

"DON'T BE SCARED, MARIE," Mr. Fleming said in a fatherly voice. "I'd like to ask you some easy questions. Is that all right?"

Marie nodded.

"Good. Tell me about your life in St. Jacques."

"I loves Mrs. Myles, Bessie, Joe, and Sam." She paused. "Even when Joe teases me. I likes school, playing alleys, and skipping rope. I have heaps of friends. Annie and—"

"Who's Annie?"

Marie explained Annie's relationship to the Myles family. "Annie treats me like her grandchild, too. I loves her coconut cream pies."

"Tell me about school."

"Mother Patrick is awful strict sometimes. That's all right, 'cause she's the best teacher in the world." Marie giggled. "The boys calls her Sister Crooked. They denies it, but they likes her and all the other nuns. They gives us milk and cookies for recess."

"What can you tell me about your Aunt Sheila?"

The smile fell from Marie's face. She lowered her head and clasped her hands until the knuckles showed white.

"Marie, I promise you that Miss Jones will never find out anything you tell me."

Marie looked at him with tear-filled eyes. "She never talks to me." Marie wiped her nose with Harry's handkerchief. "She makes me feel like I'm invisible."

"You did an exceptional job, Marie," the lawyer said, his voice a shade lower than normal. "I need a few more minutes with your aunt and Mrs. Myles. Do you mind waiting with Miss Murphy again?"

Marie's smile returned. "She's nice."

Sheila marched into the office the instant Marie appeared in the outer room. "Mr. Fleming, are you finally ready to read the will?"

"Yes." He pulled out a document from the file folder and scanned the first and second pages. "Mr. Jones made the will ten years ago. A year ago, he made several revisions."

"He came to St. Jacques when Marie was just a few months old," Nellie said.

"A difficult time for Ike," Mr. Fleming said. "He'd just lost his wife."

Sheila snorted with derision. "Why he ever chose a place like St. Jacques to live is beyond me. At least St. John's has some modern conveniences."

Nellie ignored the slight. "Marie knows very little about her mother. Did Ike tell you anything, Mr. Fleming?"

"Only that her name was Chantal and that she wasn't a Newfoundlander."

Sheila put her hand to her mouth as if to stifle a sob. "Terrible business," she said, and quickly added, "but I feel Ike would want us to move on, to get back to the will."

"To hurry the process along, I'll simply read the six major bequeaths. Item one. The house in St. Jacques, along with the contents, goes to his daughter, Marie, and cannot be sold until her eighteenth birthday."

Sheila's hands tightened on the chair's armrests.

"Item two. The St. John's house situated on Lemarchant Road goes to Nellie Myles to do with as she pleases. Also, she is allotted five hundred dollars a year for the next ten years."

Sheila's eyes looked ready to pop out of her head. "There must be some mistake," she said.

Nellie gulped and stared at Mr. Fleming. "I . . . are you sure?"

"Absolutely," he said, then turned unblinking eyes to Sheila.

"I assure you, Miss Jones, this will is quite legal and binding. Item three. A thousand dollars goes to Mrs. Annie Cluett for being the grandmother Marie never had."

Sheila's lips pressed together into a thin line. "This is absurd," she muttered.

"Item four. Two thousand dollars goes to Miss Sheila Jones.

"Item—"

Sheila laughed, a low throaty croak that resembled a frog's cry. "Now I know this has to be a joke."

"Item five. Forty thousand dollars is left to Marie. Her guardian will oversee the necessary funds for her living expenses and education."

Sheila's eyes shimmered. "That's quite a large sum of money," she said, her voice almost musical. "I'll do my utmost to look after Marie's welfare."

"The last and most important item. Ike appointed Harry and Nellie Myles as his daughter's guardians in the case of his untimely death."

"This is outrageous!" Sheila yelled, her breathing rapid. "As Marie's only living relative, I insist—no, I demand!—that she be given over to me."

Mr. Fleming replaced the document in the file folder. "Miss Jones," he said in his level lawyer's voice once again, "Ike's main concern was his daughter's happiness."

"Happiness!" Sheila shrieked. "In a backward settlement with uneducated people who distort the King's English!" She leaned forward in the chair. "Mr. Fleming, surely you understand."

The lawyer leaned forward as well. "More than you know," he said quietly. "I was born in Joe Batt's Arm, which, by the way, is even more of a 'backward' community than St. Jacques. My daughter spends every summer there and hates to return to 'civilization.'" He pulled a piece of paper from the folder. "I've arranged everything with the bank. Present this and you'll receive your inheritance without delay."

Sheila grabbed the paper out of his hand. "I'm not giving up this easily."

Mr. Fleming stood up. "Our business is concluded, Miss Jones. Good day."

"Sacred Heart of Mary," Nellie said after Sheila stomped out of the office. "I thought she was gonna explode."

The lawyer chuckled. "What a pleasant thought."

"Is it really true?" Nellie hesitated, afraid the question spoken out loud might somehow change the answer. "Marie can live with me?"

"Absolutely true. Sheila Jones was a stranger to Ike. He'd invited her to Newfoundland on many occasions to meet Marie, which she always declined with one excuse or another."

Nellie shook her head. "I pity her. She doesn't know how to love."

"Shortly after the *Marion*'s disappearance, I wrote requesting her presence at the reading of Ike's will. She showed up anxious for information about her niece."

"She wanted Marie so she could get her hands on Ike's money."

"If Sheila had made an effort with Marie over the years, Ike would have rewarded her," Mr. Fleming said.

"Why did you ask Marie questions?"

"Simple curiosity, Mrs. Myles."

"I blame Ike for what happened to the *Marion*," Nellie said.

"I admire your honesty," he replied. "However, it changes nothing."

Miss Murphy poked her head into the office. "Marie wants to see Mrs. Myles," she said.

"Send her right in."

Marie crept around the receptionist into the office. Her face was grey, her eyes heavy. "Aunt Sheila looked awful mad," she said.

Nellie held out her arms. "That's because you're going home with me."

Even Miss Murphy in the outer office covered her ears against Marie's shrieks of joy.

"The house on Lemarchant Road is fully stocked with food," Mr. Fleming said. "I'll take you there, if you like. It's only a ten-minute walk."

*

NELLIE FELT LIKE SHE'D been transported to another world when she stepped inside the regal home. The walls were painted a soft yellow, reminding her of sunshine. White lace curtains hung from every window. Light-toned furniture highlighted the dark hardwood floors.

"A woman comes in once a week to clean," Mr. Fleming said.

Nellie looked around the living room. "Has it been empty all these years?"

"Ike stayed here whenever he had business in St. John's."

Marie galloped down the stairs into the living room. "Mrs. Myles, can we sleep here tonight? It's so beautiful!"

"No problem," the lawyer said. "I'll have your luggage sent over." He hauled a chain watch out of his top suit pocket. "Time to get back to work. We'll discuss the finer points of Ike's will tomorrow."

"Thank you," Nellie said. "I still can't believe all this is happening."

"Alice won't know where to find us tomorrow," Marie realized.

"I'll tell the hotel you're here," Mr. Fleming said. "Good day."

"Let's see what we can find to eat." Nellie opened the door to a spotless kitchen that was as big as the first floor of her house in St. Jacques. Oak cupboards with glass doors lined three walls, and a square oak table graced the centre of the tiled floor. The sink captivated her attention. She turned the faucet, and clear water spilled out. "What a luxury," Nellie said. "Annie would love this."

She checked a cupboard and found bread and cheese. "I'll make us a sandwich."

"Who owns this house?" Marie asked, her mouth crammed with food.

"Goodness me," Nellie said. "I forgot to tell you. Your pa gave it to me in his will."

Marie's green eyes sparkled. "That was some nice of him."

"And he left me and Annie lots of money."

"Did he give Bessie, Joe, and Sam some money, too?"

"No, but that's all right," Nellie continued when Marie frowned. "They won't mind."

Marie looked as if she was considering something. "Did he give me any money?"

"Yes. Heaps."

Marie gave a sigh of relief. "Good. Now Joe and Sam won't ever have to leave us."

"What do you mean, angel?"

"I'll give them my money so they don't need to fish on the Banks."

"That's a lovely thought," Nellie said, her voice shaky, her eyes glistening with pride. "But you don't have to worry about the boys. Your pa gave me enough money to keep them safe."

They finished their sandwiches and explored the rest of the house. The sun was just setting when their luggage arrived. Marie ran from bedroom to bedroom before deciding on the one she wanted.

Nellie chose the room next to hers. As the night closed in, she snuggled under the covers. A cool breeze fluttered the lace curtains and the sound of passersby amazed her. St. Jacques was quieter than a graveyard after dark. Nellie hugged the pillow. Exhausted from the boat trip and from worrying about Marie, she fell into a deep sleep.

ANNIE SHOT UP IN bed and stared around the dark room. Her eyes roamed over unfamiliar objects. "Where am I?" she said to the empty night. The reason for her being in Nellie's old bedroom flooded back. "Poor, darling Marie," she murmured, and lay back down. She shot back up again and listened. The only sound was her own breathing. "Must've dreamt it."

A muffled cry, like a hand held over a mouth, fractured the silence. Annie whipped off the blankets and hurried to Bessie's room. Sam stood over the bed. Joe sat on the edge and gently shook his sister. "Bessie, wake up."

She moaned. Her head tossed from side to side.

Joe shook her harder. "Bessie, wake up." His voice sounded panicked. "You're having the Old Hag. Wake up."

Sam turned to Annie. "We can't wake her." His hands were clenched at his sides. "She'll die if we can't wake her."

"That's an old wives' tale," Annie said. "Not a word of truth in it."

Bessie's eyes opened and she gasped for air. "The hooded man," she cried. "The hooded man took Marie."

"The hooded man isn't real," Annie said. She cradled Bessie against her chest. "Marie's safe with your ma."

"He is real," Bessie bawled. "I saw him in St. Pierre." Her small fingers dug into Annie's back.

"Shhh," Annie said, and smoothed Bessie's hair. "Marie's all right. I promise ya." She looked at Joe and Sam. "Go back to bed. I'll stay with her."

"She's missing Marie," Sam said. "I don't understand why she had to leave us."

"Neither do I," Annie said. "Neither do I."

Bessie's sobs slowly diminished into the occasional hiccup as a restless sleep overtook her. Annie lay beside her and shed a tear or two herself. She was awake when the sun rose on the horizon.

Chapter 15

MR. FLEMING ARRIVED AT the house on Lemarchant Road at nine in the morning. He declined Nellie's offer of pancakes and toast.

"I never eat before noon. Which annoys my wife, because our daughter is beginning to develop the same habit. I'll have a cup of tea, though," he said. "Little Marie still in bed?"

"I let her sleep in. She's had a couple of awful days."

"Quite so." He opened his briefcase. "I have the deeds to this house and the one in St. Jacques. Also, there are a few papers you need to sign concerning guardianship of Marie and the release of money."

"I'd rather you kept hold of the deeds."

"That's not a problem." Mr. Fleming took out the papers for Nellie's signature. "You'll receive your allotment of money by post at regular intervals. Let me know whenever you require money for Marie."

"Marie needs very little," Nellie said. "She can save the money for when she's older."

"Mrs. Myles," the lawyer continued when Nellie had signed the last paper. "Will you move your family here?"

Nellie poured more tea. "I was pondering that very thing before you arrived. My youngsters and Marie have had enough . . ." She hesitated, searching for the word Mother Patrick had used. ". . . upheavals for a lifetime. We'll move here when they finish school at the convent." Nellie glanced around the huge kitchen. "There'll be more opportunities in St. John's when they're older." She stared at a spot on the wall over the lawyer's shoulder. "I loves St. Jacques. It's just that . . ."

"I do understand," Mr. Fleming said. "Fishing is extremely hard work, and dangerous, as you well know."

"Harry's father drowned on the Banks when Harry was Marie's age."

"A good mother doesn't want her children to suffer the same fate. My father was a fisherman and swore his only son would have an easier, safer life."

"If Harry was buried in St. Jacques, I could never leave him. Most fishermen's wives lose their men to the sea and never get their bodies back." Her throat hurt from the effort not to cry. "That's what tears me up the worst. I can never visit his grave and chat with him."

"The young woman who got off the boat with you is a *Marion* widow as well?"

"Married four days when Simon shipped out. She didn't know at the time that she was in the family way. We're going to see Dottie McEvoy today, another widow. She had twins a little while after the *Marion* left." Nellie explained why the two women had moved to St. John's. Mr. Fleming listened quietly while she talked about the *Marion* crew and the effect of their loss on the community.

The lawyer passed his empty cup from hand to hand, a reflective look on his face. "Even though I represented Ike, to hear first-hand about the crew and their families makes their deaths feel more real."

Marie skipped into the kitchen. "Mr. Fleming, can I have some money to buy five presents?" She counted the names off on her fingers. "Annie, Mother Patrick, Bessie, Joe, and Sam."

"Don't go throwing your money away," Nellie said.

"What a lovely idea," Mr. Fleming said. "Drop by my office." He poked his hat on his head. "I have an appointment at ten. By the way, I thought you'd both be pleased to hear that Miss Jones left for Montreal this morning with her inheritance." He chuckled, a low, rumbling sound. "She was madder than a rabid wolf."

Nellie saw him to the door and lingered as she watched him walk down the road. People rushed along the sidewalks. She wondered where they were going in such a hurry. A horse and buggy passed by; the *clip, clop* of the hooves was the only similarity with St. Jacques. She closed the door as a horse and milk wagon turned onto the street. Marie helped herself to pancakes and toast.

NELLIE HAD THE DISHES washed and put back in the cupboard when Alice and her sister-in-law, Mrs. Coombs, showed up.

"I was some surprised when they told us at the hotel that you were here," Alice said. "Where's Miss Jones?"

Nellie described what was in the will. "Sheila carried on like a greedy youngster," she said.

"That's some good news," Alice said. "Dottie'll be some glad, too. She lives on the street around the corner." Alice smiled. The dark circles under her eyes seemed to lighten. "You're neighbours."

Dr. and Mrs. Williams welcomed the women into their home, especially Mrs. Coombs, who had been a long-time patient. Nellie couldn't get over how much the twins had grown in two weeks. The doctor suggested a visit to Signal Hill as it was a warm, sunny day. Mrs. Williams insisted on watching over the twins.

"She's spoiling my youngsters rotten," Dottie said with a smile, as everyone climbed the steep, long path up Signal Hill. They'd taken the streetcar and walked from there. "Always looking for an excuse to have them to herself."

"Annie's missing them something shocking," Nellie said.

"Tell her not to fret," Dottie said. "She'll get to see them again."

They marvelled at Cabot Tower, then stopped off at Mr. Fleming's office, followed by a trip to the shops on Water Street. Marie bought a soccer ball for Joe, a skipping rope with red wooden handles for Bessie, a box of linen handkerchiefs for Annie, and a book full of pictures of Ireland for Mother Patrick. Sam was more difficult to buy for, but she finally settled on Dottie's suggestion of a book of arithmetic puzzles.

For the next week and a half, Mrs. Coombs played the role of tour guide, showcasing the city's highlights, such as the Basilica, the courthouse, and the public library. Nellie noticed that each day Alice looked paler and thinner, but Nellie kept these thoughts to herself. Just before midnight, the night before the boat was due to leave for St. Jacques and the coastal communities, Dottie came to see Nellie. Tears coursed down her face. "Mr. Coombs came for us. Alice took bad after supper."

Nellie noticed Dr. Williams for the first time, standing to the left of Dottie. "I'll keep an eye on young Marie while you're gone," he said.

As they made their way to Torbay, Nellie couldn't enjoy the beautiful maple and juniper trees lording over luscious grass and flowers. The Coombs house was centred on a flat hill overlooking the ocean. A line of clothes behind the house had been left out.

A grey-haired man of about sixty with a medical bag came out when Mr. Coombs reined in the horse to a stop. Nellie didn't need to hear the words. The expression on his face shouted out the sad truth. Alice had lost her baby.

"Physically, she'll recover," the doctor said. He looked up at Dottie and Nellie. "Go in. The poor girl needs comforting."

Alice was reclining against a stack of feather pillows, her eyes vacant as she stared straight ahead. She didn't acknowledge Dottie or Nellie.

Nellie gently reached for Alice's hand. It felt cold and lifeless, like a dead fish. "I don't know what to say," she said.

"Nothing's left," Alice whispered, her eyes transfixed on the wall in front of her. Nellie shuddered at the naked bleakness in her voice. "The baby gave me the strength to keep going. I wants to be with Simon and our baby."

Dottie whispered, "You don't mean that."

Alice remained still, her eyes devoid of all emotion.

Nellie moved closer to her. "Stop gaping at the air and look at me."

No response. No movement.

Nellie turned Alice's face toward her. "You listen to me good, Alice Whelan. No more foolish nonsense about being with Simon and the baby. He must have the shivers up there in Heaven hearing that."

Nellie pushed down the pity she felt for the young woman. "Tell me what Simon would say if he was here."

Tears moistened Alice's unblinking eyes. None fell. "He . . ."

"He what?" Nellie said gently. She strained to keep her voice steady.

"He'd be mad with me."

Silence.

"Why?"

"He said I was to go on if anything happened to him." Tears gushed over grey, sunken cheeks to form a puddle that tumbled from her chin.

Nellie kissed Alice's forehead. "Love, you have to muster the courage to do what Simon wanted."

MR. FLEMING CARRIED MARIE'S bags from the house and started down the street. Nellie and Marie preferred to walk the short distance to the wharf. Dottie, unable to bear the sight of the boat taking them away, said her goodbyes at the house.

"I'm sorry about your friend's baby," the lawyer said.

Nellie grimaced. "Another *Marion* casualty."

When they reached the harbourfront, Mr. Fleming turned to Marie. "Take good care of your new family."

"I promise," Marie said.

"I'll keep in touch, Mrs. Myles. Goodbye and safe journey." He waited for them to board, and with a final wave returned to his office.

Marie stared at the city while the boat sailed through the Narrows. "Will Alice's parents be mad she's not coming home?" she asked.

"They'll be sad and lonely for a while," Nellie said.

The sun's rays played with Marie's eyelashes and cast them in elongated, shadowy thin lines across the top of her cheeks. "Bessie and everyone else are gonna be some surprised to see me," she said.

They ate dinner, explored the boat, and read to pass away the hours. "We're here! We're here!" Marie finally said when the entrance to Burke's Cove appeared like a beacon on the horizon. She bounced on her feet and clapped her hands. As the boat manoeuvred into the Cove, Marie ducked below the rail.

"What's that for?" Nellie said.

"I wants to really surprise everyone."

While the boat laid anchor, Nellie searched the crowd. She spotted Annie and Mother Patrick. The mother superior stood tall, yet her face appeared veiled in mourning. Annie leaned into the nun. Her eyes lacked the gleam that had always bestowed a youthful look to her wrinkled face.

"Marie," Nellie said when people began to disembark. "They've suffered enough. Show yourself."

She popped up.

"Jesus, Mary, and Joseph," Nellie heard Mother Patrick gasp.

Annie held her hands up to the sky. "Please, Sweet Jesus, don't let me be dreaming."

Marie barrelled down the plank into Annie's open arms. In one long breath she told them about the contents of her father's will. "Aunt Sheila was some mad," she concluded.

"She's on the way to Montreal," Nellie said. "We've seen the back of her for good. Mr. Fleming's a lovely man. He didn't like Sheila any more than we did."

While they walked, Nellie talked about Dottie, the twins, and how Dr. and Mrs. Williams treated them like their own.

"That's some weight off my shoulders," Annie said. "It's not that I didn't believe what Dr. Fitzgerald said, but it's good to be sure."

"How's Joe doing at the plant?" Nellie said.

"Grand. He's taken to the work like a baby pigeon to the sky."

Mother Patrick stopped at the convent. "I'll see you all later. Joe wouldn't be cross with me if I missed history class," she said with a straight face.

Marie ran on ahead and disappeared from sight. Nellie and Annie neared Young's General Store. The door opened, and Nellie came face to face with Denis Burke. "Good day," she said. "I didn't get a chance to thank you for taking on Joe."

"It was nothing," Denis said, and hurried away.

Annie stared after him. "I thinks he was half-scared you were gonna smack him." She cocked an eye at Nellie. "Why would that be?"

Nellie shrugged. "Who knows why the Burkes act the way they do?"

"I don't think that was your first fib."

Marie had the dishes set out for supper when Annie and Nellie came through the door. She hugged herself and danced around the table. "I'm some happy to be home." She whirled around and stumbled into Nellie. "Mrs. Myles, can I give Annie her present now?"

"You're as good as my daughter," Nellie said. "Call me Nellie."

Marie screwed up her eyes, a sure sign that she was giving serious consideration to the suggestion. "No," she finally said. "I'll call you Ma Nellie."

Chapter 16

NELLIE PLACED A PAN of hot, soapy water on the floor and dropped into the rocking chair. Her feet still hadn't quite recovered from traipsing around St. John's. She looked out the window. The setting sun painted the cottony white clouds with a crimson hue, which darkened to blood red as the sun descended lower and lower behind the hills. Her gaze strayed from the colour display to the kitchen, where all four children sat around the table absorbed in homework. Joe had been reluctant to leave the fish plant until Mother Patrick ordered him to her office for a private chat. She suspected the good sister had lectured her son about the best way to "honour thy mother."

Nellie's eyes wandered to her wedding portrait. *I don't know what to do, Harry,* she thought. *Annie and Mother Patrick says I should move into Ike's house.* She didn't think Marie cared one way or the other.

"Josh Cabot did not discover Newfoundland," Sam said. Nellie thought he sounded frustrated. She heard Bessie and Marie giggle.

"What's so funny?" Joe said.

"Go on, b'y," Bessie said. "I knows you're joshing."

"No he ain't," Sam said.

"Then who did?" Joe said.

Marie shoved her history book in front of him. "John Cabot," she said, her finger next to the name.

Joe chewed his bottom lip. "Was Josh his brother?"

Even Sam laughed this time.

Nellie turned back to the portrait. "The youngsters are getting back to normal," she murmured. "They're becoming used to you being gone, Harry." She rested her head against the back of the rocker. *I never will.*

As if he was seated in his armchair, she could hear Harry's deep, gentle voice. *Love, what's holding you back from moving into Ike's house?*

"It's because of you, Harry," she whispered, her eyes closed. "This house breathes your presence. There's nothing of you at Ike's."

Don't fret none about me, Nellie, love. I knows you always do right by our youngsters.

"Ma," Joe called from the table. "I'm on my way to get water from the well."

Nellie heard the door open and close. Ike's house had a sink connected to a well in the fancy kitchen, the feature that appealed most to Annie, along with the latest equipment. No more lugging heavy buckets several times a day in all sorts of weather. Six bedrooms would make it possible for the children to each have one of their own. Even so, she hated to desert the home Harry and Uncle Joe had built. The children had been born here, laughed here, cried here.

Moving don't destroy special memories, love. You carry them with ya.

Nellie hauled her feet out of the pan, slipped on her shoes, and went to the kitchen. "Homework almost done?" she asked. Sam was helping Marie with arithmetic. Bessie was writing a story.

Marie finished the last division problem and closed her scribbler. "I am," she said.

"I'm taking a walk to your house. Come along with me."

The clouds had darkened to resemble stacks of coal. Nellie took her shawl from the door hook and reached for Marie's raincoat.

"It's not raining," Marie said, and skipped out of the house.

"It will be," Nellie called out.

They'd reached the bottom of the path before Marie spoke again. "Can I bring my porcelain doll display back to your house?"

"You haven't spoken about those in a while."

"I ain't so sad anymore."

The wind stirred and Nellie breathed in the salty air. She'd missed the tangy smell while wandering through the many streets of St. John's. The one thing that had caught her off guard was the brick buildings that had been built after the big fires that ravaged the city. They appeared desolate, stretching out of the ground like charred fingers. Their images flooded Nellie's head and she shivered despite the warm breeze.

They passed the Rooms. A light glowed in the Burkes' office. Jon Burke sat at his desk, his head bent over paperwork. He'd been annoyed when informed that Ike's house couldn't be sold until Marie was eighteen. Nellie smiled. *That's one thing the grab-all merchants won't get their hands on.* A twinge of guilt pricked at her conscience. At least Denis had shown an inkling of kindness. Carried out in secret, to boot. Harry had once told her there was some good in the youngest Burke brother. Nellie had laughed and said, "Sure, b'y."

Thunder drummed in the distance. Nellie increased her pace after feeling a raindrop fall on her nose. Another struck the ground, followed by another and another, giving rise to puffs of dry, thirsty earth. Rain bit into the ground until the road transformed into a mud pie.

Marie looked up to the sky. "I likes how the rain tickles me skin."

Nellie tucked her shawl around Marie's shoulders. "Let's hurry before we drown."

They scooted up the hill toward Ike's house. The garden had ceased to beg for attention. The months of neglect and the early onset of frost at night had reduced the thriving plant life to decrepit, decaying mush. The only saving grace was the trees that dotted the lawn like pieces on a chessboard. The autumn leaves displayed a cavalcade of splendour befitting a royal palace. They reached the path, which curved in an S shape to the front door. Dead leaves floated in small puddles. Halfway up the path something in the soaked ground caught Nellie's eye.

Boot prints. The shape and size of a man's. Nellie looked toward the house; there wasn't any light visible inside. The windows and front door were closed. A thought jumped into her head. "If Jon Burke's been poking his nose around, I'll put my boots to him," she muttered, marching up to the house. Marie ran to keep up with her. Nellie stopped suddenly, remembering that Jon was in his office. He could not have gotten here before her.

Wet leaves squished under their shoes. "The prints go right up to the door," Marie said. "I bet they belongs to one of Joe's friends."

"Stay close to me," Nellie said, and unlocked the front door. Clouds whisked across the sky, releasing a captive moon. Enough light seeped in to illuminate the pale-blue tiled floor.

"Look," Marie said. She pointed to the base of a window. Broken pieces of glass were strewn across the floor. Muddied boot prints, encrusted with crushed glass, tracked through the living room and down the hall toward the den and kitchen area. Nellie couldn't think who would break into the house. No one in St. Jacques would dare stoop so low. To her knowledge there weren't any visitors in the community. If it turned out to be a youngster, he'd get an earful from her. She checked the living room, then proceeded to the den. The drawers in the desk were half open. Nothing else looked out of place.

"We're gonna leave," Nellie said, turning away from the desk. Marie was gone. Nellie ran to the living room. Still no Marie. She climbed the stairs and squinted down the long, obscure hallway. Several seconds passed before her eyes adjusted to the dark. "Marie, are you up here?"

A thump came out of the darkness.

Nellie froze. "Marie," she whispered. "Is that you?" She crept forward.

Another thump.

Nellie's skin tingled. Her heart thudded so hard her ribs hurt. She reached Ike's room. The door stood ajar and she spied a figure clad in a black cape and hood rummaging through the bureau. Sweat broke out on Nellie's forehead. "Who are you?" she asked before her brain had time to assess the danger.

The hooded figure's head snapped toward her. Nellie's legs felt too heavy to move. The shadow grunted and bolted past her down the stairs. She couldn't tell if the fleeing form was male or female. "Marie!" she shouted. Her voice shook. "Marie."

Her own shallow breaths splintered the silence. A low, muffled groan penetrated her senses. She listened. A sob. Nellie gathered her strength and raced to Marie's room. The child was crouched in the corner, her face buried in her hands.

"Marie, are you all right?"

She dived into Nellie's arms. "I saw the hooded man go into Pa's room. Bessie said he wants to take me away."

"No one is going to take you away. The hooded man was a dream and can't hurt you."

Marie's body trembled. "Who was he, then?"

"I don't know. But I'll find out. Mark my words."

Marie gripped Nellie's hand. They hurried to the stairs and noticed the front door swung wide open. The rain drilled against the floor like shards of stone.

"He's gone," Nellie said, her heartbeat slowing. They rushed down the stairs and Nellie slammed the door shut behind them. The rain had stopped again by the time they reached home.

Joe, Sam, and Bessie were playing cards at the kitchen table.

"None of you take one step out of this house until I get back," Nellie ordered, and took off again. She panted and held a hand to the stitch in her side when she reached the convent.

"What in heaven's name?" the nun said and handed her a towel. "Did ye swim here?"

"Mother Patrick, you have to promise me to keep quiet about what I'm going to tell you. Annie will be frantic with worry if she finds out."

"Out with it, then. I can't promise if I don't know what you're on about."

Nellie described the broken window, the tracks, and the intruder in Marie's house.

"You went inside!" Mother Patrick said. "Have you lost your mind, maid? The fiend could've hurt the two of you."

"I thought nothing of it at first. People don't break into houses hereabouts."

Mother Patrick blessed herself. "What possessed you to go after dark?"

Nellie was all set to defend her action when she sneezed. A series of sneezes she couldn't control followed.

"Pneumonia is all you need," Mother Patrick said. "Go home and get into bed with a hot toddy. And don't take any more foolish chances." She called for Sister Thérèse. "We'll accompany you, to be on the safe side."

SAFELY CONFINED TO BED by the mother superior, Nellie mulled over the incident at Ike's house. She couldn't come up with a probable suspect and tried her best to put it aside. The next morning she went to Young's General Store to order glass to repair the broken window.

"We have the measurements from when Ike built the house," Mr. Hodder said, and filled out the paperwork. "That was some sturdy glass. How did it break?"

"Someone broke in."

Mr. Hodder looked at Nellie over the top of his glasses. "How awful. That's a first for something like that in these parts." He took off his glasses and poked them on top of his head. "Did you know there's been a stranger hanging about?"

"What stranger?"

"A Frenchman's been asking about Ike's place. I found him a mite on the crooked side."

"What does he look like?" Nellie asked, hoping she sounded casual.

"Small man. About sixty, I'd reckon." Mr. Hodder signed his name on the form. "It's gonna be a while before the glass comes. Be sure to board up the window until then."

"I will," Nellie said. She swung around and bumped into Jon Burke.

"Mrs. Myles." His voice was colder than the ocean in winter. "I don't appreciate being lied to. You should've said you don't want me to have Ike's house."

Nellie put aside her initial burst of anger and spoke in a civil tone. "What makes you think I lied?"

"An old Frenchman's been looking for the house. He said it was up for sale."

"When was this? Did he give his name?"

Jon looked down his nose. "Come now, Mrs. Myles. Don't act surprised." He scoffed. "You're selling Ike's house to the very man you claim is responsible for the *Marion*'s disappearance."

Nellie's mouth went dry. "Is he still here?" Her lips stuck to her teeth.

"His trawler is anchored in Burke's Cove." Jon gave her an indignant look. "I'm sure he's waiting for you."

Nellie yanked open the store's door and sped up the hill to the convent. Her shawl slid down her back to the dirt road. She was out of breath before long but kept going. She reached the convent gate and whipped it open, her eyes pinned on the small group of people flocked in front of the convent door.

"You're the hooded man!" she heard Bessie screech. "You can't take Marie."

"Hooded man?" Captain Maurice said. "What is this hysterical child talking about?"

Annie's big hands flanked her large hips. She glared at the small man. "Get back to where you came from and leave decent folk be."

"I want to talk with Marie."

"Ma!" Bessie ran to Nellie. "Make the hooded man go away."

Marie hovered so close to Mother Patrick she was almost hidden by the nun's abundant robes.

"I suggest we go inside," Mother Patrick said. "Before every soul on the Burin peninsula hears this ruckus and decides to join in."

Captain Maurice bowed, the gesture stiff. "As you wish, *ma bonne soeur.*"

Annie snarled. "Don't put on false airs for Mother Patrick. She's onto ya."

Sister Thérèse offered to take Bessie and Marie to the kitchen for milk and cookies.

"Ma," Bessie said when Sister Thérèse tried to lead her away, "don't let the hooded man take Marie."

"Marie's staying put, sweetie. Go along to the kitchen."

The others went with Mother Patrick to her office. "Everyone sit down and act like grown-ups," she said. "As for you, *monsieur*," she looked Maurice squarely in the eyes, "you don't walk up behind a child and scare the wits out of her like you just did with Bessie."

"I did not mean to frighten her."

Annie's chin quivered. Nellie could see she was about to jump Maurice. "Captain," she said quickly, "you know well enough we blame you for sinking the *Marion*."

He squeezed his eyes shut. "How much longer must I fight against such an absurd accusation?"

"Why are you here?" Nellie asked, as if he hadn't spoken.

"I wish to speak to Marie," he said. Nellie loved when Eloise McEvoy spoke English with lilting musical tones, but the same accent from Maurice's mouth scraped her last nerve raw.

Annie's body grew rigid. "You killed her pa along with a whole crew of God-fearing men," she said. "You have some gall coming here."

Captain Maurice turned to Mother Patrick. "I have a right to speak to Marie."

"Right!" Annie shouted. "Marie and Bessie had a right to see their fathers again!"

"Annie," Mother Patrick snapped in her disciplinarian voice. "Kindly take control of yourself."

"Captain Maurice," Nellie said softly. "Did you break into Marie's house last night?"

"Yes."

Annie's steel-hard eyes flew to Maurice. "You hated Ike so much, you won't be satisfied until his little girl suffers, too."

Nellie covered Annie's hand with her own. "Captain Maurice, what makes you think you have any right to see Marie, let alone talk to her?"

"The best reason," he said quietly. "She is my granddaughter."

Chapter 17

ANNIE LEAPED TO HER feet and stood over Captain Maurice like a brick tower. “Pay the slime fish bait no heed!” she said. “He’s nothing but a racket raiser.”

“Annie,” Mother Patrick interrupted. “We need to discuss this matter rationally, quietly.”

Nellie felt the room spin. *This is a dream*, she thought. *I’ll wake up any minute now.*

Annie remained standing. “Why should we believe this murdering slippery eel?”

Annie’s raised voice penetrated the fog in Nellie’s brain. She blinked and stared at Maurice. “But . . . but Ike would have told us,” she whispered, barely able to put a thought together.

“Annie,” Mother Patrick said. “Please sit down.” She leaned forward and folded her hands on the desk. “Captain, why haven’t you bothered with the child before now?”

Annie leered at Maurice. “S’pose you’re gonna put the blame on Ike for that.”

“*Non.* It was all my fault.”

Nellie felt the shock fizzle away and the haze lift from her brain. Another emotion boiled up in its place. She peered at the captain. “Ike must’ve had some good reason to keep you a secret.”

“Darn right,” Annie said.

“Your anger is justified,” Maurice said. “I would like to try and explain—”

"Annie," Mother Patrick said over him. "Take Bessie and Marie home right now."

"With grand pleasure," she said, and marched from the room.

Nellie glared at the captain. "Let me straighten you out about one thing. Even if what you claim is true, Marie stays with me."

Mother Patrick's right eye twitched ever so slightly. "I'm sorry, Nellie. He told you the truth about Marie."

Nellie squashed the urge to run from the office. Away from Maurice. Away from the pain he represented. Away from the truth. "How do you know?"

The nun tidied books on her desk absently. "Father Jean-Claude told me what Maurice said to Marie when he saw her in St. Pierre." Her glasses slid to the tip of her nose and she pushed them back up with a finger. "I didn't believe you were ready to hear the awful truth."

"You should've warned me, given me time to prepare for this." Nellie's breath quickened as she turned to the French captain. "Ike left Marie in my care. His lawyer said nobody, relative or no, could take her from us."

"That is not my intention."

"I need some time to think on all this. Marie's future is at stake."

Maurice withdrew a stack of white envelopes from the top pocket of his jacket. His hand trembled as he held them out to Nellie. "Please, read these."

"You stole them from Ike's house, didn't ya?"

"They are addressed to me."

Nellie snatched the letters and stuffed them in her apron pocket. "Don't go near Marie or Bessie again without my permission." She glanced at Mother Patrick. "I'll be talking to you later."

She pushed open the door to a refreshing cool breeze and took a deep breath. Her hand hovered over the pocket containing the letters. They might be addressed to the captain, but he had no right to break into someone's house and steal them. Nellie strode down the hill with long steps. The pressure of the feather-light letters against her leg was hardly noticeable, yet it felt like she carried the burden of a lifetime.

Nellie let the door slam behind her when she entered the kitchen. Annie had supper underway, muttering to herself about Maurice. The children were nowhere to be seen. At five o'clock, they all appeared and sat at the table without a word. Bessie's appetite had returned to normal after the pneumonia, yet she picked at her food today.

"Why aren't you eating?" Annie said. "You loves pease pudding."

The corners of Bessie's mouth turned down. "I don't like Captain Maurice. He's the hooded man." She swished a lump of pease pudding around her plate. "Marie said he wore a hood when she saw him in her pa's house."

"That was a raincoat," Nellie said. "Captain Maurice will never take Marie away."

Annie smiled at the two girls. "I'll see to it that promise is never broken."

Bessie poked a blob of pease pudding in her mouth. "I knows a secret about Joe," she said playfully. "He sat with Amy LaCroix in school all week. He likes her."

Joe flushed like Nellie had never seen before. "It was the only seat left," he said. His eyes bored into his plate.

Sam looked sideways at him. "No it wasn't."

"She always sits by me."

"No she don't." Sam again.

"I don't want to talk about it."

Bessie puckered her lips. "Amy wants to kiss ya."

Nellie enjoyed the pleasant bantering between her youngsters, thrilled they were acting more themselves again. *Harry Myles,* she thought. *You must be some pleased about that.*

"Joe likes Amy, Joe likes Amy," Bessie and Marie sang in chorus.

Joe gobbled down a huge piece of gingerbread. "I'm gonna cut wood," he said before anyone else finished eating.

Annie tut-tutted. "Leave the poor boy be."

After completing their homework and chores, the youngsters played cards in the kitchen. Nellie and Annie retired to the living room.

"I've decided to move into Ike's house," Nellie said, the knitting in her hands forgotten. "What do you think about that?"

Annie darned a hole in one of Joe's socks. "About time. That big house shouldn't go to waste."

"I'd like you to come live with us. It'll do the youngsters a world of good to have their nan under the same roof."

Annie pulled a hanky out of her pocket. "My darn hay fever's acting up again." She blew her nose. "I can't let the youngsters down."

"It's beautifully furnished, so we'll only need our clothes and personal things." Nellie sighed. "Now there'll be three empty houses here . . ." She looked toward the kitchen and lowered her voice. ". . . because of Ike and Captain Maurice."

Annie stuffed the hanky back in her pocket. "That French fella has some gall coming here and spilling dirty lies."

Nellie laid down her knitting and took out the letters Maurice had given her. "We have no choice but to face up to the facts," she whispered, so quietly Annie had to lean in close to hear her. "Marie is Maurice's granddaughter."

"Aren't you gonna read those?" Annie said.

"I haven't decided yet."

Annie yawned. "I'm gonna put the French fella from my mind for tonight." She stretched, spreading her bare arms out wide. "My bones are dog tired. I think I'll stay the night."

"Time for bed," Nellie yelled into the kitchen. Annie kissed Bessie and Marie goodnight. She grabbed hold of Joe and Sam when they tried to escape her embrace. "Harry and Tommy did the same," she chuckled.

Nellie headed for the stairs, but Annie remained in the armchair. "Aren't you coming up?"

"I'll sleep on the chesterfield."

Nellie hid a smile. Annie intended to protect them if Maurice sneaked into the house during the night. She got blankets and a pillow from the hall closet. "Good night, Annie."

"Things will look brighter in the morning."

Nellie dragged herself upstairs and into bed. She lay back

against the pillows and stared, wide-eyed, at the letters on the side table. Marie had never known her mother. Had she the right to deprive her of a grandfather? Nellie cringed. As far as she was concerned, Maurice had murdered every man aboard the *Marion*. She ran a hand down the side of the bed where Harry had slept all their married life.

Can you really be sure he's guilty, love?

"Oh, Harry," Nellie murmured through a sob. "I don't know anymore."

Maybe reading the letters will tip the scales for ya.

You always knew the proper thing to say, Nellie thought. She sat up, reached for the first envelope, and opened the flap. Her heart beat faster. The bedside candle had burned down to the quick when she returned the last letter to its envelope. She snuggled under the covers and fell asleep.

NELLIE CRAWLED OUT OF bed to the smell of pancakes and toast after what felt like only a few minutes.

"Got some good news," Annie said. "Maurice's trawler is gone."

Nellie looked out the window toward Burke's Cove. "We haven't seen the last of him," she said, and buttered the warm toast.

Annie stirred bubbling oatmeal. "Did you read the letters?"

Nellie placed the toast in the centre of the table. "I did."

The youngsters scurried to the table, stopping Annie from further questioning. "There's plenty of grub," she said, "so eat up."

"Before you do," Nellie said, "I have a question. How would you all like to move into Ike's house? You could each have your own bedroom."

Joe let out a sigh of relief as if he'd been holding it in for a long time. "I was scared you were gonna say that we're moving to St. John's."

"That's a decision each of you will make for yourself when you're older."

The children looked from one to the other. "All right," Marie said for the group. "When do we go?"

"Me and Annie will start moving the clothes today. She's gonna live with us."

Smiles broke out all around the table. Sam's was the brightest. "Now we'll have coconut cream pie all the time," he said.

With the children off to school, Nellie and Annie carried two sacks of clothing to Ike's house. Annie boarded up the broken window and scrubbed the kitchen floor. Nellie dusted the entire first floor and washed up the captain's muddy tracks.

"It'll take a few days to get this grand house sparkling clean," Annie said, and wiped the sweat from her forehead with a handkerchief. "It's almost dinnertime. We'd best get back and feed the youngsters." She went home and heated up chicken soup while Nellie made a trip to the post office. Two envelopes awaited her: one from Dottie, the other from Mr. Fleming.

She opened Dottie's letter the instant she came through the kitchen door. "She says the twins are growing like weeds and she can't wait for you to see them. You know, Annie, there's nothing stopping you from going to St. John's whenever you likes now." Nellie pulled the lawyer's money envelope out of her pocket.

"I'll go when everything's quieted down here. Is there any mention of poor Alice Whelan?"

"Yes. She's on her feet again. Mr. Fleming found her a job at the bank."

"Alice was always good with numbers. Like our Sam."

"She's not back to herself yet, but she's coming along."

"Poor love," Annie said. "Tim near had a fit when she wrote to say she was staying on in St. John's. Rosie's the sensible one. Gave Alice her blessing even though she misses her something shocking."

The conversation was cut short when the children arrived. "It'll be a few days before the house is ready to move into," Nellie informed them.

"It'll be some good to sleep in my own bed in my own room," Sam said.

Joe nudged Sam with his elbow. "And I won't have to listen to you snore all night."

Sam nudged his brother back. "You're the one who snores!"

Nellie had to push the children out the door so they wouldn't be late getting back to school. "I want them to be happy," she said. "Sometimes, though, I'm scared they'll forget Harry."

"It's natural they get past his death," Annie said. "It don't mean they'll forget him. Harry never forgot his parents."

Nellie pulled a heavy woollen shawl around her shoulders. "I've an errand to run. I'll tell you all about it later at Ike's."

She left for Dr. Fitzgerald's house and quickly related her request and the reason for it when she arrived.

"Of course, my dear," Dr. Fitzgerald said, and brought out his horse and cart from the stable. "Sure you don't want me to drive you?"

Nellie declined the kind offer and headed for Boxey. Guy Hays was chopping wood when the horse pulled in alongside him. "I'm some glad I caught you home," she said.

"This is a surprise, Nellie. What brings you this way?"

"I came to talk to you."

Guy helped her down and tied the horse to the fence post. "I'll get Chiselle to warm up the kettle."

The young French girl smiled sweetly at Nellie. "*Ça va? Ah . . . Pardon*. How are you?" she said in slow, very accented English.

"My missus hasn't gotten the hang of our talk yet," Guy said, putting his arm around her. "She's coming along, though."

Chiselle placed the same French pastries on the table Nellie had eaten in St. Pierre. Guy chomped on the creamy delight. "Can't beat the French for making sweets."

Nellie chewed a tiny morsel. "Guy, I want to ask you about what your cousin François said about Captain Maurice and the *Marion*."

"*Ouf!*" Chiselle said, throwing her hands into the air. "*François est fou.*"

Guy turned to his wife. "*Qu'est-ce qu'il y a?*"

Chiselle continued in French with the occasional question thrown in by Guy.

"Sorry 'bout that, Nellie," he said when his wife concluded the rant. "When she gets riled up, the smidgen of English she's learned flies out of her head."

"I take it Chiselle's not too taken with your cousin."

"She says he's a drunk and practically lives in the bar of the *Hôtel de France*. I thought he still sailed with Maurice, but Chiselle said the captain let him go after a half-dozen warnings about being drunk while fishing on the Banks."

"François 'ates *le capitaine* Maurice," Chiselle said. "One cannot . . ." She paused, looked at Guy, and continued, "*croire.*"

"Believe," he translated.

"*Oui.* One cannot believe what he say of *le capitaine*."

Nellie made it back to Ike's house by late afternoon and filled Annie in. "Didn't mean to be so late. I'm still in a fog about everything."

"For now let's worry about getting the house ready," Annie said, and took out a sack of potatoes from the pantry.

Bessie started in on Joe about Amy at supper. He suffered the teasing in silence. Nellie wasn't sure how she felt about her oldest boy growing into a man. The next day she and Annie continued cleaning Ike's house. Both were exhausted by the time they went home. Nellie had just started to go upstairs when they heard a knock at the back door. She heard Annie mumble something about being disturbed while getting supper. Annie opened the door to a familiar face.

"*Bon soir,* Mme. Myles," Father Jean-Claude greeted Nellie.

"Father Jean-Claude, is something the matter?"

Mother Patrick stood behind the priest. "We're going to Ike's house. It's time to settle this mess with Maurice."

Nellie grabbed the key from the cupboard and chased after the mother superior. "Why are we rushing like the devil's on our tail?" she said.

"I'll tell you when we're in Ike's house."

Annie and Father Jean-Claude almost ran to keep pace. "Thank heavens we're here," Annie said, a hand on her chest.

"*Quelle belle maison!*" the priest said. "What a beautiful house."

Inside, he saw the portrait of Marie's mother and stood under it. "Chantal was very lovely," he said.

The front door opened and a cold wind swept into the living room, along with Maurice. He took off his captain's hat. "*Bonjour, mon père.*"

"Take a seat," Mother Patrick said. She gazed at everyone in the room. "I sent for Captain Maurice. Father Jean-Claude is here on my bidding to help guide us through our problem."

Chapter 18

NELLIE LOOKED AT THE small man she had believed gutted her world with one vicious act. "You're a fishing captain like Ike was," she said. "Why did you resent him before you ever met him?"

Maurice gripped his hat with both hands. "Fishing is a dangerous life, and lonely for everyone in the family. I did not want that for my only child."

"Marie's the spitting image of Chantal. I will not let her be a stand-in for your daughter," Nellie said, holding back tears.

Maurice's shoulders stooped. "I have denied my granddaughter all her life. I simply want the chance to get to know her."

"Father Jean-Claude," Nellie said, "what do you think I should do?"

"As a priest, I must say that we all deserve a second chance. As a man who has known *le capitaine* Maurice for over thirty years, I feel he is worthy of that second chance."

Annie's face burned pink. "Begging your pardon, Father, but I don't agree. That man scuttled the *Marion*. He deserves nothing."

The captain's fingers tightened around his hat. "I did not sink the *Marion*." He sounded tired. "I was nowhere near the schooner when it disappeared."

A tear hung in the corner of Nellie's eye. "I need one more night to think this over," she said.

Maurice bowed his head to her. "I cannot ask for more than that. *Bonne nuit,*" he said, and walked from the room, his shoulders still bent.

Father Jean-Claude returned to Chantal's portrait. "She was a happy child," he said softly. "The artist has captured that quality in the eyes. Maurice would never have hurt the man she loved." The priest looked at Nellie. "Regardless of his hatred for him."

Not another word was uttered as they departed the house. The moon guided their silent trek along the shoreline. "Sleep well," Father Jean-Claude said when Nellie reached her front door.

"Thank you." She watched him walk toward the convent with Mother Patrick. It wasn't until they were lost among the shadows that she went inside, going straight up to bed.

She lay awake sifting through the facts gathered by the Burke brothers and her own investigation into the *Marion*'s disappearance. By morning she'd come to a decision. When the children were leaving for school, she said with more calm than she felt, "There's something you all need to be told. Marie has to hear it first, so she'll stay home this morning."

Sam kept his eyes on his books. "Is it more bad news, Ma?"

Nellie searched for the answer herself. "No, Sam," she said after a brief hesitation. "It may even turn out to be good news." The tension in the room lifted like mist broken on a sunny day. The children were down the path and on the road before Nellie spoke again, more to herself than to Marie. "Everything is changing too fast."

"I misses Pa," Marie said. "You made it a whole lot easier for me."

Nellie smoothed Marie's dark hair behind her ears and led her to the living room. Both sat on the chesterfield. "Your mother didn't want to leave you and your pa."

Marie smiled. "I knows that. Pa told me all the time."

"He was a good father who wanted the best for his little girl."

"Pa told me that, too. Why are you talking so much about what Pa used to say?"

Nellie licked dry lips. It had seemed easy enough last night when she'd gone over in her head how to tell Marie about Maurice. The reality was tougher. She swallowed. "You've heard folks talk about Captain Maurice."

"He frightened me at Pa's house."

"He didn't know you were there. He was looking for letters his daughter had written to him. The last letter she wrote talks about you."

Marie's expression went from surprise to confusion. "The captain's daughter doesn't know me."

Nellie took Marie's hands in hers and held them to her heart. "The captain's daughter was your mother."

"That can't be right. Pa would have told me." Marie scrunched up her nose. "I don't understand what you means."

"It's hard to explain."

Marie's eyes flew wide open. "He didn't tell me about Aunt Sheila because she's mean." She pulled her hands free of Nellie's. "That's why he didn't tell me my mother was the captain's daughter! The captain's mean, too."

"The French captain loved your mother and was awful sad when she died. He shut down his heart so he wouldn't hurt anymore."

Marie sniffed. "You said he scuttled the *Marion*."

The energy seeped from Nellie's body. Could she speak aloud the possibility she had only been able to consider in her thoughts? Father Jean-Claude's belief in Maurice chimed in her head like church bells. "I was wrong. So is everyone else. Maurice didn't scuttle the *Marion*. He's sorry for being mad at your pa and wants to see you."

"Will you be with me?"

"Whatever you want," Nellie said. She glanced at the wedding portrait.

Nellie, love, you understands Ike now, don't ya.

Nellie understood now that he wanted Marie to know her grandfather.

Marie clutched Nellie's arm. "You promise?"

Nellie hugged her. "I promise. This is what your pa wanted most of all for you."

"I can feel your heart pounding," Marie said. "Are you scared, too?"

Nellie held the child closer. Marie couldn't know that she had never been so uncertain about anything. "I'm beside myself with excitement for you."

"When do you want me to see him?"

"We'll go to the convent right now, and Mother Patrick can send for him. Is that all right?"

Marie nodded. "As long as you stays with me."

"Before we go, I want you to read your mother's last letter to Captain Maurice." Nellie handed her a sheet of faded blue paper.

Mon chère Papa,

I am saddened beyond what words can express that you have refused to read any of my letters. I will persist and pray that one day you will change your mind. I miss the kind, gentle man who was my father and loved me as I loved him.

In a few short months you will be a grandfather. Ike has promised we will move to the Burin peninsula after the baby is born. To visit, you will only be a boat ride away. Forgive me, Papa, for marrying without your consent, but I love Ike. He is a good man and wishes as much as me to include you in our family. I cannot bear for my child to never know its grandfather. My heart aches to see you, to talk about everything and nothing like we used to do.

If my baby is a boy, Ike has agreed to call him Pierre Maurice. Please, Papa, give my husband the chance to show you the kind of man he is.

I miss you more with every passing day. Come to St. John's. Having you with me when mon bébé is born will fill me with much comfort and joy.

Your loving daughter always. Je t'aime.
Chantal

"My mother sounds some nice," Marie said when she finished reading the letter. "She loved her pa like I loved mine."

Nellie took the letter and kissed the top of her head. "You're a smart girl," she said. "Let's go."

Marie held Nellie's hand as they walked to the convent. "Will the captain try to take me away like Aunt Sheila did?"

"No. Besides, he knows it wouldn't do any good if he tried." Marie's hold slackened. Nellie hadn't noticed until then that the child's grip had numbed her fingers. They passed Young's General Store. "We'll stop off for a treat on the way back."

"What about school?" Marie said.

"You can miss one day."

"Can we buy chocolate for Joe, Sam, and Bessie, too?"

Nellie was about to answer when Denis Burke come out of the convent and scooted off down the road. Mother Patrick waved to her from the door.

"He donated fifty dollars for school supplies." The nun folded her arms inside the large habit's sleeves. "Whatever you said got through to him." She switched her attention to Marie. "Now, missy. You don't look sick. Why aren't you in school?"

"I'm gonna see Captain Maurice here."

Mother Patrick's eyes twitched, the only sign that she was shocked. "And what makes you think that?" she said, leading the way to her office.

Nellie closed the door. "I thought this would be a safe place for the meeting."

Mother Patrick sent a nun to Eloise McEvoy's house to fetch the French captain. "As for you, young Marie," she said, "go to the kitchen and tell Sister Assumpta I'd like a nice cuppa tea."

"Why did you send her off?" Nellie said once they were alone.

"Have you heard the fuss everyone's making over the captain staying with Eloise?"

"Not a word. But I'm not surprised."

Mother Patrick sat behind her desk. "Mrs. LaCroix called her a traitor to Fred's memory. Five of her ten youngsters were with her and chanted the word over and over. She even wrote to Dottie about it. The next day Billy Evans's mother crossed to the other side of the road when she saw Eloise. The poor girl is beside herself with worry, and came running to me with her eyes red and swollen from crying. She's doing her pa a favour by allowing the man to stay there. To make matters worse, Seth is due back tomorrow. I told Eloise not to worry, that I would deal with Maurice and the townspeople."

Nellie had no doubt that she would.

Marie came back the same moment that Maurice was shown into the office, his hat crumpled up in his hands. "You sent for me, *ma mère* Patrick?" he said.

"It was me," Nellie said. "Marie's agreed to talk with you if I stay in the room. She has read your daughter's last letter."

"I'll wait outside," Mother Patrick said, and turned to Maurice. "I want a word with you about Eloise McEvoy before you leave."

"I realize I have caused a problem for her. I will leave immediately."

"Glad to see you have a spark of common sense," the nun said, and closed the door behind her.

Maurice sat in the chair next to Marie. "*Tu es jolie comme ta mère.* Pardon me. You—"

"You said I was pretty like my mother. Pa was some happy when I did good in French," Marie said with a smile.

Maurice cleared his throat and whipped out a handkerchief. He blew his nose with a loud honk. "You are eleven years old," he said.

"My birthday was in June."

Maurice rubbed sweat from his face and hands. "I am a stupid old fool who let his child and grandchild down. If it isn't too late, I would like to be a part of your life." His voice quivered. "*Mon petit chou*, can you ever forgive me?"

Marie sat still, her fingers intertwined on her lap. She glanced over her shoulder at Nellie, who sat behind the desk.

"Say what ya feels."

Marie fidgeted on her chair. "Captain Maurice, did you scuttle the *Marion*?"

He leaned forward and stared into eyes as green as his. "*Non.* I did not sink the *Marion*."

"I'm some glad. It would be awful if my grandpa killed my pa."

"It's near noon," Nellie said. "I have dinner to get ready."

Maurice stood up. "When may I see Marie again?"

"That's up to her."

"Marie, would you like to visit me in St. Pierre? You can meet other children and practice French," the captain said.

"Can Bessie come, too?"

"*Bien sure.* And Mme. Myles, thank you for your kindness and understanding." Maurice shook Nellie's hand. "My crew will come for me today, but I will return on Friday for Marie and Bessie."

"They're not going without me."

"That is not a problem, Mme. Myles."

Nellie hauled the letters out of her pocket and gave them back to the captain. "I feel like I know Chantal now. You better not hurt Marie."

Nellie and Marie arrived home a half-hour before Joe, Sam, and Bessie stormed in from school.

"Ma," Sam said, "what did you have to tell Marie this morning?"

"Captain Maurice is my grandpa," Marie said, getting straight to the point with one simple statement.

"Sure, b'y," Joe said, "and I'm Father Curran's grandfather."

Sam gaped at Marie. "I thinks she means it," he said.

Bessie turned pale. "He killed our fathers," she said. "He's the hooded man and wants to steal you away."

Nellie dished out cabbage hash. "I was upset too, at first. Now I understand. Captain Maurice isn't the hooded man and he isn't responsible for the *Marion*'s disappearance." The look of absolute disbelief and hurt on her youngsters' faces seared into her soul. She related the reasons why she'd changed her mind, praying they made sense to the children. "Marie is part of the family now, and the captain is her grandfather. How do you feel about that?" No one spoke. The silence pounded in her ears.

Joe threw down his fork. "I hates that Pa's gone." He stared down at the table and seemed to be absorbed in his thoughts. Sam and Bessie looked away. Finally, he raised his head. "It doesn't hurt so bad knowing he wasn't killed on purpose."

"Me too," Sam said. "I couldn't get it out of me head how Pa must've felt when the trawler rammed the schooner."

Bessie's colour returned. "Marie, are you happy the captain's your grandfather?"

"He scared me in St. Pierre, but not anymore."

"Ma," Joe said, "all our friends are gonna be some mad when they finds out."

"I've been giving some thought to that. I'll ask Father Curran for a meeting in the church to talk to everyone. Mother Patrick will want to help."

Marie produced a chocolate treat from Young's General Store. Joe cracked off a chunk of the thick, creamy bar with his teeth. "Ma, I don't want to go back to school today."

"All right," Nellie said, and gave him a key. "All of you get some of your belongings together and bring them to Ike's house. I'll be over when I'm done cleaning up here." She washed the dishes and swept the floor, her mind on Maurice. Had she really convinced the youngsters of his innocence? A suspicion of his guilt remained lodged in a far corner of her brain. *No*, she thought. *It's more than that.*

The suspicion soon warped into a funny feeling that more tragedy was in store for her family. A soft tap at the door became a loud thump before she heard the noise. She turned toward the kitchen door, but realized the *rap, rap* was coming from the front of the house. No one ever used the front door. She hurried to answer it.

"Hello," Mr. Fleming said. "I have an urgent matter to discuss with you."

Chapter 19

"THE COASTAL BOAT IS not due for another week," Nellie said. "How'd you get here?"

"The mere mention of a boat makes me seasick," Mr. Fleming said. "I took the train, then hired a horse and cart."

"When did you arrive?" Nellie asked, delaying for as long as she could the urgent business that could only pertain to Marie. "Where are you staying? Would you like a cuppa tea?"

The lawyer smiled. "May I come in?"

"Goodness me," Nellie said. "Where are my manners?"

The lawyer followed her past the stairs and down a hallway painted a soft cream colour. A portrait of each of her children hung in a neat row along the wall. He paused outside the living room and stared at the wedding portrait. "You and your husband made a handsome pair."

Nellie steeped tea and enquired about the weather in St. John's, his daughter, Dottie, Alice, his trip to St. Jacques, anything but the matter at hand.

Mr. Fleming answered each question with polite patience. "I must apologize," he finally said when she ran out of questions.

Here it comes, Nellie thought, and wrapped cold hands around her hot mug. "Marie's gonna be taken from us," she said. Her voice echoed hollowly in her ears.

The lawyer gaped at Nellie and tea slopped over the rim of his mug. "Of course not," he said. "I apologize for giving you the impression that something was wrong. At times, my lawyer's mind takes control." He pulled out a letter from an inside coat pocket. "Sheila Jones notified me that she intended to fight for custody over Marie." He hurried on. "I sent a copy of Ike's will to her lawyer, who notified me at once that he will convince his client she's wasting her time and money."

Nellie allowed herself to breathe. "You could have written and saved the long trip."

"I have a good friend in Belleoram. This was a good excuse to visit, since I've never been to the Burin peninsula." Mr. Fleming asked for more tea. "I was surprised to hear you hadn't moved into Ike's house yet."

"We're in the middle of packing up everything."

The lawyer produced a sad smile. "Change is difficult," he said. "Especially when it's a result of circumstances out of our control." They chatted for a while more, and after he said his goodbyes, Nellie went to Ike's house. The youngsters had each staked their claim to a bedroom and had spent the rest of the time exploring the house.

After supper she asked Mother Patrick about setting up a meeting to inform the community what had occurred with Maurice and Marie. The nun tapped her foot and folded her arms across her chest. "Like I told you earlier, let me deal with any comments or concerns on the subject."

Overtired from a stressful day, Nellie went to bed before the youngsters that night. She blew out the bedside candle and got under the blankets. Sleep wouldn't come, as one single thought tormented her. "Harry," she mumbled into the sheets. "Mr. Fleming's encouraging news hasn't taken away my funny feeling." The moon's shadow bobbed on the harbour water.

Nellie, love, you only get the bad feeling before someone dies.

THE NEXT MORNING NELLIE dragged herself out of bed, the bad feeling fouling the air like the stench of rotted fish. She chatted with the children during breakfast to occupy her mind, and made dough for bread when they left for school. The mid-October weather was unseasonably cold. The sky was overcast and the wind moaned against the window, rattling the glass like skeleton's bones. To Nellie it sounded like a death wail.

She poured hot water into a pan for the dishes. Someone whisked open the back door. The sudden movement startled Nellie, and she splashed soapy water onto the counter and down her apron.

"Mme. Myles, you must come right away!" Sister Thérèse held the door open. The icy wind chewed at her reddened fingers. Her veil spiralled out like a schooner's sail. "Mrs. Cluett has had an accident."

Nellie's bad feeling stirred, like ripples on a smooth pond. "Please God," she whispered. "Not Annie." A black haze swarmed in front of her eyes. She shook her head to dispel the sensation. "Is she all right?"

"She is unconscious. Dr. Fitzgerald is with her."

Nellie stood transfixed.

"Please hurry," the young nun said. Sister Thérèse reached out and grabbed her by the arm. "There is no time to waste!"

Nellie threw on her coat and raced down the path, the open door abandoned to the whims of the wind. She prayed all the way to the convent.

Mother Patrick was pacing in front of the graveyard fence when Nellie and Sister Thérèse arrived. The wind beat the heavy robes against her legs.

Nellie rushed toward her and almost knocked her over. "What happened? Is Annie all right?"

Mother Patrick pulled her inside the convent and hurried down a side corridor to the kitchen. Hot tea awaited them both.

"Denis Burke found Annie at the foot of a ladder outside her house. Can you believe she was cleaning windows in this weather?"

Nellie shoved aside the steaming tea. "Is she here?"

"Denis helped Dr. Fitzgerald carry her to his house."

Nellie sprang to her feet.

"Sit down. Denis will let us know when the doctor says it's all right to see Annie. He doesn't want us underfoot acting like scared youngsters while he's examining her."

"Sweet Jesus," Nellie said. "I knew something awful was gonna happen."

"What!" Mother Patrick stared at her. "Please tell me you don't have one of your bad feelings."

Nellie fell limp into a chair. "It's a curse. I couldn't save Harry or Tommy either."

Sister Thérèse stood in the doorway. "M. Burke was just here. You may go to see Annie now." The young nun darted to the side in time to avoid being trampled by the two anxious women.

"We must remain calm," Mother Patrick said when the doctor's house came into view. "Hysterical women only get in the way." Nellie heard the edge of panic in her friend's voice.

Hattie Fitzgerald met them at the door. Her face was grey, solemn. "Conrad will be with you in a few minutes," she said, and showed them to the den.

Neither Mother Patrick nor Nellie enquired after Annie. Both knew the doctor's wife would not comment on any of her husband's patients.

"Good day, ladies," the doctor said just after his wife departed to make tea. "I'm afraid the news isn't good."

"Sweet Blessed Virgin," Mother Patrick cried out. "I refuse to hear that good woman is gone."

Nellie had a sensation of floating. The nun and doctor looked like shadows on a wall. Dr. Fitzgerald patted her hand. She looked at him. Why did he seem so far away? Water dribbled down her chin.

"Drink it," a voice ordered.

She swallowed the cold liquid. The shadows took on solid form.

"Nellie, how do you feel?"

Nellie shook her head and stared around the room. "What happened?"

"You fainted," Dr. Fitzgerald said.

Nellie rubbed her face with both hands. "I'm all right now. How's Annie?"

"Annie suffered a serious concussion, as far as I can tell. She hasn't regained consciousness."

Mother Patrick tapped her foot. “Isn’t there some way to bring her around?”

“No. We have to wait for her to wake up.” Dr. Fitzgerald sat down, his movements slow. “There are several things that can happen in the meantime. She may lapse into a coma, from a blood clot, or her brain may swell.”

Nellie trembled. “Can they do anything for her in St. John’s?”

The doctor heaved a great sigh. “Even if they could, it would take too long to get there, and I dare not risk moving her.”

Mother Patrick slid into an armchair. “What can we do?”

The doctor ran a hand through his hair. “She could really use your prayers right now.”

Word about Annie’s accident reached every corner of the community. By dinnertime, most of the people had crowded to the doctor’s house, only to leave, disheartened by Annie’s condition. Sister Thérèse took it upon herself to pull Marie and Nellie’s youngsters out of class to tell them before they heard it from a neighbour. Mrs. Fitzgerald made a pot of chicken soup in anticipation of their arrival. She insisted they eat when they stampeded into her house, anxious to see Annie.

They’d gobbled down the soup and ran to the den in time to hear Dr. Fitzgerald’s update. “Annie’s condition hasn’t changed,” he said to the frightened faces staring at him.

“It’s been hours,” Mother Patrick said. “Surely that isn’t a good sign.”

“It’s not. The longer she’s unconscious, the less chance there is for recovery.”

Sam sat down next to his mother. “Is Annie in pain?” he said.

“No, son. She doesn’t feel anything.”

“Conrad,” his wife called from the top of the stairs. “Come quickly!”

“Stay here,” Dr. Fitzgerald said, and ran from the room. His wife had gone back to attend to Annie by the time he climbed the stairs two at a time.

*

THE DOOR TO HER room was ajar. Hattie leaned over the prone figure on the bed. There was no sound, no movement.

"What happened?" Dr. Fitzgerald said, his breathing deep but steady.

His wife stepped aside.

Annie lay back against a pile of pillows, her eyes open. "How'd I get here?" she moaned.

The doctor moved to the bed. "You fell off a ladder and struck your head."

Annie closed her eyes. "On a ladder? What was . . . That's right. I wanted all the windows cleaned before I moved to Ike's house." She tried to sit up. "Ohhh. My head feels like Joe used it for a soccer ball."

The doctor opened his medical bag. "That's to be expected."

"Don't fuss over me," Annie said when he tried to take her pulse.

"I don't want to hear any more complaints, Annie Cluett. I'm examining you whether you like it or not." He checked her eyes and held up two fingers. "How many do you see?"

Annie squinted. "I have never had such an awful headache in my life."

"How many?" Dr. Fitzgerald repeated.

"Two."

"Excellent. Are you dizzy?"

Annie shook her head. "Ohhhhhh," she groaned. "Shouldn't have done that."

"Do you feel like vomiting?"

"No."

"You're very lucky to be alive with such a severe concussion."

"I wants to go home."

"You're staying right where you are until I say otherwise. Hattie will be up shortly with a light soup."

Annie made to object. A low moan came out instead.

"Lie still and behave yourself or I'll send Mother Patrick up to look after you."

"All right," Annie grumbled.

Dr. Fitzgerald soaked a cloth in a pan of water on the bedside table and placed it on Annie's forehead. "This should make you a little more comfortable. Let me know right away if you feel dizzy, get blurred vision, or feel sick to your stomach." He waited for his wife to come up with the soup. "Hattie, call me if she gives you an ounce of trouble."

Hattie smiled. "I'm sure she'll co-operate." The doctor took his leave and returned to the den.

"YOU TOOK LONG ENOUGH," Mother Patrick snapped.

"Your prayers worked, Mother Patrick. Annie's awake."

"Blessed be the saints! Is she up to visitors?"

"Not for a day or two. She needs rest and care for at least two weeks."

Bessie looked at Dr. Fitzgerald with huge eyes. "Is Annie really all right?"

He smiled again. "It looks that way. She's staying here tonight. You children go on home."

"Go ahead," Nellie said. "There's dough on the counter for toutons. I'll see you in a little while."

"I wants to stay," Bessie said.

Joe took her by the hand. "We can have the toutons ready when Ma gets home. She'll like that."

"I would indeed," Nellie said.

As soon as the youngsters were out of the house, Mother Patrick turned to the doctor. "Is Annie out of danger?"

"Not yet. People with severe concussions who lose consciousness and stay out for as long as Annie did usually develop one of the life-threatening conditions I described. She's strong, but her age is against her." He clicked his tongue against the roof of his mouth. "Thank the good Lord she's beaten the odds this far."

"Years of good, hardy work kept her strong and healthy," Nellie said.

Mrs. Fitzgerald poked her head in the room. "Conrad, Annie's resting as best she can under the circumstances."

"Thank you, Hattie, dear. I'll be up in a minute. As for you, ladies," he said, addressing Nellie and Mother Patrick, "if there's any change in Annie's condition, I'll send for you both right away."

"Come along," Mother Patrick said. "Let's not pester the good man any more."

They walked as far as the Rooms. "Nellie, is there something else besides Annie troubling you? You haven't opened your mouth since we left Dr. Fitzgerald's house."

Yes, Nellie thought. The answer came out as no. Her bad feeling gnawed at her stomach like a hunger not quite satisfied.

Chapter 20

THREE WORRISOME DAYS AFTER Annie's fall from the ladder, Dr. Fitzgerald gave her permission to leave his home, with strict orders to do nothing more strenuous than get in and out of bed for at least a week.

"Nellie's going to St. Pierre with Marie and Bessie today," she said. "I must look after the boys for the weekend."

"Not necessary," Mother Patrick said. "You and the boys will stay at the convent."

"Nonsense. I don't need no one to coddle me."

Mother Patrick tapped a foot impatiently. "I won't hear another word about it. You're coming to the convent."

Nellie helped Annie with her coat. "Give in without a fight. You knows what Mother Patrick's like when she's made up her mind."

"Indeed I do," the nun said, and linked arms with Annie. "Nellie's brought a few of your things to the convent. Come along. Steve Marsh is waiting outside with his horse and cart.

"I ain't riding in no cart," Annie said as Mother Patrick led her out of the room. "There's nothing wrong with my legs."

Nellie smiled at Dr. Fitzgerald. "I wonder who'll win that little tug-of-war?"

"My dear Mrs. Myles, is there really any doubt about that?"

Annie eased into the seat next to Mother Patrick. She was flushed; sweat dribbled down the sides of her face and her breathing was heavy. She looked at Nellie and massaged her temples. "I thought it wouldn't hurt just this once to accept a ride."

"Your room is ready and waiting," Mother Patrick said. "I baked a rhubarb pie especially for you this morning."

Nellie hid a smile and scrambled into the cart. *What would the youngsters say about the crusty old mother superior if they could see her fuss over Annie?*

Steve Marsh climbed into the driver's seat. "It's some good to see ya up and about, Annie," he said. "Gave the whole community a scare."

"Take us home," Mother Patrick said. "And for goodness' sake, man, watch out for the bumps in the road."

Steve saluted her with two fingers to the side of his cap. "Right-o."

Annie grunted with disgust. "You wouldn't know but I was a babe in arms."

Steve directed the horse to go as slowly as possible. "Old Winnie usually listens to me, Mother Patrick," he said, "but she's got a mind of her own."

Denis Burke hurried out of his office to see Annie when they passed by. His bright smile at her recovery caused Nellie a pang of guilt for ripping into him about the *Marion*'s loss. "It's too bad his brothers aren't more like him," she said after they drove past.

Steve glanced over his shoulder at the women. "Never thought I'd hear words like that uttered around here about a merchant."

"Never thought I'd be the one to speak them," Nellie countered.

The cart stopped numerous times for well-wishers to have a few words with Annie. "We'll get you straight to bed," Mother Patrick said when they finally rolled up to the convent. "And I'll bring you up a nice tray for supper."

"I am a mite tired," Annie admitted, bringing a hand to her forehead. "A rest would do me good." Steve lifted her down as best he could without jostling her.

Mother Patrick linked arms with her once again. "I'll mix up some herbs for that headache."

Annie didn't turn her head to look at the nun. "That would be lovely."

Nellie kissed her cheek. "Me and the girls will see you Sunday afternoon."

Annie mumbled a response and permitted herself to be led inside.

On the way back home, Nellie saw Captain Maurice's trawler chug into Burke's Cove. Bessie and Marie had eaten supper and placed their packed bags by the door. "We made fish cakes," Bessie said, pointing to the table with excitement. A plateful sat at Nellie's place.

The food looked delicious, but the knots in Nellie's stomach prevented her from enjoying it. "Captain Maurice's trawler is here," she said. Marie poured tea for her.

"We knows," Bessie said breathlessly. Marie almost danced the teapot back to the stove.

Nellie sipped at the tea, holding the mug with two hands. "Did Joe and Sam have supper yet?"

"They're playing soccer in Ned's Field," Bessie said. "Mother Patrick told them to go to the convent for supper."

"We'd best get the dishes done," Nellie said. "The captain will be here soon."

Nellie was right. Maurice arrived minutes after they swept the floor. "A crewman is waiting at your wharf," he said. "We will go to the trawler by boat, if that is not a problem."

"I don't mind," Nellie said, thrilled she didn't have to walk through the community with the man.

THE YOUNG CREWMAN SMILED as he helped Bessie and Marie into the boat. Nellie noted he was two or three years older than Joe. *Too young to face the sea's treachery and its lonely life.* As soon as they boarded the trawler, they departed for St. Pierre. A moment of panic overwhelmed Nellie. She'd put her trust in a man she hardly knew, one she'd believed had killed seventeen defenceless men. The moment passed, and soon she breathed easier.

The crossing was smooth, with no wind or rain to delay them.

The captain gave Bessie and Marie a tour of the ship, while Nellie opted to sit on deck and savour the evening air. Wrapped in a blanket, provided by the same young man who'd rowed them to the trawler, she tried to imagine a fisherman's life on a schooner. Harry never talked about his time on the sea, a sure sign it was a back-breaking, desolate experience. He never encouraged his sons to follow in the tradition. On the contrary, he'd displayed disappointment when Joe expressed a keen interest.

"We arrive soon," a voice thick with a French accent said.

Nellie looked up into the face of the young crew member. "Thank you," she said.

"*Le capitaine* wants that you know."

"Have you been long with the captain?"

"I sail one time." The young man paused. Nellie could see he was searching for his words. "I come from France two month ago." He smiled. "*Excusez-moi, Madame.* I have work to do."

Nellie watched him walk away, not sure what she'd hoped to learn about Maurice. She turned back to the water. The lights of St. Pierre twinkled under the stars, and the island floated on the horizon with the sway of the ship. Her mind came back to Harry. What had he thought whenever the tiny French community came into view? Had he wished it was home? She shook herself to free her mind. Maurice, Marie, and Bessie walked toward her.

"We dock in ten minutes," the captain said.

The bliss she saw in Marie and Bessie's faces soothed her misgivings about going to the captain's home. The harbour was half-full with foreign vessels, and the wharf bustled with fishermen and dock workers.

Mme. Dubois, Maurice's housekeeper, had tea and pastries laid out on the dining room table. She insisted the guests eat before being shown to their rooms. The captain joined them and chatted with Nellie and the children about St. Pierre, as if they'd known each other for years.

"*Le capitaine est tellement exciter de vous avoir içi,*" the housekeeper said when the children were in the backyard with Maurice.

From her smile and gestures, Nellie gathered that Mme. Dubois had said the captain was as excited as they were. "*Oui,*" Nellie said, the only French word she knew.

Mme. Dubois collected the dishes and left Nellie alone. She inspected the room for the first time, amazed at how much it resembled Ike's dining room. Happy voices filtered in through the open window. Maurice sat on a wooden bench with the children, acting like any grandfather with his grandchild.

"*Mme. Myles, je vous amène à votre chambre.*"

Nellie picked up her bag and followed Mme. Dubois upstairs to a room at the end of a long hall. Three walls were pale green; yellow wallpaper patterned with white carnations completed the fourth. The open bay window was framed by soft cream lace curtains that fluttered in the wind. A pale green bedspread, white bureau, and wardrobe accentuated the polished medium-dark hardwood floor. Nellie wondered if this had been Chantal's room. She took off her shoes and lay down to ward off the headache threatening to explode behind her temples. Nellie drifted to sleep to the faraway sound of Bessie and Marie's laughter.

More stars sprinkled the sky as evening progressed into night. The full moon's face deepened, the only witness to Nellie's slumber. She shivered and hugged her knees to her chest. The cold air tugged at her face and woke her. The house was quiet, peaceful. Nellie got up to close the window, undressed, and slipped under the covers again, asleep almost the second her head touched the pillow. The next sound she heard was Bessie entering the room.

"Ma, wake up. Breakfast is ready."

Nellie peeled her eyes open and squinted against the blaring sun. "What time is it?"

"Seven. The captain wants to get an early start to the day. There's so much he wants to show us."

Nellie sat up. "I'll be down in a minute." She slid off the bed as her daughter skipped down the hall. A decanter of fresh water had been placed on the bureau with a cloth and scented soap. Ten minutes later, Nellie appeared in the kitchen.

"*Bonjour*," Maurice said with a smile. "I asked Mme. Dubois to make blueberry pancakes. The children told me it is their favourite."

Nellie didn't realize how hungry she was until the first mouthful. Chocolate sauce and whipped cream made the meal even more pleasurable.

"This morning we are going to visit the *boulangerie*, the bakery. M. Ledoux will show us how he makes bread and croissants fresh every day. Then we go to the *patisserie*, the cake shop, to see how the delicious pastries you have eaten are made."

The morning passed quickly and Nellie was surprised how much she enjoyed the excursion. The bakery and cake shop owners treated Bessie and Marie like royalty. The girls left each place loaded down with bread and pastries given as gifts to the "*jolies Terreneuviennes*."

"*Jolies terreneuviennes?*" Nellie said outside the *patisserie*.

Bessie grinned. "That means pretty Newfoundland girls."

"All the shops and businesses close from twelve to two," Maurice said. "We French take time to appreciate and digest our food."

The afternoon was less hectic, with only a visit to the graveyard planned. Maurice showed Marie where her grandmother was buried. "She would have been so thrilled to know you," he said. "I will tell you about her. At least you will understand the kind of person she was." As they walked, he described her likes and dislikes, how she felt about children, how she loved St. Pierre.

"Oh! Oh!" Marie said. "I collects porcelain dolls, too."

"Your grandmother had a room filled with them. I will show you after the evening meal."

"Ma loves dolls, too," Bessie said.

After a nap, Nellie paid Father Jean-Claude a visit while Maurice went to the Lavier home to see Louisa.

"I heard you and the children were in St. Pierre," the priest said. "I was about to have tea and a pastry. Please join me."

Nellie relaxed in the big armchair in the den. "It never occurred to me in my wildest dreams that I'd be here as Maurice's guest," Nellie said. "To tell the truth, it feels awkward. Marie and Bessie love every minute here, though."

"Since Maurice has accepted Marie as his granddaughter, he is a different person. A happier, gentler man."

Nellie frowned and gazed out the window.

"Tell me what's bothering you," the priest said after a long pause in the conversation.

"Captain Maurice has been bitter and angry for all of Marie's life and caused a lot of trouble for Ike's crew. It'll take a lot of time for me to get past that."

Father Jean-Claude smiled. "At least you are willing to try."

"Marie deserves to know her grandfather." Nellie described what they had done so far. "It's time I got back. I don't want to insult Mme. Dubois by being late for supper."

Roasted chicken with baked potatoes, carrots, green beans, and the best gravy she'd ever tasted filled their bellies. Bessie and Marie, unable to keep their eyes open, toddled off to bed right after the meal. The captain invited Nellie to sit with him in the den. She was tempted to say no, but reconsidered for Marie's sake. She stared at the wall of books behind him, avoiding eye contact. She hadn't gone through any of the books in Ike's den. *I must do that when we move in,* she thought.

Maurice lit a pipe. "We had a wonderful day," he said, puffing out a cloud of smoke. "Marie is a happy child like her mother was."

Nellie nodded in agreement. "She's always been like that."

"Your daughter treats her like a sister."

"My boys do, too."

Maurice laid his pipe in a marble ashtray on the side table. "Mme. Myles, thank you for giving me the opportunity to spend time with my grandchild. I will treasure these memories forever."

You don't deserve it, Nellie itched to say.

"Marie's happy. That's what matters." Nellie yawned. "Think I'll go to bed. See you in the morning, Captain."

"*Dormez bien,* Mme. Myles. Sleep well," he added in English.

NELLIE HEARD MAURICE CLIMB the stairs. The floor outside her door creaked when he passed by. The grandfather clock in the entranceway chimed eleven times. She rolled over onto her side. Two hours in bed, eyes closed, trying to empty her mind, and she still couldn't sleep. The grandfather clock chimed midnight. She got out of bed and decided to go to the den to see if there were any books written in English. A lantern glowed at the end of the hallway and brightened the way down the stairs. Another shone in the hallway to the den. The house was warm despite the cool night.

Moonlight flooded in through the den window and shone on the bookcase. Nellie began at the top shelf and ran a finger along each book. All French titles. She continued downward in the same manner until she came to the bottom shelf. Two English books: *Huckleberry Fin* and *Treasure Island*. She chose *Treasure Island* and blew dust from the cover. She turned and caught her toe on the edge of the rug, stumbling into the desk. A half-full cup of tea sloshed around. Some of the cold liquid seeped into the papers on the bare desk and dribbled down into the top drawer.

Nellie scooted to the kitchen for a cloth. She wiped down the desktop and pulled open the drawer, relieved that it was empty. Very little tea seemed to have spilt inside. To be sure, she hauled the drawer wide open. An object the size of the palm of her hand was wrapped in a linen handkerchief at the very back. She was about to close the drawer when something about the shape made her pause. Nellie unfolded the handkerchief. Her heart thudded like a herd of frightened, runaway horses. Her mouth dried up. Sweat broke out all over her body.

She sprinted to her room and dressed quickly, sneaked out the front door, and raced through the streets. Her ragged breathing was the only sound audible in the quiet night. In the darkness and in her haste, she tripped often and almost tumbled into a ditch on the side of the road. She reached her destination and pounded on the door.

A groggy Father Jean-Claude opened the door. "Mme. Myles, what has happened?"

Nellie struggled to catch her breath.

The priest gently took her arm and led her inside. "Come in. I will get you something to drink." He sat her down in the den and got her a brandy. "Drink this," he said, and put the glass into her shaking hands. "Then tell me why you are so terribly upset."

Nellie gulped down the alcohol. It burned her throat. She laid the glass down and took out the object she'd found in Maurice's desk. She couldn't find the right words.

"Is that what has you upset?"

Nellie nodded.

"It is a pretty sculpture," the priest said, as if talking to a young child. "Too bad the right flipper is missing."

"This is the proof that Maurice killed the *Marion*'s crew," Nellie blurted out. She jumped to her feet and paced back and forth in front of Father Jean-Claude.

"Please, Mme. Myles. Sit down and explain what you mean."

Nellie obeyed and sat on the edge of the armchair. "This wooden seal belonged to my husband, Harry." Her voice shook. "His father made it for him when he was a boy."

"I do not understand. Why has it upset you?"

Nellie held the seal to her heart. "Harry had this with him on the *Marion*." Tears ran down her face. "I found this tonight in Maurice's desk."

"How did you come—"

"We both knows how it got there!" Nellie interrupted. "Maurice rammed the *Marion* and killed the crew." She glanced at the wooden seal. "He took this from Harry."

"Why would he do that?"

"Because he's a hateful man who doesn't care what happens to innocent people," Nellie snapped. "He lied to me and to Marie, even used his dead daughter's letters to get what he wanted."

She stood up and paced once more.

"Maybe we should confront *le capitaine* with this. Give him a chance to explain."

Nellie spun around to face Father Jean-Claude, her eyes dark, her cheeks ablaze. "He took the seal from my husband when he killed him. He doesn't deserve to spend another second with Marie."

The priest got to his feet. "Please forgive me if I appear to side with Maurice. I only hope for the sake of Marie that you are mistaken." He blessed himself. "From what you have told me, *le capitaine* may well be responsible for the disappearance of the *Marion*."

"I best get back before he suspects anything," Nellie said.

"What are you going to do?"

"I don't want Maurice to know I have the seal. I can't think about any of this until I'm home in St. Jacques."

"In the morning I will ask Maurice if I may go with you to visit *la mère* Patrick."

"Thank you, Father. I'll feel safer with you on board."

The priest accompanied Nellie to Maurice's door. The house was quiet and wrapped in darkness; he was reassured her absence hadn't been discovered, and then returned to the rectory. Nellie put the seal back in the drawer with the intention of retrieving it again just before she left the house for good.

The next morning, when Nellie woke from a restless sleep, the sky was overcast and there was a moderate wind. Nellie was more tired than she had been when she went to bed.

"We will attend mass at ten," Maurice said at breakfast, "then depart for the trip back to Newfoundland."

Nellie felt anger and disgust at the very thought of the captain inside a church. However, she made it through the meal without drawing undue attention to herself.

Father Jean-Claude approached Maurice outside the church. "I have a favour to ask. May I come along with you to St. Jacques this morning?"

"I am surprised by the request, Father. You rarely go there."

Nellie held her breath.

"I would like to visit Mother Patrick."

"She's not well," Nellie said, to save the priest from inventing an excuse. "It's nothing serious. I told Father Jean-Claude she'd like to see her dear friend."

"Of course," Maurice said. "We leave in one hour."

The sky was still overcast when they set out, and the wind had died down to a gentle breeze. Father Jean-Claude kept Marie and

Bessie occupied, which allowed Nellie time to think. Would the authorities in Newfoundland or St. Pierre accept the wooden seal as proof of his guilt? Nellie doubted it. Who would take the hysterics of a grief-stricken widow over that of a rich and powerful French captain?

"The girls are busy with their small round coloured glass," Father Jean-Claude said, and sat on the bench next to Nellie. "How are you doing?"

She looked around to make sure they were alone. "My family was happy before Captain Maurice took it all away."

Chapter 21

MARIE AND BESSIE BOUNDED across the deck of the ship. "Ma," Bessie said, "I can see home from here."

Maurice smiled at the girls. "Would you like to help me steer the ship into the harbour?" They shrieked with excitement and followed the captain.

The trawler docked with smooth precision and the girls droned on and on about their role in it.

"Mme. Myles," Maurice said as she prepared to disembark, "I have to deliver cargo to Montreal. I will be away for two weeks." He looked at Father Jean-Claude. "How much time would you care to spend with *la bonne soeur*?"

"I will return in an hour or two if that is agreeable," the priest said.

"*Très bien.*"

The priest assisted Nellie with the bags and headed straight for the convent. Joe and Sam crooned over the chocolate and pastries.

"How's Annie?" Nellie asked, once seated with Father Jean-Claude in Mother Patrick's office.

The nun rolled her eyes. "She's improved, through no fault of her own. I practically had to tie her to the bed. Don't think me rude, Father Jean-Claude, but what are you doing here?"

Nellie took the wooden seal out of her pocket.

"Wait a minute," Mother Patrick said. "That belongs to Harry. He never went anywhere without it."

"I found it hidden in Maurice's desk. He acted saintly with the girls, like he was the Holy Pope himself."

Mother Patrick paled. "Sacred Heart of Jesus," she said. "Could Marie's grandfather really be a cold-hearted killer?" She stared from the priest to Nellie. "Maybe Harry lost it in St. Pierre and Maurice found it?"

"It was wrapped and hidden in the back of a drawer," Nellie said.

"What can we do?"

"Maurice won't be back for two weeks. That'll give us time to decide." Nellie stood up. "I don't want Annie to hear about this."

"Not a problem," Mother Patrick said. "She's in the first room at the top of the stairs.

Annie looked much improved after a mere two days. "How's our mother superior been treating ya?" Nellie said.

"Like I was two years old. Now that you're back, I can go home," Annie said with relief.

"We'll be ready to move into Ike's house in a day or two." Nellie grinned. "Why don't you stay here until then?"

Annie leaned back into the pillows. "I knows you're fooling with me, so I won't get mad at ya."

Nellie gathered up the youngsters and sent them home. Steve Marsh waited for her and Annie with a horse and cart. "Mother Patrick's orders. Annie isn't strong enough to walk."

"I should've known," Annie griped.

"Have you heard about the *Sherman*?" Steve asked. "She was fired on by a German war boat. The men escaped in the dories and were picked up a day later by a Portuguese schooner. Most of the crew is from Heart's Content."

"Praise the Lord," Annie said. "Anyone hurt?"

"Guy Hays broke his leg real bad. His missus is some glad, 'cause now he'll be on land for two months. Two men near drowned and another caught pneumonia. He's in the hospital in St. John's." Steve grew quiet. "I wonders if the *Marion* met with the same fate?" he said after a long pause.

No! They were murdered, Nellie's mind screamed.

"Don't s'pose we'll ever know," he added.

Steve pulled on the reins to slow Winnie. She neighed and stopped at the bottom of the path to Nellie's house. The horse chewed on the tall grass while Steve assisted Annie to the house.

"Mother Patrick's orders," he said with a wink when Annie tried to protest. With a cheery farewell after a cup of tea, Steve went home.

Nellie prepared salt fish and potatoes with drawn butter for supper. Joe and Sam ate like they hadn't seen food in a week. "Didn't Mother Patrick feed you?"

"Loads," Sam said. "But it didn't taste all that good."

"After supper we're taking the rest of our stuff to Ike's house." Nellie looked around the kitchen with a great sigh. "This'll be our last night here."

By nine o'clock most everything had been delivered to Ike's house, and the children, along with Annie, snoozed in bed. Nellie made up the chesterfield. Tired from the long day, she fell asleep almost right away. The next morning she woke early, started breakfast, and went to the youngsters' rooms to get them up for school, taking care not to disturb Annie. With the house peaceful once again, Nellie brought a tray up for Annie. She snored, her lips puckered like she was ready to bestow a kiss. Nellie laid the tray on the bedside table.

AT TEN-THIRTY THE YOUNGSTERS spilled out of school for recess. Several of them gathered around a tree stump near the cemetery. Elsa LaCroix, twelve years old and tall for her age, whispered to the group, her eyes on Marie and Bessie, who walked toward them.

"You can't play with us," Elsa said.

The others mumbled agreement.

"Ma said the old French captain that scuttled the *Marion* is your grandpa."

Bobby Noseworthy, a fourteen-year-old, joined in. "He killed my pa."

Marie burst into tears. "No he didn't!"

Elsa snorted. “He did so. Everybody knows that. You even went to St. Pierre on the trawler that scuttled the schooner.”

Bobby sneered at Bessie. “You’re some traitor, going with him and all. You don’t care what the Frenchie’s done.”

“I’m not a traitor,” Bessie cried. “And I loved my pa.”

Joe and Sam ran over. “What’s the matter?” Joe said.

Bessie sobbed. “They’re mean to us because of Captain Maurice.”

“You’re all dirty traitors,” Bobby spit out.

Joe stepped in front of Bobby. “Take that back,” he said.

“Dirty traitor,” Bobby said again, and the others began to chant the two words.

Joe lunged at Bobby. Another boy joined in to help Bobby. Sam tried to pull him off his brother’s back, but soon a brawl broke out between all the boys. The girls yelled while Elsa tried to kick at Joe.

Mother Patrick stormed across the grass to the children. “Stop this right away,” she bellowed. As if a bucket of icy water had been thrown over the children, they froze, entangled in each other’s grip. “Get back to class this minute.”

They moved past the nun in single file, avoiding her eyes. Nellie’s boys stood back and waited for the others to move away. Joe sported a bloody nose. Blood dripped from a cut under Sam’s right eye.

“Wait, you two,” Mother Patrick said when they started for the convent. “Go to the kitchen. Sister Assumpta will take care of those cuts.” She followed the boys inside and made for the classroom. Amid tears and sobs from Elsa and Marie, she got to the heart of the matter. Instead of a severe lecture, as every child expected, Mother Patrick assigned a written page on the dangers of fighting. Sister Thérèse supervised the class while the mother superior set out for Nellie’s house.

Nellie was making bully beef hash for dinner when the nun arrived. “I need a quiet word with you,” she said. Nellie was almost in tears herself when Mother Patrick concluded her story about the fight at school.

"I don't blame Elsa LaCroix for feeling like she does. It must seem like we're buddies with Maurice despite what he's done."

"Maybe you should have a talk with Mrs. LaCroix and explain why you thought the captain was innocent."

Nellie went cold all over. "It wouldn't do any good." She mashed the bully beef in with the potatoes, her tears teetering on the surface. "I was going to help out the widows with some of the money Ike left me. Now they'll think it'll be because I feel guilty about associating with Maurice."

"Good point," Mother Patrick said. "I'll give the youngsters a good talking to after dinner."

Joe and Sam walked in, followed by Marie and Bessie. Nellie put dinner on the table. "I heard all about the ruckus," she said softly.

"We saw Mother Patrick leave the house," Sam said. The skin around his eyes was puffy, and signs of bruising were already visible along his upper jawbone. Joe would have two black eyes by morning. Nellie chewed her food and noticed Marie sneaking glances at the others, guilt and shame obvious on her face. She couldn't scold her boys for defending Marie.

"Why does Elsa think Captain Maurice killed her pa?" Bessie asked, her eyes fixed on the table.

Sam fingered his cut and winced. "She'll feel different when the truth comes out," he said quietly.

Joe gave Marie a lopsided smile. "We'll sort it out."

The tension lifted from Marie's face. "This bully beef hash is some good," she said, and shoved a huge forkful into her mouth.

Nellie marvelled at her youngsters' wisdom. They had seen Marie's pain and reassured her with a few heartfelt words.

Joe pushed back his chair. "Come on. We can't be late for school."

"See you later," Nellie said as the four youngsters marched out the door, heads held high. She checked on Annie, who lay under a pile of blankets. Nellie wrote a brief note to say she would be at Ike's house, transporting the last of her porcelain dolls.

When she returned, Annie sat in the kitchen with a plateful of bully beef hash. Nellie ordered her back to bed after the last mouthful, and told her they were having fried codfish for an early supper. She wanted to settle into Ike's house before dark.

Annie rested on the chesterfield while the last of the belongings were carted away by the youngsters. "I hate to leave, " Nellie said. "This has been my home for fifteen years."

Annie sighed softly. "We'll make Ike's house our home for the next fifteen."

Nellie frowned. "We should stop calling it Ike's house."

The door opened and the children ran back in. "All done," Joe said. "We even chopped wood and cleaned up the backyard."

Nellie took one last look around the room. The square patch of paint where the wedding portrait had hung was a stark contrast to the faded walls. "I believed I would live here for the rest of my life," she whispered. "Your coach awaits," she said to Annie. "I asked Steve to come by with his cart.

Annie turned up her nose and marched past Nellie. "Then he'll have wasted a trip."

Steve was nowhere in sight. "If he says he'll be here," Nellie said, "he'll be here."

"I can't wait all night," Annie said, and started down the path with Nellie.

A third of the way to the new house, Steve caught up. "Evening, all," he said, and smiled at Annie with his usual charm. "I'm surprised you didn't wait for me."

"Well now, Mr. Marsh. You've come all this way. I might as well do the neighbourly thing and accept a ride."

Steve had tea steeped on the stove and three cups on the table when Nellie arrived. "I don't mean to poke my nose in where it doesn't belong," he said after the children scurried to their rooms, "but have you heard the talk 'round the community about Marie and the French captain?"

Annie slurped her tea. "I for one don't like him, but he's Marie's grandfather."

Steve sucked on a tooth. "It's a nasty affair," he said. "My missus was yakking with Mrs. LaCroix this afternoon. She gave Elsa a tongue banging for causing a brawl at school."

Annie leaned her elbows on the table. "I feels some bad for her. She's rearing ten youngsters with little to no money coming in. Now we're chummy with the man she thinks took her husband away."

Nellie explained to Steve why they'd agreed to let Marie associate with Maurice.

"To be honest, b'y," Steve said, "I don't see how that will make one iota of difference to the widows."

Nellie sat up straight. "One good thing, anyways, is that Maurice doesn't live here."

Steve slapped his hat on his head. "Well, if I stays much longer, my missus will think me and Winnie rode into the harbour. Good night, ladies."

"I'm off to bed," Annie said. "Don't want Dr. Fitzgerald harping on me for overdoing it."

"Me too," Nellie said. "It's been a long day."

"Try not to worry," Annie said as they climbed the stairs. "Everything will work itself out in the end."

"Sleep tight, Annie," Nellie said, and proceeded down the hallway. Her new room was twice the size of the one she'd shared with Harry. She turned up the wall lantern next to the door and studied her surroundings. The room contained a large brass bed with a hand-carved oak table with curved legs, shipped over from France. A wardrobe and bureau were nestled together against the side wall and a settee sat in the corner. Green velvet curtains, which matched the bedspread, draped the large bay window.

She crossed the room to the bed and stared at her wedding portrait, which she had hung over the bureau. "Oh, Harry," she moaned, "I'm in some pickle." She took the wooden seal out of her pocket and caressed it. "What am I s'posed to do about Maurice now?"

Give it time, love. The answer will come.

Nellie undressed and climbed into bed. Big and comfortable though it was, she longed for the familiarity of their bed. She ran her hand along the side where Harry would have slept, the familiar indentation in the mattress missing. The last physical evidence of her husband's presence had been abandoned to the past. She bit her lip.

Nellie heard a soft creak and looked toward the door.

"Ma," Bessie said. She sniffed and wiped her nose with the sleeve of her nightgown. "Can I sleep with you tonight?"

Nellie threw down the blankets. "Of course, sweetie."

Bessie crawled into bed and snuggled next to her mother.

"Have a bad dream?" Nellie said.

"No . . . I felt Pa around me in our old house. He's not here."

Nellie pulled Bessie closer to her. "That's because all your memories of him are there. You keep your pa in your heart, right?"

Bessie nodded.

"Then he's in this house because you're here." Nellie kissed the top of her head. "Your pa will always be with you no matter where you go."

Bessie looked up at Nellie with Harry's blue eyes. "I miss Uncle Tommy. Do you?"

"He was like my little brother."

"Sometimes I don't feel sad. Then other times I want to cry all the time. Like the time Shelly Drake brought cupcakes to school. Uncle Tommy made the best cupcakes." Bessie's eyelids drooped. "Joe cries when he thinks no one's around."

Nellie gave a sharp intake of breath. "Does he know you see him?"

"No," Bessie mumbled. "Boys should cry. It makes you feel better."

Nellie felt her daughter's body go limp as she drifted to sleep. She pondered Bessie's words and realized that children were far wiser than adults gave them credit for. At dawn, she carried Bessie back to her bed and checked on the others. Wide awake now, Nellie knew sleep was out of the question. She dressed and went downstairs. Joe and Sam had filled the wood container to capacity, and she lit the stove. Blueberry pancakes would be a nice treat for their first breakfast. The smell of cooking soon wafted into the hallway.

Annie ambled into the kitchen. "I came down early to make breakfast," she said. "Didn't expect you up this early."

"Bessie missed her old room and spent the night with me."

"From the dark circles under your eyes, I'd say you didn't get a wink."

Nellie poured another batch of pancake mix into the frying pan. The familiar sizzle made her long for Harry and her former life. "It'll take me a while to get used to the change." She passed Annie the teapot. "You, on the other hand, look fitter than you have in days."

"I didn't stir the whole night. That darn concussion took the good clear out of me." Annie sipped a cup of tea. "I'll take over. You go get some sleep."

Too exhausted to argue, Nellie went to her room and lay down on her unmade bed. The sun peeked through the sides of the curtains and warmed her face. Would she ever consider this house a home? She was vaguely aware of the children's footsteps tramping down the hall.

Chapter 22

MARIE CHEWED ON A hard-boiled egg. "The two weeks are up," she said. "My grandfather should be home any time now. I can't wait."

Nellie didn't feel hungry anymore.

"He promised to bring me back a surprise," Marie continued.

Bessie smiled. "I bet it's gonna be a porcelain doll. He knows how much you loves them."

Nellie pushed her plate away. She glanced at Marie, then at each of her youngsters. She knew they'd all be devastated by the truth about Maurice.

"Whatever the surprises are," Annie said, "I won't stand for him spoiling either of you girls."

Nellie went to the stove for the teapot. "Annie's right. Now get off to school with the lot of you."

Marie waltzed out the door with Bessie. Sam trailed after them with a shake of his head. "Girls are some foolish."

Annie cleared the plates off the table. "What was all that about?" she asked.

Nellie filled the sink with water and feigned ignorance. "What?"

"Come on, Nellie. It's me you're taking to. You became crooked as hell when Marie blabbered on about the French captain."

"It's been grand not to have him around. Even if he didn't scuttle the *Marion*," Nellie hastened, which only added to the skeptical look on Annie's face. "I don't like him." Nellie realized that she'd better learn to hide her resentment of Maurice.

Annie sponged down the table with a wet cloth. "He ain't my favourite person in the world either."

The sun played across the kitchen and the wind rattled the window. "It's a perfect day to hang out clothes," Annie said. "I'll get right to the washing."

"I'll do it," Nellie said. "Scrubbing clothes is too much for you yet."

"I'm not gonna sit on me arse all day and do nothing."

Nellie took her hands out of the soapy water. "You do the dishes, then." She lifted the corner of her apron to dry her hands.

Annie face grew pale as she looked at the floor by Nellie's feet.

Nellie looked down. "Dear Jesus," she moaned, and snatched up the wooden seal.

"Where . . . How did you get that?" Annie's voice sounded thick.

"Sit down first," Nellie said, frightened by Annie's pallor, and tried to lead her to the table.

Annie pulled away. "Harry never went anywhere without that seal. He had it with him on the *Marion*."

"Annie, try to calm down."

"I'm not a child. Tell me where you found that."

Nellie took a deep breath to steady her nerves. "In Captain Maurice's house."

Annie's big hands balled into fists. "The murdering sea scum! All sweetness and kindness to our Marie." Spittle fell on her chin and red blotches covered her face. "I'm gonna rip his scrawny head from his shoulders and feed it to the sharks!"

"Believe me, Annie, I know how you feel, but we have to think this through."

Annie thumped a hand on the table. "There's nothing to think through. We take the sculpture to the authorities."

"What's that gonna prove? They'll say Harry dropped it in St. Pierre and Maurice found it. I've thought about nothing else since I found the seal." Nellie sighed. "I keep coming back to how this is going to affect Marie and the youngsters."

"That's why you turned crooked when Marie brought up the devil's name. I knew something was up."

Nellie placed the wooden seal on the table. "I have to hide it away from the youngsters." She wiped a tear from her cheek. "Part of me wishes I never found it."

"It'll be safe in my house. Heaven help the little rat if he comes near me."

"I'll go, and you get dinner started," Nellie said. She waited for Annie to cool down, which took several minutes. "Will you be all right while I'm gone?"

Annie nodded.

Nellie grabbed her coat from the hall closet and rushed to Annie's house. *If Maurice ever discovers the seal is missing, what then? No,* she thought. *You don't have anything to hide. He's the one with the awful secret.* She reached the convent and turned for Annie's house.

"Mme. Myles," Sister Thérèse called out, interrupting her thoughts. "I was just on my way to see you."

"Is one of the youngsters hurt?" Nellie asked.

"*Non.* Mother Patrick wanted you to know that *le capitaine* Maurice is here."

Nellie's first instinct was to rush inside, but she controlled herself, thinking about the consequences for Marie if she didn't behave like everything was normal. Her heart thudded as she followed Sister Thérèse into the convent. She felt the weight of the seal tucked deep in her dress pocket when she entered Mother Patrick's office.

The captain rose. "*Bonjour*, Mme. Myles. I have only now returned from my trip and stopped off to see Marie before heading home to St. Pierre." He looked down at his granddaughter.

Nellie smiled. Her cheeks hurt from the effort.

Marie held out a box wrapped in blue paper tied with a white ribbon. "It's a late birthday gift," she said.

"That's lovely."

"Grandpa said I'm not allowed to open it until I gets home."

"Proper thing," Nellie said, and noticed sweat glistening

on the captain's forehead. He rubbed his hands on his knees as though they were clammy. His breathing had become heavy, shallow.

"My crew is waiting." Maurice swayed and grabbed the back of his chair.

"Are you unwell?" Mother Patrick said.

"I have missed a meal, that is all."

"Would you like something to tide you over?"

"*Non, merci.*" He kissed Marie on both cheeks. "*À la prochaine, mon petit chou,*" he said, and hurried from the office.

"What did he say to you?" Nellie asked.

Marie stared at the pretty box. "Goodbye, until the next time," she said. "*Mon petit chou* is another way of saying sweetie."

"Back to class, young lady," Mother Patrick said.

Marie gave the present to Nellie with an exaggerated frown. "It's gonna be a long morning," she said.

"I wonder why Maurice took off like that all of a sudden?" Nellie wondered aloud, once Marie had left the room.

"One thing's for certain," Mother Patrick said. "He's a strange little man."

"I must go," Nellie said. She dashed to Annie's house and hid the seal under a loose floorboard in the living room. She made it back to the house in time to help Annie with dinner.

Annie eyed the blue box. "What's that you have there?"

"Captain Maurice came to the convent and gave Marie a late birthday present."

"He's got some gall."

"We can't let on to the captain that we changed our minds about him."

"I allow he'll come and go here as he pleases without a thought for anyone but himself." Annie clenched her teeth. "He doesn't deserve to be alive."

Later, Marie ran into the kitchen and snatched the box from the table.

"Open it. Open it!" Bessie said. "I can't wait a minute longer."

Joe and Sam pretended to be uninterested in the box, but Nellie caught them sneaking a glance in its direction.

Marie untied the ribbon and opened the paper one flap at a time. Bessie bounced on her chair. Marie took the lid off the box beneath the paper and pulled out a small linen tablecloth. She spread it out to reveal a word embroidered with blue thread in the centre and blue bells along the edges. *Chantal.*

"It's a tablecloth for a child's play table and chairs," Nellie said. "It's beautiful." She smiled at Marie. "It must've belonged to your mother when she was a little girl."

Joe and Sam looked at each and groaned. "Can we eat now?" Joe asked.

Nellie served pea soup topped off with gingerbread and tin cream, the only luxury she permitted the family with Ike's money. It wasn't easy to break a lifetime's habit of scrimping to make every penny stretch to a dollar.

Annie cut a slab from the gingerbread loaf and slapped on two spoons of cream for herself. "Any more trouble with the other youngsters at school about Maurice?" she asked.

Joe shoved an oversized portion of gingerbread into his mouth. Cream coated his top lip like an old man's fuzzy moustache. "No," he said, his mouth full. "Mother Patrick had a long talk with everyone."

Bessie giggled. "She took the whole afternoon."

"Elsa said she was sorry. She cries all the time about her pa," Marie added.

"'Tis enough to break your heart," Annie mumbled, and remained quiet for the rest of supper. She stayed at the table after the children had gone.

"You all right?" Nellie said.

Annie played with a button on her blouse. "Marie will be devastated if she finds out the truth about her grandfather."

"Bessie, too."

Annie sniffed. "I'm dead tired," she said. "Perhaps a little rest will set me right."

*

NELLIE ROCKED IN HER chair and knitted for the first time since she moved in. The grandfather clock in the entrance bonged twice. *This chair makes me feel close to ya, Harry*. She wished there was something she could do to make Elsa and her ma feel better.

Nellie, love, what are you gonna do with all that money Ike gave ya?

An idea popped into her head and she bounded from the rocker. She threw on her winter coat. The early November air hinted at snow, and her nose and cheeks glowed cherry red as she approached her destination.

Denis Burke half rose from his chair when Nellie walked into his office. "Mrs. Myles. What have you come to tell me off about today?"

Nellie saw the hint of a smile in his eyes. "I have a favour to ask. Before you starts preaching about how business works," she added, "you won't have to part with a penny of your money."

"Please sit, Mrs. Myles," Denis said, and leaned back in his chair. "I can't think what sort of favour you'd want from a Burke."

"I've racked my brain for weeks and came up with the idea not an hour ago."

"How can I help?"

Nellie unbuttoned her coat. "The pile of money Ike left me every month will last until I'm old and grey."

Denis nodded. "That was quite generous of him."

"I want to start a fund for the *Marion* widows."

"That's a grand idea, but what does that have to do with me?"

"The widows have their pride," Nellie said. "They'll see my money as charity."

"I see your point," Denis said. He folded his hands under his chin. "If the money comes from the Burke brothers, the widows will see it as their right."

"Exactly," Nellie said. "Will you set up the fund in your family's name with the money I give every month for as long as I can?"

"My brothers won't mind at all taking the credit." Denis paused, a pensive look on his face. "It won't sit well with me, though."

"All I want is for the widows and their families to have a better life."

"If that's what you want. I'll talk it over with my brothers and get back to you."

"Remember," Nellie said, "only you and your brothers are to know. I haven't even told Annie or Mother Patrick."

"You have my word, Mrs. Myles. No one will hear about this from any member of my family."

"Thanks, Mr. Burke." Nellie turned to leave, and paused. "Harry said you were different from your brothers. He was right." She walked away before Denis could respond, and she passed Jon on the way out of the building.

JON WENT STRAIGHT IN to see his brother. "I saw Nellie Myles just now," he snarled. "What sort of trouble was she trying to stew up this time?"

Denis looked up into his older brother's eyes. "Shut up," he said. "Sit down and listen good to what I have to say."

He paid a visit to Nellie very late that night. Over gingerbread and cream they finalized the details of the Widow's Fund. On Nellie's instructions, a simple handshake sealed the deal, with no paperwork involved.

The next day the Burkes called a meeting in the church to announce their generous offer.

"Well, well," Mother Patrick whispered. "It's about time the Burkes did something for someone besides themselves."

"Indeed it is," Annie said with a smile.

Nellie saw by the glint in Annie's eyes that she hadn't been fooled, not even when Skit Kettle's wife stood up and said, "I'll be! What a grand gesture."

Jon Burke smiled. "It's the least we could do to help out the community."

Denis went red in the face and excused himself from the church.

Chapter 23

SNOW FELL THE NEXT week and coated the hills like white icing on a chocolate cake. The first signs of ice shimmered on the water. Nellie looked out the kitchen window into the backyard. She missed the view of the main road and the harbour from her old house.

Annie and Mother Patrick came in and went straight to the stove to warm themselves. Annie blew on her fingertips. "It's cold enough out to freeze your breath," she said. "I'll allow winter's here to stay."

Nellie turned away from the window. "Don't worry yourself sick," she said. "The coastal boat will get Dottie and the twins here for Christmas."

"You're right," Annie said. "I shouldn't look for problems." She poured tea for herself and Mother Patrick.

The nun carried the steaming liquid to the table. "Don't you think it odd Maurice hasn't been back to see Marie since the day he gave her that lovely tablecloth?"

"It's only been a few weeks," Nellie said.

Mother Patrick breathed in the steam rising from the tea. Condensation gathered on her nose. "You must be delighted your bad feeling amounted to nothing."

"It hasn't exactly gone."

Annie choked down a mouthful of tea. "Why haven't I heard about this before?"

"What does that mean, Nellie?" Mother Patrick asked.

Nellie thought for a moment how to answer the question. “My bad feeling comes and goes like the tide, always there.” She wrapped her arms around herself. “It feels like high tide today.”

Mother Patrick tapped her foot. “No more dreary talk,” she said. “Have you heard that Dr. Fitzgerald’s oldest son, Charles, is here for a short visit?”

“I did,” Annie said. “Steve Marsh will take the pair of them to St. Pierre tomorrow for the weekend.” She chuckled. “Hattie is staying put. She gets greener than you on water.”

“I almost forgot,” Mother Patrick said. “The good doctor said he’d be happy to deliver a letter for Marie to Maurice.”

“I’ll tell her,” Nellie said.

MARIE WROTE A TWO-PAGE letter. “Thank you, Dr. Fitzgerald,” she said with a smile when he arrived after supper.

“My pleasure, Marie.”

She skipped out of the kitchen to her room.

“Annie, you’re doing quite well,” the doctor said, following a brief examination. “My best advice to you is never to climb another ladder.”

“I’m cured of any more foolish risks,” she said, to Nellie’s surprise.

“I’m off,” Dr. Fitzgerald said. “We leave at dawn for St. Pierre.” He wished the women a good night.

“Have a safe journey,” Nellie said, showing him to the door.

The doctor put on his coat. “Isn’t is marvellous about the Widow’s Fund?” He winked. “The whole community knows how generous the Burkes are.”

“I . . . who told you?”

“Hattie saw you come out of the Rooms the day before the big announcement.” He patted her hand. “My dear, what you wish to do with your money is entirely your concern.”

Nellie prayed no one else would figure out what she’d done.

STEVE LED DR. FITZGERALD and his son Charles to the *Hôtel de France*. “Join us for a drink,” the doctor said.

"Don't mind if I do," Steve said. "I'm staying overnight anyways."

Close to noon, the bar was empty. They ordered drinks and sat at a corner table. "Isn't the Widow's Fund a godsend?" Charles said.

Steve downed a rum and water. "Can't see the Burke brothers offering help to anybody," he said. "Specifically if money's involved."

"I agree, Mr. Marsh," Charles said. "It's been six months since the *Marion* disappeared. What took them so long?"

Steve smacked his lips together. "To be honest, b'y, I think Nellie Myles had a hand in the Widow's Fund." He grinned. "We all knows once she gets started on something she don't stop. Ike gave her a load of money. I believe she's the fund's source." He ordered and paid for another drink. "The Burkes wouldn't give away shit from thrown-away fish carcasses, let alone money. Nellie's a good woman and understands how we feels about charity."

"Well," Charles began. "If you've reached that conclusion, so will everyone else."

"I ain't in dire need of money. Widows like Mrs. LaCroix are too desperate to worry about where it's really coming from."

Father Jean-Claude came into the bar with Maurice. The priest nodded to Steve and sat with the captain at the opposite end of the bar.

Steve finished the second drink and stood to leave when Father Jean-Claude and Maurice walked over. "Hello, M. Marsh," the priest said. "It is good to see you again."

"Likewise, Father." Steve introduced the doctor and the doctor's son.

"Mother Patrick speaks very highly of you, Dr. Fitzgerald."

"Gentlemen," Maurice said, "I would be honoured for you to join me in my home for the noon meal."

"We'd be delighted," the doctor said. "And a good opportunity for me to give you a letter from Marie."

Mme. Dubois smiled politely as she served chicken sandwiches, French bread, and a variety of cheeses, tea, and custard pastries. After dinner the men adjourned to the den for a smoke and a glass of sherry. Steve tasted his, made a sour face, and laid it aside. He smoked one cigarette and doused the butt in the fancy glass ashtray on the side table. "I'll be on my way," he said.

"We should as well," Dr. Fitzgerald said. "Thank you for a lovely meal, Captain. Please give our regards to your housekeeper."

"You are—"

Suddenly, Maurice clutched his chest and sagged forward with a loud cry. His glass of sherry smashed to the floor.

Dr. Fitzgerald dropped to his knees beside the captain. "Can you describe how you feel?"

"My chest . . . is tight." His skin was grey. Sweat soaked his face. "My left arm is numb."

"Charles," the doctor said. "Help Steve get him to bed." He turned to Father Jean-Claude. "Have Mme. Dubois send for his doctor. He'll know the captain's medical history." He grabbed his medical bag and followed his son and Steve up the stairs.

Dr. Renard arrived shortly after.

"How is he?" Father Jean-Claude asked.

"He suffered a massive heart attack," Dr. Fitzgerald said. "He is as comfortable as possible, under the circumstances. Dr. Renard said he has had two mild attacks over the past three years."

"Will he survive?" the priest asked.

Dr. Renard shook his head. "Too much hurt to his heart," he said in his limited English. "Little time left to him."

"He wishes to see Marie," Dr. Fitzgerald said.

"I was planning on spending the night here," Steve said. "As time's important, I'll go back now. We should be back around dinnertime tomorrow."

"That is most kind of you," Father Jean-Claude said.

Dr. Fitzgerald and Charles parted for their hotel with condolences to Father Jean-Claude and Mme. Dubois.

NELLIE SHIVERED AND RUBBED her arms. Despite the sun's rays, which stretched to every nook of the kitchen, the bad feeling lingered in the air like the smell of day-old fried fish.

"You can't be cold," Annie said. "The heat from that stove is enough to stifle ya."

Nellie swished the water in the sink to make it soapy. "I ain't cold."

Annie passed her five dirty plates. "It's the bad feeling again, right? Try to put it aside and think about what to buy the youngsters for Christmas."

"I'll try."

"Tell you what. Forget the dishes. Go to the post office. Maybe Dottie's written us."

Nellie smiled. "I'll get some of the cocoa you likes at Young's, too."

The wind off the water, mixed with the salty air, aggravated her uneasiness. She turned her thoughts to the Widow's Fund. Most of the widows had taken advantage of the money with no concerns or suspicions raised about the source.

"Good day, Mrs. Myles," the postmaster said, and handed Nellie three letters, two from St. John's, one from Montreal. "I hope that Jones woman ain't trying to start trouble again."

"Me too," Nellie said, and paused outside to open the letters. Her hands stopped trembling when she stuck the last letter back in its envelope.

"Not bad news, I hope," Father Curran said, stopping to say hello.

"Not at all," Nellie smiled. "Sheila Jones's lawyer wrote to reassure me there's no way she can take Marie from us."

"Lovely," the priest said, and went on his way.

Nellie stopped by Young's for the cocoa and dashed home.

"That's one pain in the arse gotten rid of," Annie said upon hearing the news about Sheila.

Nellie handed over the envelope addressed to Annie and opened the other from Ike's lawyer. "Mr. Fleming asked the lawyer in Montreal to write me. This is a surprise." She read on. "He wants to buy a house here as a summer home. He wonders if I'll look into it for him."

Annie looked up from her letter. "Well then, missy. Who's house will we sell?"

"Tommy's," Nellie said softly. "I ain't ready to let go of mine."

"Dottie wants me to come to St. John's for Easter," said Annie.

"Proper thing. Maybe me and the youngsters will come along."

THE FULL MOON GUIDED Steve Marsh into Burke's Cove. He docked his boat and headed for Ike's house. Nellie answered on the first knock.

"Mr. Marsh, what are you doing here?" A knot formed in her chest. "Dr. Fitzgerald said you were s'posed to stay overnight in St. Pierre."

"Would you mind if I came in, Mrs. Myles? I have a bit of bad news."

The knot tightened. "Where's my manners," Nellie said. "I'll put the kettle on."

"Much obliged, ma'am."

"I'll heat up some fish and brewis and scruncheons left over from supper."

"That's kind of ya. I haven't eaten since dinnertime." Steve took off his coat and drank tea while Nellie prepared the food. "Here you go," she said, placing a hot plate in front of him.

"Lovely," he said, and dug in.

Nellie's mind was racing. What bad news could Steve have brought her from St. Pierre? Mother Patrick would be the one to tell her if something had happened to Father Jean-Claude. It couldn't be about Eloise's parents. They were almost strangers to her.

Annie strolled into the kitchen. "Thought I heard the door," she said. "I didn't expect to see you here, Steve."

"Father Jean-Claude sent me." He looked toward the hallway. "The youngsters in bed?"

Nellie and Annie nodded.

"Captain Maurice had a heart attack. Me, the doc, Charles, and the priest were at his house when it happened. The French doctor agreed with Dr. Fitzgerald that the captain ain't got much time left."

"He wants to see Marie, doesn't he?" Nellie said quietly. *Funny,* she thought. *I don't feel anything at all.* She glanced at Annie. The older woman's face told nothing of how she felt.

"I came back tonight so we could leave tomorrow morning, if that's all right with you."

"That's awfully good of you, Mr. Marsh," Nellie said.

Steve smiled. "Just helping out my neighbours. Just like you are." He wiped his mouth with his handkerchief. "Is eight o'clock tomorrow too early?"

"Whatever's good for you."

"I'll see myself out. Good night, then, ladies."

Annie finally sat down. "It couldn't happen to a more deserving man," she said.

"Annie," Nellie said softly, "it's not like you to be so unchristian."

"That devil took away our menfolk." Annie's voice was thick. "I feels some bad for poor Marie, though. She was starting to love the old bastard."

Nellie wrung her hands. "Should I wake Marie and tell her or wait until morning?"

"Let the child sleep," Annie said. "There's not a thing she can do about it tonight."

Chapter 24

NOON THE FOLLOWING DAY, Nellie and Marie climbed out of Steve's boat. The circles under his eyes and his unshaven face testified to his exhaustion as he carried their luggage to Maurice's house.

"My missus said I have to wait for you, even if it takes a couple of days."

Mme. Dubois opened the door, her eyes also bloodshot from fatigue, and showed them to the den where Father Jean-Claude sat drinking tea.

"How's Grandpa?" Marie asked. It was the first time she'd spoken since leaving St. Jacques.

"I am very sorry, my child. Dr. Renard does not give your grandfather much more time. He wishes to see you right away."

"I'll come with you," Nellie said.

"Mme. Myles, he wishes to see her alone." The priest showed Marie to the captain's room. "I will wait with Mme. Myles in the den."

"*Merci,*" Marie said, and opened the door to her grandfather's room.

MAURICE OPENED HIS EYES and smiled. "Ah, *mon petit chou,* come in," he said in a weak voice. "I am so very happy that you came."

Marie sat in the chair by the side of the bed. "I don't want you to die," she said. "It's not fair."

Maurice smoothed a tear from her cheek. “It is my fault we do not know each other well.” He paused to catch his breath. “*Mon enfant*, you will make me a promise, *oui?*”

“All right,” Marie said. “What is it?”

“Do not allow anger and stubbornness to rule your life. Forgive and let your heart guide you. If I had done this, we would have shared many years together.” Maurice reached for her hand. “Do you promise, *chérie*?”

“*Oui, mon grandpère.*”

Maurice smiled and closed his eyes. “*Je t'aime.*”

“I love you, too,” Marie whispered in his ear.

A soft knock came at the door. “*Mlle. Jones, voulez-vous quelque chose à manger?*”

“*Oui,* I would love a bite to eat,” Marie answered.

Maurice opened his eyes. “Mme. Dubois is an excellent cook. Go eat and ask *le père* Jean-Claude to come up.”

“I'll come back as soon as I finishes.”

MME. DUBOIS BROUGHT IN a tray of French onion soup, bread, pastries, and tea for Marie and Nellie.

“Thank you,” Nellie said.

“She's some sad,” Marie said.

Nellie stared at the departing French woman, amazed that such a cruel, evil man could inspire such love and loyalty. “I wonder if Mme. Dubois has family here?”

“*Non,*” Father Jean-Claude said, coming into the room. “She is a widow. Her only child died of consumption many years ago.”

“What will become of her?”

“This house will belong to her with a yearly allowance for the rest of her life.”

“A generous man,” Nellie said with a slight trace of sarcasm.

Father Jean-Claude looked toward Marie, who slurped at the French soup, seemingly unaware of the conversation. “*Le capitaine* is capable of generosity, amongst other things.”

As soon as Marie and Nellie were done eating, Mme. Dubois

took the tray and showed them to the same rooms they had stayed in during their last visit. Father Jean-Claude left for the rectory and assured them he would be back within the hour. Nellie went to check on Marie and found her with Maurice.

"I'm sorry to bother you," she said, standing in the doorway. "I came looking for Marie."

"I am very happy you brought her here," Maurice said.

Nellie managed to keep her shock in check. Maurice seemed to have shrivelled to half his size. His face was grey with black circles under hollowed eyes. His voice sounded old, feeble. For a moment she experienced a pang of sadness.

"I wants to stay until he goes to sleep," Marie said.

Nellie quietly closed the door and went back to her room. Marie would grieve the death of the man who had taken away her father. She paced the room. Fate had played a nasty trick on the child.

Nellie heard movement in the hallway and opened her door.

"Grandfather's asleep," Marie said. "I'm tired. Can I stay in your room for a while?"

"We'll both catch a nap before Father Jean-Claude and the doctor come back."

Nellie closed the curtains to darken the room and found a blanket in the bureau. Marie dropped off to sleep with hands clasped under her cheek. Nellie carried the child back to her room.

NELLIE'S EYES FLUTTERED OPEN. She rolled onto her side and looked toward the window. The sun had disappeared, and faint glimmers of stars filled the sky. She leaned on her elbow. The house was quiet and cold. Nellie slipped from under the blanket and tiptoed from the room so as not to wake Marie. Everything was shrouded in darkness. She didn't bother to turn on any lanterns as she went downstairs. The den was empty, as were the library and kitchen. She made her way back up the stairs and was about to go into her room when she noticed the door to Maurice's room was open. She treaded softly down the corridor and heard a low voice come from the captain's room.

Nellie turned to leave, but something inside her wouldn't let her move. The voice spoke again, low, soft.

"I have a question to ask before I give final absolution," Father Jean-Claude said.

Nellie wondered why he had switched to English.

"Did you sink the *Marion*?"

"I know the fate of the *Marion*."

Nellie heard Father Jean-Claude gasp. She clapped her hands over her mouth to stifle her own cry of shock.

"*Non, mon père.* I was not responsible. The *Marion* was half sunk in the water when I came upon her." A pause. "Most of the crew were dead. Some drowned. Some from injuries."

Nellie leaned against the wall to keep from falling over.

"What sort of injuries?"

"In the distance was a German warship." Nellie could hear Maurice struggle for breath. "It had attacked the schooner. It burned to ashes. My men brought aboard one survivor." A long pause this time. "He was wounded badly in the head and died a few hours later."

"Did he tell you his name?"

"No. He was not very lucid. He pressed a wooden seal into my hand and spoke. Sadly, I could not make out what he said."

Nellie slid to the floor and covered her mouth to hush her sobs.

"I gave the poor man a decent burial at sea."

"Why did you not bring him home to Newfoundland?"

Maurice coughed. Several more seconds passed before he could talk. "I knew the people of St. Jacques would accuse me for the destruction of the schooner. I was correct."

"You kept the wooden seal?"

"*Oui.* It must have been very important to the young man."

"What became of *le capitaine* Ike?"

"He lay over a man with three fingers on one hand. Ike must have tried to protect him from a beam that had broken free."

Father Jean-Claude began to mumble in French the monotone rhythm of absolution. Nellie gripped the wall to get to her feet and hurried to Marie's room. She sat on the bed and took deep breaths to slow her racing heart. Harry and Tommy had been murdered by unknown enemies from another country. An enemy with no name and no face. Harry had survived long enough to pass on the wooden seal, an object that meant the world to him. What had he said to Maurice?

Nellie, you know what I said.

"I love you too, Harry." She held her head and sobbed faintly.

"Mme. Myles," Father Jean-Claude whispered through the door. "May I come in?"

"Yes," Nellie called.

The priest stood before her. "*Le capitaine* has passed."

"I'm awful sorry, Father. I really am."

"I know that," he said. "Marie will also be saddened."

Nellie wiped her eyes. "She's asleep. Should I wake her?"

"There is time enough for the child to learn of her grandfather's death."

Nellie got off the bed. "How did you know I was in Marie's room?"

"I heard you cry." The priest followed her into the hall. "For an old man, I have exceptional ears." He looked at her with wise, kind eyes. "They miss nothing." They stared at each other a long time. "*Excusez-moi.* Mme. Dubois is terribly upset. I must go for Dr. Renard."

You wanted me to know the truth one way or another without breaking the seal of confession, she thought. "Thank you," she murmured to herself, regretting she could never say it out loud to him.

THREE DAYS LATER, PIERRE Maurice was laid to rest in the crypt with his wife. Grey clouds skidded across the sky. A cool wind blew. The air was moist with the promise of snow. Only Father Jean-Claude and Nellie remained at the gravesite. Steve had taken Marie back to the captain's house.

"I wonder where Ike buried his wife?" Nellie said as she gazed into the crypt.

The priest looked at her in surprise. "Chantal is buried here with her parents. Ike wanted her to be with her mother."

"Why didn't Maurice tell Marie that?"

"He did not want her to know about the animosity between himself and her father. Also, Maurice was ashamed of his behaviour and the way he had hurt Chantal."

Nellie shook her head. "I misjudged Ike some lot. I saw things one way when they were the other."

"Do not be too hard on yourself, Mme. Myles. Ike was a very secretive man."

Nellie sighed. "I s'pose."

THE NEXT DAY, STEVE took them back to St. Jacques under a sunny sky and calm seas. "It's some good to be home," he said when he rounded the hills into Burke's Cove.

"I can't thank you enough for everything, Mr. Marsh," Nellie said. "I know you've lost a bit of 'trading' time."

Steve grinned. "Never you mind about that, Mrs. Myles. Knowing what really took the *Marion* makes it all worthwhile."

"Do you think anyone will believe the story?" she said as Steve tied the boat to the dock.

Steve puckered his lips. "Hard to tell." He glanced at Marie dragging her suitcase from the boat. "I believes it. Are you gonna tell everyone?"

"I don't know as of yet, Mr. Marsh."

"The secret's safe with me, if that's what ya wants."

"I'm hungry," Marie called.

"We made it in time for supper," Steve said as they made their way to St. Jacques.

The convent was quiet when they reached it. "I have to get something at Annie's house. Wait here," Nellie said, and hurried down the road. The sunshine warmed her face, bringing a smile to her lips. She took the wooden seal from its place of concealment and headed for home.

Annie and the boys had just sat down to eat. "What a sight for sore eyes," Annie said, hopping up from the table and hugging Marie.

Sam looked at his mother. "Is Captain Maurice all right?"

"He's gone," Nellie said. She placed the wooden seal on the table. "Harry gave this to him to bring home to us."

NELLIE SAT IN HER rocker after the others had gone to bed. She was surprised that she'd actually missed Ike's house. It felt like her home for the first time. She rocked and knitted a scarf for Bessie, humming softly.

Joe came into the room.

"I thought you were in bed," Nellie said.

"I couldn't sleep, thinking about pa, fishing . . . and this." He held out the sculpture. "Pa always promised he'd give me the seal on my first trip to the Banks. He said it brought him good luck."

Nellie sighed. "Not in the end."

"I think it did. If you hadn't found it in Maurice's desk, we wouldn't know how Pa and Uncle Tommy died."

"How do you figure that?"

"Father Jean-Claude asked Maurice about the *Marion* because of the wooden seal, right?"

Nellie put down her knitting. "You want to tell me something, don't you?"

He nodded. "Fishing on the Banks was hard work, Ma, but I don't want to do anything else."

"I only ask one thing." Nellie picked up her knitting and finished off the row. "Wait until the war is over."

Joe smiled and went off to bed. Nellie turned out the lantern, got into bed, and stared at her wedding portrait. "Harry Myles," she whispered, "thank you for finding a way to ease my mind and heart about the *Marion*'s disappearance."

Nellie, love, the whole community needs to hear the truth.

Acknowledgements

I would like to thank Paul Butler for his encouragement, and whose guidance kept me on the right track. Special thanks to my mother, Alice, who always believed without reservation that I would one day be a published author. Many thanks to Garry Cranford for allowing me to fulfill a lifelong dream.

LINDA ABBOTT was born in St. John's, the eighth in a family of ten children. She is a graduate of Memorial University, with a Bachelor of Arts and Education. She holds a Certificate in French from Laval University, Quebec City, and attended the Frecker Institute in St. Pierre. She is a recently retired French Immersion teacher, having spent most of her career at Holy Trinity Elementary School in Torbay. She resides in St. John's.